Brainchew

WOL-VRIEY

Burning Bulb

PUBLISHING

Other Books By Wol-vriey:

The Bizarro Story of I

Meat Suitcase

Chainsaw Cop Corpse

Vegan Zombie Apocalypse

Boston Posh (Bud Malone #1)

Vegan Vampire Vaginas

Vagina Mundi

Melanie Nemesis Catchpole

Bizarro 101: A Basic Primer

Boston Corpse (Bud Malone #2)

Dr. Orgasm

Boston Lust (Bud Malone #3)

Pussy Transmission

Hell Dancer

Girls Are Not Smiling

Novellas and Short Stories By Wol-vriey

Big Trouble in Little Ass

Forever Ago Sunshine

Brainchew

WOL-VRIEY

Brainchew
By **Wol-vriey**

Burning Bulb Publishing
P.O. Box 4721
Bridgeport, WV 26330-4721
United States of America
www.BurningBulbPublishing.com

Cover artwork by Anton Rosovsky.
Author Photo: Lolade Akinsowon © 2014.

First Edition.

Paperback Edition ISBN: 978-0997773040

Printed in the United States of America

CHAPTER 1

Kat and the Gang

It was Wednesday. 11 p.m. on a warm July night in east Massachusetts.

There were four people in the gray Ford Focus sedan that cruised the darkness into the town of Raynham, MA. One of them was bleeding to death.

Kat glanced back worriedly from the driver's seat. "How's he holding up?"

Summer shook her head back at her. "He ain't; he's bleeding like a stuck pig. Except we find a doctor soon . . ."

Lance, his eyes focused coldly ahead, his fingers tight on the gun in his lap as he rode shotgun to his wife, scowled. "Fat chance of us finding a doctor at this hour. And even if we did, that's a bullet wound Chuck's got: the doc will insist on calling the cops after treating him. Shit! Shit!"

"We need to do *something*," Summer insisted. "He won't last much longer if we don't."

At that moment the car hit a bump and the wounded man let out a loud groan that seemed to rattle the Ford's frame. Chuck lay spread across the car's back seat with his head in Summer's lap. She was holding a blood-soaked napkin pressed against his belly. It wasn't doing much good: her latex gloves were bloodstained and more blood kept seeping through the napkin to stain the leather upholstery. Kat wondered how much blood was draining off inside of Chuck, like his belly was a reservoir being filled up by the severed arteries or veins.

Likewise, because she'd been handling Chuck since he'd been shot, Summer's clothes were all red too. Her white *Manhattan Transfer* T-shirt had a massive red patch on it.

"I mean it guys," she said, her face and voice tinged with worry. "Chuck needs a frigging doc, and right now at that."

"Shit!" Lance growled again, still not looking back at Chuck.

His wife instinctively took her right hand off the steering wheel for a moment and squeezed his arm. She looked his way; their eyes met across the darkness of the car's interior. Then, her eyes troubled, she focused again on the road ahead.

No one said anything for a while after that. The only sounds heard inside the car were the hum of its engine, their accelerated breathing, and Chuck's groans of pain.

All four of them were wondering how something so simple could have gone so wrong.

***

It was an odd, though straightforward enough deal: Boston billionaire Ellis Drake had hired the four of them to rob Mr. Frank Thomas, an Attleboro, MA antique dealer who kept refusing to sell him something he wanted.

They'd not met Ellis. He was out of the country at the moment, in Europe. Everything was being handled by his personal aide Bella Novak.

At Ms. Novak's request, they'd met her in Raynham, at the Sunflower Motel.

She'd rented a room for the night, and had apparently also paid the couple that ran the place extra so they raised no eyebrows when her four visitors (who did have a somewhat sleazy look to them) showed up.

They'd sat in the spacious room drinking and sizing each other up for a while:

Bella Novak was a small, compact woman of about forty-five. She had shoulder-length black hair, gray eyes, a slightly crooked nose, and a large mouth painted purple. She was attractive, but her comeliness was dulled by the air of ruthless efficiency she projected. In Kat's practiced estimation, Bella's white pantsuit cost at least five thousand dollars, and her matching brown designer handbag and high heeled sandals likely much more than that. Clearly a VERY wealthy man's representative, Bella Novak reeked of second-hand money.

"Please just call me Bella," she'd introduced herself on meeting them, speaking in clipped tones and with a controlled smile, "and this is Mr. Drake's chauffeur, Rafael."

Rafael was middle-aged and looked Spanish or Mexican. He too was well dressed, but his clothes were nowhere near as expensive as Bella's.

And then there was the gang themselves: co-leaders Kat and Lance Somerset, Summer Wallace, and Chuck Baker.

Kat Somerset was an attractive gray-eyed blonde. Short hair, average height, and curves just under the overweight limit. Kat handled the driving, she could fit their car into the smallest spaces if need be.

Kat's husband Lance was dark, stocky, and not good-looking. What stood out about him was the fierceness he projected. Anyone meeting Lance Somerset for the first time instinctively understood that he was dangerous. Generally, only those who had to transact business with Lance hung out with him.

Summer Wallace was tall, also a blonde (though blue-eyed as opposed to Kat's gray), and had large breasts well out of proportion with her slim body. The breasts were an attention-grabbing recent purchase (amongst other surgeries) paid for by their last knock-off job. She was much more attractive than Kat. (Kat only tolerated having her in the gang because she was so good at what she did.) Most times Summer was a calm and pleasant woman, but she also had an extremely violent streak to her. In marked contrast to Lance though, she was all peaches and cream till it was time to get her knife out. But once it was out, her switchblade hardly ever returned into its handle without blood being spilled.

The fourth member of their gang, Chuck Baker, was the handsome one and the ladies' man. He had black hair, dark eyes, a Roman nose, and smiling sensual lips. Chuck was also their safe cracker and all-round geek technician.

"Two hundred thousand dollars the job is worth to you guys," Bella Novak explained easily between sips of wine. "C.O.D., and with no questions asked as to *how* you get it done. All Mr. Drake wants are the matching set of diamonds in the safe."

Lance sipped some beer and leaned forward. "From what you said over the phone, Ms. Novak—"

"Bella please."

"Yeah, alright . . . Bella. Look, from what you've been saying so far, all your boss wants us to get for him are two small rocks." He scratched his chin. "Now, see here, we ain't dummies here. I very much doubt that those diamonds will cost you as much to buy as you're paying us to steal them. What's the catch? And don't jerk us about by saying there ain't any."

"Mr. Drake's interest in the stones shouldn't concern you. He's a billionaire, and like all extremely rich people must be permitted a few eccentricities. In Ellis Drake's case, rather than trying to start the next world war simply for its news value, or buying the Boston Red Sox, he collects beautiful things . . . whatever catches his fancy. We his employees never question either his fancy or purchases, and neither should you."

Bella's speech was brusque, its tone more forbidding than the Berlin Wall.

In a disgusted voice, she added: "Thomas, the man who owns the diamond set, is an old fossil, so set in his atrophied ways that even carbon 14 can't date them. We've made all sorts of financial overtures to him, but . . ." She winced, then tapped her violet lips with a perfectly manicured finger. "Please spare me the long explanation here. The bottom line is—Thomas *won't* sell to us. Which is why we wish to hire you to get them for us." Her lips compressed in a frown. "You four come with the highest recommendations. Still, the choice is yours: if you're not interested, we can forget it. I'll make an alternative arrangement."

"We're interested alright," Kat said, glancing sideways at Lance's cold face then back at Bella's ice-cool expression. Interest aside though, something about this steal—something impossible to put a finger on—was already making her uneasy. She had a red flag to walk away from this. However, that was easier said than done. Kat wasn't stupid; one didn't throw away a seemingly easy two hundred grand without good reason. The important word here though was *seemingly*. "But my husband's right," she finished. "Something smells fishy about this. We don't want to walk into a trap."

Bella rolled her eyes. "There is no damn trap. We just need to get this done *discretely*, and I've heard that you four are the best out there at being discreet."

The chauffeur Rafael now spoke for the first time. His voice was calm, though to Kat's alert ears it also appeared to betray a hint of worry. "We're *not* setting you up to frame you—"

"You'd better not be," Summer said. "Or else . . ." She made the universal gesture of drawing her thumb slowly across her throat. "My knife would love to get on intimate terms with your neck."

"Please stop being vulgar, Miss Wallace," Bella said. "For heaven's sake, we're not hiring you four to kill Thomas for us."

"And we are not setting you up," Rafael repeated with finality. "Like Bella just explained, we've made several overtures to Mr. Thomas to get him to part with the pair of diamonds, but he refuses to." He flashed them a smile that dripped irony. "So finally we had to resort to hiring *you*."

There was grim distaste in Rafael's words, like he disliked them all intensely, disliked hiring them, and would prefer to have nothing at all to do with either them or the plan to rob Thomas.

Again Kat felt that bad vibe. The chauffeur's clear unease now gave the meeting a creepy undercurrent that she had to fight to clear out of her mind. First, though, she examined Bella Novak closely, trying to determine something suspicious about the woman. However, Bella seemed normal enough, merely another right-hand-bitch hiring others to do her employer's dirty work. Kat believed she understood the reasoning process at play here. It was common enough with the idle rich. If they coveted something enough, they got it by any means necessary, even if the final means of achieving their end was downright dastardly and dirty. Most likely, Ellis Drake had seen the desired diamonds in a catalogue somewhere and decided he wanted them as a present for some lady he wanted to fuck—custom gem-set earrings to go with a designer dress; or a pendant.

Kat finally managed to shrug most of her disquiet off. She wasn't judging either Bella or her employer. Men like Ellis Drake made the criminal world go round. Besides, she understood the thrill of making a steal like this. *Oh, I'd love to be that rich. It must be great to have the cash at one's disposal to indulge one's pettiest whims.*

"So will you do it or not?" Bella asked after a swallow of wine, her gray eyes like a winter dawn.

Lance looked around at the others for dissent, his eyes resting longest on Kat's. No one said anything. "Yeah, we'll do it," he replied finally. "Let's have the details."

"Wonderful." Bella's icy gaze thawed and she smiled coolly. She looked at Rafael and extended her perfectly manicured hand. He nodded, and handed her a photograph. She in turn handed the photograph to Lance. He took it, stared a moment at the silver-haired man it depicted, then turned it over to read the writing on its rear.

"That's the address on the back," Rafael said. "Gardner Street, Attleboro. You do the job next Wednesday."

"Why *then?*" Summer asked, her eyes studying Rafael so intently that Kat was unsure if she wanted to have sex with him or kill him. Summer could be crazy like that.

Rafael replied, "Next Wednesday is Thomas's daughter's wedding anniversary. He's a widower and she's his only child. He's certain to be at her house until the early hours of the morning, same as every year. You do the job then. Get in say, by nine, and get out before he gets back."

Bella nodded and leaned back in her chair. She crossed her legs, a smile on her violet lips. Kat understood that pleased smile: it was satisfaction at seeing money doing its work. *The rich always get what they want.*

But still, Kat had that niggling bad intuition about this job.

She looked around at the others—her husband, Summer, and Chuck. Rafael was explaining details about the house. (The pair had already had Thomas's residence cased—they'd apparently been planning this steal for ages). Her three companions were listening attentively, though Chuck was also busy putting the make on Bella Novak, making suggestive eyes at her.

She smirked to herself. Ha, ha, this was just typical Chuck; he had to attempt to bed every female he met, even if, like Bella Novak, she looked as frigid as a snowwoman in winter. Since the meeting started, Kat had been wondering how long it would be this time before Chuck attempted to seduce Bella. She didn't think he'd succeed though. Ms. Novak seemed way too controlled, and also, too used to being around big money to slut herself on the cheap.

But, oh gosh! Just looking at Chuck, Kat instantly felt a stab of pain in her breasts and a rush of heat between her thighs. Chuck was super-handsome. She regularly lusted after him herself. If she didn't love her husband so much—and heaven knew that she *really* loved Lance—she'd be leaping into bed with Chuck at every opportunity she got. And Chuck wasn't the kind to say no to such offers.

She concentrated on the discussion: Rafael's explanations, with Bella occasionally clarifying a point on request.

Laid out like they were doing, the deal made sense. They hit Thomas for the diamonds, gave them to Bella and Rafael, and got paid. Easy squeezy. *These two clearly have zero intention of screwing us over. They're doing it for the boss, and the cash is guaranteed—Ellis is worth over a billion bucks. So why the hell do I feel so wrong about this?*

"The only caveat here . . ." Rafael coughed apologetically.

"Yeah, here it comes," Summer said. "I knew there was a catch to all this."

Rafael shot her a look tinged with fear; Kat wondered if maybe he was imagining her actually slitting his throat. "Ladies and gentlemen, if you screw this up . . . *you* take the fall. You don't involve us at all. I mean, if you get the police involved in this matter, Mr. Drake has never heard of you. And Bella and I will never have met the four of you in our lives."

"That goes without saying," Lance retorted coldly. "We're responsible if we screw up. But we won't screw up, okay?"

"I'm just saying," Rafael said quietly, undeterred by the other's anger. "Just so you understand."

Lance said nothing. He understood. As did Kat and Summer and Chuck, who was grinning at Bella (who to Kat's surprise seemed to like the attention; so maybe this power chick liked slumming too). All four of them knew the score here: the behind-the-scenes man, Ellis Drake, was wealthy enough to get away with murder if he wanted.

"And whatever you do, don't blow up the stones," Bella pleaded nervously. "I know it's a maximum security safe and all, but . . . just don't fucking damage the merchandise?" Her handsome face scrunched up as if she could already see both the diamonds and their safe and Mr. Thomas's entire downstairs antiques establishment and his overhead living quarters blowing apart all over Gardner Street. "We'll be incensed if you do."

"No problem, Bella. They haven't yet built a safe I can't get into," Chuck assured her with a laugh. He was still making sexy eyes at her. "And I get safely in and out of a lot of other tight places too."

Caressed by his gaze, she smiled back coyly and preened herself. "I really hope so. The boss wants those damn rocks; you've no idea how badly." She flashed Chuck a smile loaded with future carnal promise then nodded to Rafael. "Time to go."

He got to his feet and extended a hand to help her up.

Bella Novak waved back at them from the motel room door, a glossy and expensive ice queen, the perfect advertisement on the benefits of being employed by the super-rich. "So, everyone, here's to a happy jewel heist. If all goes well, we'll meet here again next Wednesday night. And you'll all be a whole lot richer. Ta ta!"

And then she'd exited into the night, and her reek of second-hand money with her. Kat found that odd about her—like she'd hung around Ellis Drake's wealth for so long that its aura had stuck to her.

"I don't trust that Rafael guy," Lance said once they'd heard Bella's black Cadillac Escalade drive off and there was no chance of their being overheard. He polished off his beer while scratching his chin. "He's shifty, more edgy than a snake whose tail someone's been stepping on all night."

"Me neither," Summer agreed. "Something about him just doesn't sit right with me."

Kat took that to mean that the pair had also picked up on Rafael's unease. Which, now that she thought about it, seemed to be what had been unsettling her too all along.

"I think he was just nervous," she said. "Maybe Ellis Drake likes yelling at them. Guys, you saw how Bella just went on a rant about us not blowing up everything."

Lance nodded grimly. "As if you can blow up diamonds anyway. Damn, what an airhead."

There was an air of celebration in the motel room now. This was a big score, and one they'd not have to work too hard on. Hell, the clients had even cased the joint themselves. All they had to do was get in and get out again and get paid.

"Screw Rafael," Lance decided finally. "If he makes trouble for us, we'll send him to the morgue with fatal lead poisoning. Bella Novak don't strike me as an emotional sort of lady. I hardly see her calling the cops or caring too much if the world's short one jerk. She'll just hire fresh help for their boss."

Chuck laughed and cracked open a beer. "Yeah, man. It's Ellis's money—he's the only one that matters." Then he leered broadly, and spread his hands wide. "But damn, guys, did you see *the ass* on that woman as she walked out the door? I'd love to bury myself somewhere in her Mississippi Delta. I won't even mind the crabs or gators."

Summer rolled her eyes in disgust, then pouted. "Dammit, man, you gotta get your brain out of the gutter. You're such a frigging slut."

Chuck laughed louder still. "Yeah? Summer, it takes one to know one."

***

That was a week ago.

So, today, they'd travelled down from their Boston base to Attleboro, to Thomas's place. This was a drab two-story brownstone on Gardner Street with a weatherworn 'Antiques' sign hung over a wide display window. The house had an attached garage, from which (Bella had informed them) a side door led directly upstairs to the living quarters. And just like they'd also been told, the ancient roller shutter garage door was left up—Thomas no longer had the strength to raise and lower it, and he was apparently either too stingy or old-fashioned to replace it with an electric model.

There was no sign of Thomas's car in his garage. The old man was clearly out celebrating with his daughter and her family.

They'd been cruising slowly, keeping an eye out for the police. Not noticing any, Kat parked the car beside the antiques store so they could look in its window.

The four of them regarded the shop display of vases, old clocks, lamps, spyglasses, and other miscellaneous curios. Behind those, in the dimmed interior, they made out some period furniture, gilt mirrors, framed photographs, and rolled-up rugs.

Most of what they could see looked inexpensive.

"Are you sure this is the right address?" Kat asked. "What reason would this guy have for *not selling* his diamonds to Ellis Drake?"

"Yeah," Summer agreed. "I mean, if Bella's offering us two hundred G's to steal them, she might have offered him half a million to sell them to her."

As Kat put the car in motion again, she mused on the puzzle some more. "Guys, Thomas is old. Old timers are stubborn as mules sometimes. And he's a widower too. The diamonds may be a heirloom, or they belonged to his late wife and he thinks it's sacrilege parting with them."

"Heirloom or not, he'll part with them when he dies," Chuck said.

"He'll part with them tonight," Lance corrected as Kat swung the Ford into a left side street. "And then he'll wish he'd sold the diamonds to Bella and taken the money."

Their completed circuit of the block had revealed no cruising patrol cars, although the Attleboro Police Station was just a short distance away on Pine Street, up around the corner of the third block.

Back on Gardner Street again, Kat stopped two houses away from the antiques shop, by the awning of a closed-for-the-night grocers on the other side of the road.

Now her feeling of unease returned. "Guys," she said, "I googled Ellis Drake. He's way, way younger than Thomas, just thirty-one. If I were him, I'd simply wait for Thomas to kick the bucket and buy the diamonds off the daughter. She's his only child, he's sure to leave them to her if they're that valuable. Besides, that way there's zero chance of the girl raising a stink if she recognizes the gems on some rich widow while browsing the society pages or *Vogue* magazine."

Summer laughed, the sound seemed to warm up the vehicle's cool interior. As always, she and Chuck were seated in back, while Lance rode shotgun to his wife. "Ellis Drake *wait?* Trust me, girl, you don't know these kind of high society people like I do. Remember I told you I once worked as a PA too?"

"Yeah," Kat said. "You never did say why he fired you."

Summer made a face as if from a bad memory. "The old bigot didn't like me dating his son—he said I looked too much like Barbie." She scowled. "Aw, forget that, it's old history. Back to my point: See, the rich are only patient when they're planning revenge. If you hurt them, they don't mind waiting thirty years to get even with you. Everything else though, they want done at least by yesterday. Even their babies want to drive before they can crawl." She exhaled an exaggerated sigh. "Oh, to be so damn rich as to steal stuff I don't need on a mere whim."

They all laughed at that, then Lance leaned over and kissed his wife. "Okay, babe, you know what to do. Park almost opposite the house and buzz my phone if you notice anyone suspicious. If the cops drive by, flatten yourself out of sight."

She nodded back, feeling the familiar tingle of anticipation.

Lance looked at the others. "Guys, let's get this over with."

They each pulled on a pair of latex gloves. Then, all dressed similarly in T-shirts and jackets over denim pants and sneakers (with

Chuck also carrying a backpack containing his tools) the three of them got out and made their way towards the antiques shop.

***

They forced the inner garage door and climbed the steps up to the overhead apartment. Then they proceeded straight through into the bedroom.

Chuck hadn't been lying when he'd bragged to Bella about opening whatever safe Thomas had without the need for explosives: safes *were* his baby. He understood them and, as good as his boast, he could break into just about any of them. Once inside Thomas's bedroom he was disappointed to find that the safe there was an old non-digital model, one that had an air of itself being a family heirloom—it looked to have been built around 1920.

Chuck shrugged; he'd been expecting more of a challenge. "I'll have this open in two hours max," he calmly informed the others, while snipping the wires that fed the clunky alarm. He tapped the large metal cube, which stood on four curved legs in a corner. "I could do it in way less time, but there's always a chance he's upgraded the interior with some other fancy circuitry that'll call the police station."

"We got time, man," Summer said. "Go to it." She sat on the bed and watched him set up his stuff. Tiring of that after a while, she walked around the bed and rifled through the collection of paperbacks in the old man's bookshelf. She shortly quit on that too and went back to sitting on the edge of the bed and watching Chuck work. She liked how, squatting like he was, the curve of his buttocks looked a 'w' written in female handwriting.

Across the room, Lance had settled into a chair by the window, one from which he could see down into the street. His grip on his gun never wavered. His eyes were fixed specifically on their gray Ford, where Kat waited at the wheel.

It was now four minutes past ten. The street was deserted except for the occasional straggling vehicle which rolled over the blacktop with headlights gleaming like a predator's eyes.

Lance's gaze flicked from the window to where Chuck had his ears in a stethoscope and was listening to the click of the safe's tumblers. "How's it coming along? How you doin' for speed?"

Chuck grinned and gave him a thumbs-up. "Half-done already. At this rate we'll be out of here in thirty minutes, not the two hours I first thought."

"Good, good." Gun in his lap, Lance resumed watching the window. Down in the street, a patrol car cruised past without stopping, which meant Kat had kept out of sight and all was cool. His phone buzzed. Slightly alarmed, he checked the text message—*Birds of prey just flew past*—then relaxed.

Summer got up as he wrote a reply to Kat. "Guys, I'm off to have a drink of water in the kitchen. Or a beer if he's got any."

Lance nodded and resumed writing.

"And . . . we're in," Chuck announced to a soft click. "Safe's open. Thirty-eight minutes, twelve seconds. Damn, am I good or what? A new world record for me."

Lance grunted and got out of his chair; he was used to Chuck patting himself on the back. He strode over to the safe and crouched down beside the man. Chuck's strategically placed light let them see all the metal box's contents. He smiled. "Hmmm. Looks like we ain't done too badly this time."

Chuck pulled out one of six wads of hundred dollar bills stacked just inside the safe door. "Talk about collateral benefits," he said, flipping through the wad so that Benjamin Franklin seemed in rapid motion—in a hurry to spend himself. "There's sixty G's in here." He paused, dropped the bills back inside the safe, and pulled out a small brown box instead. "And here . . . this must be what we came to Attleboro for."

He held the box up for Lance's appraisal. Lance stuck his gun in his belt, then took the box from him and turned it over under the gleam of a penlight. The brown box was made of two halves of carved wood, which split along a middle seam to reveal two large diamonds on a purple velvet cushion. The stones, identical in size and shape, broke apart the flashlight beam into a kaleidoscope of rainbows.

Nodding with pleasure, Lance closed the jewel box and put it away in his jacket. Then, as a chill breeze moved the window drapes, he walked back over to stare out the window. Down in the street, Kat caught his gaze and gave him a cautious thumbs up. Lance gave her a thumbs up of his own and returned to stand beside Chuck, who was emptying the safe of its monetary content.

"Leave a few thou for the old guy's hospital bills," Lance said. "He's certain to have a stroke when he finds the safe empty."

Chuck laughed. "Yeah. Anyone who keeps this much spare change at home won't believe in health insurance either." He split the last wad of hundreds in two, flung half back into the safe, and clicked it shut. "Okay, time to . . ." He paused in zipping up his bag of tools and gave Lance a look of concern. "Hey, dude, why the hell is Summer taking so long getting herself a drink of water?"

"I'll go see." Lance turned toward the bedroom door, then froze.

Old Mr. Thomas was standing there in the bedroom doorway pointing a gun at them.

"Aw, shucks," Chuck said. "Look what the night brought home with it."

"Put everything back in the safe," Thomas said in a scared yet resolute voice. Then he quickly flicked on the bedroom light and moved into the room to cover them better.

Lance stared at the old man. Now that the lights were on, he decided the antique dealer perfectly complimented his downstairs store. Thomas was tall but slight, with gray hair gone bald in front. His eyes were pale behind his thick glasses. He wore an old suit and had a look of both fear and intense determination on his face.

"I mean it," Thomas repeated. "Put everything back in the safe. Especially the diamonds. You can't have them."

Lance, caught unawares with his gun stuck in his belt, was puzzled. *How in the hell did he get in without us hearing him? And without Kat seeing him? When I looked downstairs just now Kat was wide awake in the car. A frigging back door? A secret passage? And ain't it too early for him to have left his daughter's anniversary party? And where the hell has Summer gotten to? How long does it take for her to get a glass of water, or has this old guy knocked her out? Shit!*

Lance (and Chuck beside him) had no end of questions. Whatever the case though, Thomas was here now and had a gun trained on them. And worst of all, the old man was clearly scared, which meant he might shoot. This had to be handled carefully. Lance didn't want Thomas shooting him.

He stared Thomas down. "Hey, old timer, put the gun away before you get hurt."

Thomas didn't budge. "No. You two leave my house right now or I'm calling the police." Sweat was pouring off his brow now. With his free hand, he began fumbling in his pocket for his cellphone.

Okay this crap has gone too far, Lance decided. No way was he letting Thomas dial the cops.

"I wouldn't try that if I were you," he warned Thomas.

"I'm calling the police. Those diamonds you're stealing are too precious to let go of. They've belonged to the women in my family for two hundred years, and I'm keeping them here for my daughter Maria." The old man had his phone out now and was trying to dial 911 with his free thumb.

And that was when Summer returned from wherever she'd vanished to.

"Hey, guys, I—"

Thomas started turning to see who'd just entered the bedroom. Seeing the old man distracted, Lance rushed at him to disarm him. Thomas, however, caught the charge out of the corner of his eye, spun back towards Lance and . . . fired.

There was a sound of thunder like a miniature earthquake in the bedroom.

Lance had almost reached the old man when the gun went off, but he was on Thomas's right, out of the line of fire.

The bullet hit Chuck, who was just getting to his feet, in the belly. With a loud squeal, Chuck fell back against the safe. Then, his face contorted in pain, he slid to the floor.

Lance stared at Chuck. Chuck stared back at him in disbelief as blood spilled from the front of his T-shirt.

Lance pulled out his gun then turned to gape at Thomas. "Old man, are you frigging nuts?"

Thomas was staring at Chuck like he didn't believe he'd just shot him. His gun-hand had dropped to his side and he was shaking. "I didn't mean to. I didn't—"

Then Thomas's eyes widened in further confusion . . . and pain. Summer had slid her hand around his neck from behind and slit his throat from ear to ear with her switchblade. "Fuck you for that!" She severed the flesh so deeply that blood didn't just *jet* from Thomas's neck, it *flowed*, like lava spilling from a volcano.

Gripping his sliced-open neck with both hands, his blood gushing thickly through his fingers and staining everything it touched, Thomas nonetheless spun around to see who'd attacked him.

Summer shook her knife at him. "That's what your stupidity just earned you, old man. You should have stayed at your damn party."

Thomas gaped at the beautiful blonde with the bloody knife. She brushed him aside like a fly, so he fell on the bed, then she hurried over to Chuck's side.

Lance shook his head down at Thomas. The life had just left the old man's eyes. Then he too rushed over to Chuck's side. Summer was helping Chuck to his feet. Chuck was grimacing, his eyes squeezed tight in agony.

"How you doin', man?"

Chuck opened his eyes and spat blood. "Worse than poop that's been floating in the New York sewers for six months."

Lance glanced at Summer. Her face was strained. She shook her head. "He ain't good at all. That old fool"—she flung a glare of pure hatred at the corpse on the bloody bed—"got him bad. He needs a doctor."

They got Chuck to his feet. Momentarily leaving him supported by Summer, Lance hurried over to the window and signaled down to Kat, then he picked up Chuck's bag (which was now all soaked in his blood) and helped Summer move their wounded friend out of the room.

Lance's primary hope now was that no one had heard the gunshot. If they were lucky, no one would discover Thomas's corpse till morning, by which time they'd be well away from here. Which made it imperative too that they leave as little blood as possible on the sidewalk downstairs.

"I'm really sorry, man," Summer told Chuck as they started down the stairway, "after drinking some water, I had to take a crap too, so . . ."

***

On hearing the single gunshot, Kat's heart instantly leapt up into her mouth.

Oh no, it's started! Though she'd not mentioned her fears to even her husband, her initial intuition warning her to leave this job alone had

15

only grown stronger during the past week. And now, it felt like things had indeed begun going wrong for them.

She immediately switched on the ignition to warm up the engine. Then she sat glancing up at the second-story bedroom window over the antiques shop. Her emotions were very unsettled. In addition, her belly suddenly felt as upset as if someone was driving a monster truck through it.

Someone's been shot, her thoughts raged. *But who shot who? Oh no—please, God, please don't tell me Chuck and Lance had one of their crazy spats again!* It was inconceivable to Kat that anything else could be the case. *Or did one of them shoot Summer?* But that was hard to credit: Summer always minded her own business. She hardly ever argued or bullshitted. So what the . . . ?

She was relieved when Lance stuck his head out of the window. At least she wasn't a widow yet. But his frantic gesturing meant something was amiss.

She waved back at him, then drove the Ford across the street and parked it neatly in front of Thomas's garage.

A few moments later, Lance and Summer burst out of the garage, dragging the wounded Chuck between them. She helped them get the rear driver's-side door open, then waited till everyone was in the car before asking, "What the hell happened up there?"

"Thomas came home early and shot Chuck, then Summer killed him."

"What?" She looked at Summer for confirmation.

Summer nodded back. "Get us out of here, Kat. The fuzz might be on the way already."

"We got Mr. Drake's bloody diamonds for him, if that's what you're worried about," Lance added, patting Chuck's tool bag. "And a sackful of money besides."

Kat flung a single alarmed look back at Chuck, who was now coughing up blood, then faced the road again and floored the gas pedal. Then, just before making the left turn at the end of the block onto Oneil Boulevard, she slowed again. If the police weren't yet after them, she didn't want to attract any unnecessary attention. Not with a gut-shot man in the back of the car.

***

Now they were in Raynham, Kat was pensive as she drove. This could still work out alright, but they needed to tend to Chuck as fast as possible. But how to do that if they couldn't take him to a doctor or ER?

After steering the gray Ford onto Carver Street, she glanced across at her husband. She was shocked: Lance was playing with his phone at a time like this?

"Look, guys, we *really* need to do something about Chuck," Summer groaned from behind them.

Kat nodded grimly. As to what they could do, she had no idea. "Lance, frigging say something, will you? You're our damn leader. And stop fooling around with that goddam cellphone!"

"Yeah, yeah." Lance looked first at her, then back at Chuck, who seemed to be asleep, though his face was creased up with discomfort, and his mouth was as bloody as if he had red lipstick on. "I'm not goddam *playing* on the phone. I was checking out where the nearest hospitals are."

Kat groaned. "Hospital?"

"Look, it's better if Chuck goes to jail than if he dies, right? What we're gonna do is, we'll drive down to the nearest emergency room, leave him outside, then drive off. It's out of our hands then."

Kat slowed the car and parked. She thought she saw some sense in that. "That might work, if it isn't already too late."

But then Summer asked: "And what about when the cops question him? Remember he'll be facing a murder rap."

Lance said, "C'mon, girl, Chuck knows the score. He'll keep his mouth shut. Besides, we've enough cash to hire him a smart-ass lawyer who'll plead self-defense. He'll get a manslaughter conviction, be out in five or six years."

"Self-defense? How on earth do you figure that?"

Lance frowned. "Simple logic. You slit Thomas's throat from ear-to-ear right?"

"Yeah. So?"

"Well, Thomas obviously couldn't have shot Chuck *after* his neck's been ripped open that bad, so he clearly must've done it *before*, see? . . . Then Chuck, fighting to protect himself against being shot again, grabs a knife and . . ."

"Can a burglar claim self-defense?"

"If we get the right attorney, he can."

"And how then do *we* explain bringing him to the hospital? We just found him bleeding by the roadside?"

"We don't explain anything. We just drop him outside the door and . . . look, for goodness sake, stop nitpicking, Summer. You're the one who's been bawling me out for twenty minutes that he's gonna die on us."

"I just wanna be sure—"

At that moment, Chuck gave an almighty twitch where he was, his back arching up off the seat. Then he let out a loud moan of pain, collapsed back down again, and lay limp.

They all froze and stared at him, then Summer gingerly felt Chuck's neck for a pulse. Then she checked his wrist. She took her time doing it. Finally though, she sighed and shook her head.

Kat stared at the prone man, his head still resting in Summer's lap like he was sleeping. The pain that had lined his face for the past quarter-hour was now all smoothed away in peace.

She didn't dare ask the obvious question. Lance tried to: "Is he . . . ?"

Summer sighed again, then nodded, wiping tears from her eyes. "Yeah, he is. Forget about finding Chuck a hospital bed. What he needs now is a bed of earth in a cemetery."

"Shit!" Lance looked pissed off. Then he shrugged, opened the front passenger-side door, got out, then opened the rear door on Summer's side also. "Alright, we'll bury him later, after we check in at the motel. For the moment though, let's get him stashed in the trunk in case of the cops."

Kat turned from the wheel and watched them move Chuck out of the rear seat and into the Ford's trunk. As she watched, her eyes misted with tears and her heart pumped a mingled ichor of sorrow and fear through her.

Oh no! This made two corpses already, and in a space of just an hour.

And worse yet, she still didn't feel any easing of her bad intuition, any sense of relief that their troubles of tonight were over. But if not, what the hell could still possibly go wrong tonight? Were the cops going to catch or kill them all?

Her face was grave and teary when Lance and Summer got back into the car.

"Fuck!" Summer said, throwing the duffel bag she'd just taken from the trunk across to the far side of the rear seat, away from the spilled blood. The bag contained the spare clothes and shoes they kept in the car in case of emergencies. "I need to change my top before we check in." She at once began wiping the bloody seat down with a rag as a prelude to doing so.

Lance waited till she'd ditched the rag out the window, then slammed his door shut. "Let's go," he growled, the sound torn from his throat like it came from a wounded bear. "At the moment I'm so angry I could kill someone."

His words did nothing to quell his wife's unspoken and rising fear.

CHAPTER 2

Dusty

Damn, what a slow night, Dusty Rowland thought.

She was seated behind the Sunflower Motel's reception desk, flipping through a copy of *Marie Claire* that she'd taken from her sales rack of fashion magazines, and wondering why some women had all the luck. Here she was, thirty-six years old and largely dissatisfied with her life, while all these young girls—just look at them all, grinning like they hadn't a care in the world—wined and dined with the rich and famous, and did photo shoots on exotic runways from Milan and Paris to Tokyo and L.A. and Berlin.

Dusty, a pretty brunette with a good figure, was a failed catwalk model herself. She'd run away from Raynham to New York at age 22, specifically to avoid the life she now had—running the Sunflower—but then . . .

She turned the magazine page and scowled at the next set of photoshopped bodies and faces preaching the gospel of anorexic femininity to her.

She hated remembering how her own modeling dreams had slowly crumbled to dust—like she was the stock index collapsing during the Great Depression—till finally she'd wound up stripping at Sapphire on East 60th Street.

For Dusty, the worst part of being a stripper hadn't been the drunken club patrons stuffing beer-soaked dollar bills in her G-string, but the fact that each time she left work to walk home, she could see her dream within touching distance—supermodels on billboards advertising perfume, lingerie, and such like—but was herself unable to make the crossing into the boat of fashion success.

And she'd really tried. She'd worked her ass off trying to break into the supermodel class. All the top agents had agreed that she had the right face and the right body for the game. She was sexy enough and should have been a legend in her own right.

But she was clearly missing something, that indefinable 'something' required to make the big league. Dusty didn't know what it was that she didn't have, but there was always some other girl—someone nowhere as pretty as she—who'd get the big photo shoot call instead of her.

And once she'd hit thirty, the dream was really over anyway even if she couldn't admit it to herself. (Except you were a supermodel, it was a 'young girl industry'—fresh flesh for the body sharks.) Then, once she'd begun regularly doing drugs to cope with her depression over her failure, that was it. Her baby-pure looks had flown out the window in six months flat, and her grand dream of gracing the catwalks of Europe and Asia officially ended.

She'd resigned herself to a lifetime of shaking her flesh for dollars. At least she could dance, and she'd been stripping for so long at Sapphire that she almost had tenure at the club. (The money wasn't bad either, so long as one didn't mind the occasional accompanying feelings of sexual degradation. On her bad days Dusty felt like she was a dripping piece of red meat dangling itself before hungry wolves.)

The one thing Dusty wasn't ready to do was return home to Raynham and her father Clint Duggan. That would be an admission of failure. (She'd not seen her father in nine years, though she always called him on his birthday and at Christmas.)

She also had enough reservations from her Catholic upbringing to be unwilling to do porn, unlike lots of the girls at the strip club, though they all said it was easy money—way easier than dancing one's ass off for spare change—and she'd gotten quite a few offers herself even during her modeling days. There was an additional inducement to do porn: Sapphire devoted its weekend entertainments to 'adult' actresses, so Dusty could have made a financial killing there if she'd been willing to suck dick on camera.

And then she'd met Shane Rowland, another failed model who'd just been employed as the strip club's bartender, and while each bemoaning the evil fickleness of the modeling industry to the other, they'd fallen in lust and love.

And then, three years ago, just as they'd been planning their wedding, Dusty's father Clint had died, and had left the Sunflower Motel to her and her older brother Ambrose.

(The circumstances of Clint Duggan's death were nothing if not doubly tragic. His granddaughter-in-law Cherry Duggan had been ripped to bits by some animal, then stuffed in a trash bag by psychopaths and thrown away in the neighboring woods for the raccoons and possums to eat. Cherry, who was married to Zak, son of Dusty's eldest brother Clint Jnr.—himself a casualty in a boating accident the previous year—had worked at the Sunflower. The old man had been exceptionally fond of the girl, and once her body was found, had had a stroke and passed on to the great beyond.)

On hearing of her father's death and her inheritance, Dusty had sat down by herself and taken cold, hard stock of her life. It was time to face the facts: all that was happening to her in the Big Apple was that she was growing older day by day. Soon she'd be too old to strip for a living, and then what?

A half-stake in the family business was something solid; something she could build a future on.

So, Dusty Duggan had agreed to return home and co-manage the Sunflower . . . so long as Shane came along also. (This final condition was important to her, as like most handsome men, Shane Rowland had a roving eye, and Dusty had twice had to give another girl a black eye to make her keep her distance from him. So, she knew if she left NYC, he'd be bed-hopping in no time at all. And—'unliberated love-slave' or not—she wasn't leaving him behind to return to the 'boonies.' She loved him way too much for that.)

Thankfully, Shane was as tired of New York as she was. He'd agreed to relocate too, and once here in Raynham, he'd found a cab-driving job and they'd gotten married.

She sighed. *And so here I am now. Mistress of all I survey.*

Which (she was honest enough to admit to herself) was actually quite a lot. The Sunflower had a reputation in the area as a nice getaway spot and got consistently good reviews on online tourist websites spotlighting eastern Massachusetts. True, Raynham was a 'just passing through' kind of town, but they got their fair share of stopover visitors.

Business could be a lot worse, and with Dusty being the forward-thinker she was, things were certain to get better. She planned on building a large restaurant behind the reception building, and after that to also add a swimming pool. So yeah, the future was gonna be bright for herself and Shane.

And where is Shane anyway? He only said he was going to check out . . .
Then she heard flushing from the inner toilet and relaxed.

She looked up from her magazine and stared out through the
lobby's glass door, at the dimly lit parking lot and at the right edge of
the motel driveway, its far end illuminated by streetlights. This *was* a
quiet night. The motel currently had just five guests in its two rear
blocks, and one in Room 3 in the larger, more luxurious, front block.

And then there was that front block reservation for Room 8.

Dusty sighed again and returned to the companionship of her
memories:

Her father's death had had one ironic benefit—it had provided her
a reason to return home without the attached stigma of failure.

Shane's coming along had also helped paint her with a veneer of
success. Dusty's high school friends—without exception all married
and overweight and each with four or five kids now—were green with
envy over how handsome her husband was. And of course, when all
her stripper and model friends came north for the wedding (including
two who'd made some adult films; Kendra Lust had promised to
attend, but had come down with the flu the day before the wedding)—
the little town of Raynham, MA hadn't seen a glossy wedding like that
in . . . they hadn't ever, period.

Of course, her husband being so hot did present Dusty with the
problem of several of her friends—like that little slut Tricia
Crawford—constantly making plays for him. Dusty knew that if she
didn't keep a vigilant eye on Shane, he'd be slotting his love muscle
between their fat adulterous thighs in no time, and she didn't want to
lose him. Most men she knew were pussy-hounds too (including her
fat friends' husbands). Dusty figured WAGs just had to know how to
keep their men in line. It was either that or sack them only to find
yourself in the same irritating situation again. She had no idea how
many women her husband had slept with while he'd been driving that
taxi.

Which was why it was good that . . . no it wasn't good—she
wouldn't wish what had happened to her brother on her worst
enemy—it was just fortuitous that that horrible nonsense had
happened to knock Ambrose out of shape. Ambrose had been on a
wild drunk ever since he lost his family . . . and in no shape whatsoever
to do more at the Sunflower than work as its janitor.

So, with her brother out of mental commission, Dusty had prevailed on Shane to quit driving his damn taxi and take over Ambrose's responsibilities . . . and most of his share of the motel's profits.

She saw nothing wrong with that—she saw to it that Ambrose had more than enough cash for his boozing, and besides, what did a drunk need a lot of money for anyway?

Alright, yeah, there was sex, too. Even a wino like her elder brother needed to blow a load into a prostitute every now and then or he got unruly. (Otherwise . . . she had a recurring nightmare of him raping some big-brained co-ed on holiday from Boston and herself being stuck with a stack of lawyer's bills.) So she saw to it that Ambrose had enough money for hookers as well.

And while Dusty Rowland didn't actually pray for anything horrible to happen to her brother again, she wasn't exactly entreating God that he'd stop drinking himself to death either. (By her estimation, his liver had to be shot several times over by now.) She just liked how things had worked out nicely for herself and Shane.

And if Dusty could just be certain that Shane wasn't screwing their cleaner Melissa each time she drove into town to buy stuff, her post-model life would be, if not perfect, at least very tolerable.

***

The lobby door swung open and they walked in. Black jackets, T-shirts, and denim.

Dusty, once again engrossed in her copy of *Marie Claire*, first gave a start, then relaxed. It was *them*—'the crooks' she'd dubbed them—the four who had tonight's reservation for Room 8. There were only three of them now though. The second guy—the handsome one who was as good-looking as Shane—wasn't with them; he was likely outside in the car.

Across the lobby, the wall clock showed 11:11 p.m.

Dusty regarded the trio as they approached the lobby desk: two blonde women and that man, Lance, who reminded her of a pit bull—he was dark and thickset, and had a seemingly ugly disposition to him.

He was polite to her, of course, but she just knew he was a bad egg. She'd seen lots of his type while stripping in NYC. They came into the club, laid good money on the girls, but they weren't actually there in spirit—watching the strippers was simply an alibi for them. Sooner or later, the rest of the gang would show up and they'd vanish into one of the back rooms to talk dirty business.

So she had this Lance Somerset down pat. And the other two, his wife Kat, and Summer, the plastic surgery reject wearing the pink flip-flops? (Dusty could barely hide her distaste for Ms. Summer Wallace: Wow, hadn't anyone thought to tell her that her breasts were two sizes too large? With her slim frame, she needed 'B' cups not the DD's she had.) These two women were also bad, but in a female way. (Dusty wasn't sure if that was better or worse than male badness. Most likely worse: at least, as a woman, she almost always saw male misbehavior coming a mile off.)

Still, she gave the three of them a warm, welcoming smile. In addition to reserving one of the Sunflower's best rooms for tonight, a middle-aged man named Rafael Marquez had paid Dusty and Shane six thousand dollars in hush money—three grand for last Wednesday, three grand for tonight—which meant these three crooks and their handsome friend out in the car were never here. Not last week and not tonight either.

Dusty hadn't thought twice about taking the money. Particularly not after Shane had told her he'd recognized the woman who'd come to meet with the four in Room 8 last week.

"It was Bella Novak," Shane had said. "You remember her—the chick who did all those *Play by Givenchy* perfume commercials?"

Oh, did Dusty remember her! But Bella looked filthy rich now, like she'd struck oil in her backyard after retiring from the modeling game. Dusty recalled what Bella had been like back then. She'd been a snobbish and polished bitch, one of the chosen few who Dusty had aspired to be like out on the catwalk. Even back then when she was young and hot, Dusty had been way below Bella's league.

And disappointingly, despite a few attempts to get to know her, she doubted that the older woman had ever realized she existed.

And now Bella was rich? Dusty was so envious, she could have pooped green eggs. She wished to God she could get her hands on that kind of money.

Oh, my dear Lord in heaven. You just watch what I'll do with it! I'll have the Sunflower upgraded in no time whatsoever to the best travel-stop in the state . . . Hell no, what kinda crap am I thinking!? If I get my hands on that kinda cash,

I'm outa here like a flash. I'm gonna have me a continual party. And I'll be draggin' Shane along with me . . . by the dick!

So no, Dusty hadn't thought twice about taking Bella Novak's hush money. She suspected that what her chauffeur Rafael had paid them for their silence wasn't even Bella's cat-food budget.

The three 'crooks' had by now arrived at the reception desk, bringing an aura of unease along with them. Dusty quickly realized that they were upset about something. Last time they'd all been smiling, even 'pit bull-man'; now they weren't. They looked sad, like someone had shot their collective dog.

"We've a reservation," Lance said in his gruff voice. "Same room as last time."

"Yes, of course," Dusty agreed and began fumbling to get their room key for them. She was suddenly worried. The two women were staring at her like she was the poltergeist apparition on one of those TV ghost-hunts. She hated the vibe in the lobby now, it felt like a skeleton was caressing her neck.

Hey, where the hell is Shane?

To her relief, he stepped into the lobby at that exact moment. She drew strength from his good looks—he was tall, with black hair and winning blue eyes, and a nice nose, and those sensual lips she just loved to kiss, or have kissing her all over. (That was the problem though: lots of other women wanted those lips kissing them all over too, particularly in the wet haven between their legs.)

Shane didn't seem to sense the odd feeling in the lobby. "Hi, people," he said brightly, then raised a finger in memory. "Ah yes, you've a reservation for tonight, paid for well in advance; which is what we hoteliers like. Let me just get you your key."

He'd found it in five seconds and given it to Dusty. Then, while Lance and Kat were busy filling in forms under his wife's supervision, he got to work flirting with the top-heavy Summer, who'd wandered over to the magazine rack and was leafing through a copy of *Elle*.

Dusty just managed to control her anger as she watched her husband chatting up Summer. Both of them had their voices down and were giggling.

She looked forward again. With Kat grim as the reaper by his side, Lance was grunting as he filled in the registration card, staring at each line of questions coldly then stabbing the words onto the form like he was killing it. Dusty noted that Kat's eyes were red, like the blonde had been crying. Then, regarding Lance again, she wondered why she'd given him a registration card anyway. The motel wasn't supposed to keep any records of their being here tonight: the booking had been made over the phone, money already paid upfront.

I'll have to tear it up later, she realized, too flustered already by both the man's preoccupied visage and her husband's prospective philandering to simply stop him wasting his time. Thankfully he wasn't objecting; best to let rabid dogs bite in peace.

Over by the magazine rack, Shane was still chatting up the big-breasted blonde. Now Summer was laughing softly at something he'd said. Dusty smirked at the pair. At least he'd cleared up her blues. Her two friends could do with a dose of whatever he'd just told her. Then her thoughts darkened again. Oh, how she'd like to beat Shane black-and-blue when they were done frolicking together.

Then apparently, Summer decided to buy some fashion magazines, so Shane took her money—a hundred dollar bill—and bent down behind the reception desk to get change for her.

Dusty took the opportunity to knee him in the ass. He gave her a hurt look then straightened up again. He handed Summer her change. "Well, here we are."

Lance and Kat were done with the forms. Still stuck in silent mode, both were walking towards the outside door. Dusty realized now that they'd hardly each spoken a word since getting here.

To Dusty's relief, Summer made to follow them. Then she turned back to Shane. Dusty fumed with anger on seeing the unconcealed lust in the woman's blue eyes.

"I'd really love to hear the rest of that story, man. That was so hilarious."

"You haven't heard the half of it," Shane replied. He was grinning, which normally would have had Dusty mad as hell. But not now. She sensed disquiet behind his mirth; his eyes didn't match his lips. "It gets even funnier," he continued. "I mean, me and Jack were so drunk at that point that . . . Okay, maybe later tonight, when you guys are all settled in, I'll—"

A sharp burst of car horn from the lot cut him off.

"Oops, I gotta go," Summer said. She fluttered her long eyelashes at Shane. "Yeah, maybe later. That would be great; I'd *love* to hear the rest of it." She waved to Dusty then hurried out the door.

The emphasis she'd put on 'love' incensed Dusty. With grit teeth she watched Summer run off across the lot. Then, once Summer was out of view, she spun around to face Shane. He was staring after the departed woman with a troubled smile on his face.

You're thinking of fucking her, aren't you?" she asked icily. She was still mad at Summer, and the perplexed look in her husband's eyes could just as easily have been a daze of lust. "Don't bother denying it. I could see your eyes eating up her overinflated chest."

Like she'd expected—like he always did—he pled innocence. "What the hell are you talking about, Dusty? I was just being friendly with the lady. We're in the hospitality business right?"

"Hospitality my butt. You want to jump in the sack with her." This time he didn't reply. He was staring past her and out of the lobby at the empty lot.

She jabbed him in the chest with a finger. "Look at me when I'm talking to you, mister, or I'll . . ."

He looked down at her, like he'd just realized he wasn't alone in reception.

The expression on his face startled Dusty. She'd rarely seen Shane like this before. What was wrong with everyone tonight? *First the crooks come in and they're all silent like I'm dead and they're at my funeral. And now Shane's looking like Miss Fat-Tits just spooked him too.*

Shane had meanwhile turned away from her and was searching for something on the upper inner shelf of the reception desk. Still troubled, Dusty looked away from him, wondering what he'd been looking at outside. She almost expected to see a ghost signaling to her in the glass rectangle of the lobby door.

She leapt with fright at a strong touch on her shoulder, then spun around to face her husband. "Don't you dare scare me like that! And what the hell is wrong with you?"

Shane didn't reply; his eyes were extremely thoughtful. She saw that he was holding out something to her: the hundred dollar bill Summer had paid for the magazines with.

He shook it at her, indicating that she take it. She did so and instantly realized that the note felt odd. Turning it over revealed a wide red stain that wasn't quite dry yet.

She looked up at Shane with a question in her eyes.

He nodded back. "That's fresh blood. And I'm sure you noticed that one of them isn't here tonight, and how Lance and his missus were both acting all subdued. Someone's been shot, maybe even killed. That other guy is most likely dead."

She was still considering his words, when he added: "Babe, looks like we're about earning that damn hush money Bella paid us."

"Yeah," Dusty said finally, the germ of a plan taking root in her mind. "And from the look of things, if she turns up tonight—and I suspect she's gonna—we just might talk her into paying us a whole lot more for our silence."

Shane grinned broadly. "Now don't be greedy, dear."

Dusty grinned back. "Who's being greedy? The woman has cash to burn; we'll just convince her that it'll be in her best interests to part with some of it, make a generous donation to our upgrading the motel."

The sound of a car interrupted their conversation. Together they peered out of the lobby at a red Volkswagen Beetle convertible just disappearing from view round the left side of the building.

"It's just Raynham's number one hooker," Shane dismissed. "Here to screw Ambrose again."

CHAPTER 3

Crystal & Ambrose

Ambrose Duggan got up and opened the door of his motel room. Crystal Parr grinned, kissed him on the lips, then walked in past him to sit on the bed.

Crystal was a lovely, stacked brunette in her late thirties, with large breasts and a fat ass now barely covered by her white tube top and blue hot pants. Her face, however, was just starting to show the sag of aging.

Crystal was a prostitute—had been since dropping out of college twenty-one years ago, and had no intent of ever quitting the business. She was popular with the guys, and made good money at the body-sliding-into-body game.

Ambrose was her favorite client.

As always, she winced at the mess in his place: so many empty whiskey and beer bottles and cans that the room could pass for a recycler's collection point, McDonald's and Subway takeaway bags galore, sandwich wrappers imprisoning moldy crusts of bread, and an endless dotting of cigarette and joint butts.

She winced, her nose wrinkling up in disgust. "Dammit, Ambrose, you really should let Melissa clean this place."

"Dusty told her not to bother anymore," Ambrose burped over his shoulder at her. "It's either that or maybe I groped her while drunk."

He stood in the doorway looking out across the lot to the front block. Ambrose lived permanently in Room 26, the last room on the second (middle) block. Across the gravel on the right of his room were the woods that made up most of this part of Carver Street, nature's fortification between the buildings. His room had originally been Room 32, back when the Sunflower had forty-eight rooms. But then, just before his father died, the whole front block had collapsed in a freak accident—Ambrose had seen the mess, it was like one of those Middle Eastern towns after ISIS or the USAF had bombed it—and had had to be rebuilt. He and his sister Dusty had decided to do a deluxe number on the new front block—there was enough insurance money—so it now had only ten rooms, each of them almost double the size of the others in the motel. Sort of mini-presidential/penthouse suites, just at ground level.

Crystal regarded him from where she sat. With the room lighting playing on his rear and the walkway light on his front, Ambrose Duggan resembled to her a Greek god long fallen from grace, with beyond him, her red car as his divine chariot.

Ambrose was tall and handsome, with dark hair like his sister's and similarly dark eyes. He was thin and muscular, but now showed the start of a beer gut. Ambrose's hair was currently shoulder-length, in addition to which he had both a mustache and a long beard. Shaving was too much of a problem: nowadays he was hungover most of the time between drunks.

Crystal couldn't fault him either for being hungover or for drinking so much. She understood how it felt to have life's rug suddenly jerked out from beneath one's feet. If she didn't have her bed-hopping job to fall back on—the soul-numbing endless rounds of sexual congress with endless male bodies—she might crack up too. Even without the constant threat of mindless violence that hung over everyone, and having to navigate one's way around crazy people like rats in God's existential lab maze, everyday life was enough in itself to drive one nuts.

**

Ambrose finally shut the motel room door and came to sit beside her on the bed. He belched, then ran his fingers through her chocolate curls. "How's the day been, sweetheart?"

"Shitty. I gotta take my car into the garage tomorrow for a checkup—the brakes seem to be failing."

Ambrose (who'd lost his driver's license three years ago after a third DUI, when he'd rammed a streetlight) nodded understandingly, then got to his feet and shambled over to the fridge to get them beers. He liked Crystal, she was his one real friend at the moment. Sure, she sold her body to pay her bills, but then no one was perfect, were they?

And she clearly liked him too—their relationship wasn't just him renting space between her legs. There was a lot more to it than that: Crystal was as fractured as he was; they made a good suffering pair. She'd had some tragedy in her life too.

Grinning at their similarities of misery, he handed her a cold can of Coors Light.

"Thanks." She grinned back, a red lipstick curve that made his groin twitch.

Too bad she's a hooker, he thought sadly through his fading hangover. *She'd make a great wife if she weren't such a dedicated slut.* And though still pretty, her face already had those hard lines women got through sexual overuse. (A woman couldn't perform endless fellatio without her mouth attempting to maintain that 'O' shape even when there wasn't a penis in it.)

But Ambrose had a lined face too. He'd begun drinking like a fish after his wife and son died. It wasn't their murders that had traumatized him—could they even be called murders?—as much as *how* they'd happened.

No one ought to die like that, like . . .

He tore his mind off the painful memories and refocused them on his beautiful companion. She was staring in distaste at the mess he'd made of his place, the bottles and wrappers and potato chips all over the bed and everywhere. It was a beautiful mess in a way, one a drunk could be proud of. It was something he'd created himself, something that had required a diligent effort of neglect to bring about.

For a moment while watching Crystal, Ambrose tried to remember: *Did I actually molest Melissa?* He sort-of remembered the cleaning girl underneath him with her clothes still on, and her kicking and screaming, or . . . No, it was impossible to reconstruct that past event so well dissolved in alcohol. Besides, it might all just be in his mind: With the exception of never coming in to clean his room again, Melissa was still polite to him and giggled when he grabbed at her. *Besides, she looks a bit like Crystal with all that brown hair, so maybe it was Crystal I was fighting with on the bed, or I mistook her for Crystal, or Crystal for her . . . And were we actually fighting . . . ?*

He quit the mental battle. The strain of thinking was about turning his hangover into a migraine.

***

Crystal was meanwhile peeling her tube top off. Damn, this room was hotter than hell. Didn't Ambrose feel the heat?

Once she had the garment off, she fanned herself with it. She was naked beneath and her breasts swung free. "Hey, turn up the air conditioning."

She watched him snap out of some kind of drunken daze. "Yeah, sure."

As he turned to adjust the AC, she wondered about tonight. She felt restless tonight. She had a sense of big things happening to her, but had no idea of what they could possibly be. Or maybe it was just the horniness? One thing about being a *good* hooker was that the customer *always* came first. Literally. The sex was always about *their* pleasure, not yours. There was an unspoken understanding between you both that *your* pleasure was their money. So, on days like today/tonight when all her work had been blowjobs on sweaty trucker penises, she was feeling a deep buzz of sexual frustration.

And to take care of that, she was in the right place. By his own admission, Ambrose *liked* fucking her in particular (like it took his mind off his empty day). And whenever he'd drank too much, he couldn't come. He'd keep thrusting forever.

And that was what she needed right now.

He'd turned away from the air conditioner now and was staring at her again, his eyes sad while his lips smiled. He winked at her and downed a gulp of beer.

She leaned back and slipped out of her hot pants. As part of her 24/7 'happy and hard-working hooker' prostitute ethic, she never wore panties. She spread her thighs toward him, showing him the wet vivid-pink lips that split her wild brown bush.

Though still sad, his eyes widened in appreciation of her sexual display and he grabbed his crotch.

She in turn grabbed both her breasts and made a slow show of squeezing them, then of lifting them to lick each nipple in turn. His animal grunts as he watched her delighted her, serving to stoke the embers of her genital frustration into a full sexual fire.

She let go of one breast and crooked a finger at him.

"Get over here and do me," she said. "No charge tonight."

He was already stepping out of his dirty jeans. Like her he wore no underpants, and his manhood stood hard and proud, pointing at her like the barrel of a shotgun.

He kicked the denim away and came to her. She instantly grabbed his penis and deep-throated it. The gasp that exited his throat was the cry of a suffering, trapped animal being comforted and freed to range the wild again. His manhood stank of sweat, but not worse than the four or five others she'd already had in her mouth tonight. Or was it six? (It wasn't that Crystal was bad at math, just that on some days, the men all blurred into one—blowjob to blowjob on one expanding and deflating penis—particularly the truckers and bikers who all tended to be burly muscular types and smelt the same. On days like this, the only way she could tell how many men she'd had sex with was by counting her earnings. She charged $60 for a blowjob . . . *So let's see—how much do I have in my purse . . . no, that other C-note was for anal with Joey . . .*)

She sucked hard on Ambrose's penis for a while, while he trembled and gasped and ran his fingers through her hair, then she slipped her lips off him. She wanted him inside her and unable to come, not ejaculating in her mouth.

She quickly got a condom from her handbag and tore the wrapping, then slipped it on him, rolling it expertly down to his pubic bone.

"Nicely wrapped up sausage," she quipped, then attempted to lie back and spread her legs.

This proved unwise. Ambrose had way too much junk on his bed. She was instantly reminded of that by a can stabbing her in the spine.

So (while he watched her over his retrieved Coors Light) she got up, rolled all the junk up into the bed covers and flung the covers—bottles and uneaten sandwiches inclusive—down on the floor. That left the bed clear, though with the blue mattress discolored in patches like Ambrose had pissed himself in bed in the middle of a drunken sleep. The freed stink bore witness to that too, but she was too horny to be picky about fuck-locations.

"Alright," she said, getting down on her hands and knees (though with her head away from any of the piss-patches) and presenting her buttocks to him. Her vagina now felt like a hungry beast between her legs threatening to eat her up if she didn't feed it a man instead. "Come inside me, Ambrose. Hurry up!"

For Ambrose, seeing Crystal bent over like that was an irresistible view. He quickly drained the rest of his beer, then got on the bed behind her.

She moaned as he slid himself deep inside her. Oh, yeah, this was gonna be good.

And then the trashed motel room was filled with the sound of their bodies smacking together and the slurps of Ambrose entering and exiting her, and with their conjoined gasps and moans.

And yes, she'd been right, *it was* good. Exactly what she needed.

CHAPTER 4

Kat

Room 8 was exactly how Kat remembered it—a seeming acre of blue-wallpapered space containing a huge bed, a living room area with duplicate brown leather couches and a massive TV on the wall, and off towards the back, a cunningly concealed kitchenette. In addition to air conditioning the room had two ceiling fans: one oversaw the living room area, the other the bedroom. The floor was covered with brown carpet with three Oriental rugs as additional decoration. The bathroom and closets formed the rest of the room's rear and were opposite the kitchen area.

It was a complete apartment in a single room. As far as luxury went, grade A+. But then, considering their employer's wealth, should they really expect anything less? And Bella Novak hadn't struck Kat as being the sort of woman who skimped on her personal comfort either.

"Well, here we are again," Summer said. She walked across and plumped herself down on the bed, then kicked off the flip-flops she'd changed into in the car.

"Yeah," Kat agreed. "Only this time there's one less of us. I still can't believe Chuck got killed that easy."

For Kat, the first shock of Chuck's death was now past. Now, the nature of their collective loss had begun eating its way into her soul. This should have been the time for tears for a good friend who'd just died. Kat had *really* liked Chuck, though she'd contented herself with sneaked kisses at parties when Lance was too drunk or stoned to notice. Though more handsome than George Clooney, Chuck was too happy-go-lucky and womanizing for her, while Lance was stability itself. And besides, Lance had actually *asked her* to marry him, something Chuck wouldn't have done in a hundred years.

And now Chuck was dead. Dead as the gravel in the parking lot outside, dead as the walls of this motel room, dead as the air between these four walls.

She forced her grief aside. She'd weep her heart out later, when they were out of the woods. She viewed that both figuratively and literally—this motel was surrounded by trees.

She noticed her husband studying her with a moody gaze that she found unsettling.

"Yeah," he said finally, "Chuck's at the moment suffering from a bad case of rigor mortis."

Kat looked away from him. The statement, though normal Lance in its tough-guy insensitivity, seemed out of place now. Also, something about the tone of his voice additionally worried her: it might just be her imagination, but he sounded almost satisfied in a way. Or—she had a scary thought—had Lance suspected her sexual feelings for his friend—*their* friend? (Maybe he'd not been as stoned as she'd imagined at all those parties?)

"What do we do now?" she asked simply, keeping her sudden nervousness out of her voice. Then, when he didn't immediately answer, she turned her attention to Summer, who now lay barefoot in bed with her legs crossed and was staring musingly at the ceiling. Summer she felt her anger could handle.

"Hey, what was that about back there in the lobby? You were all over that guy, like melted butter on lobster."

Summer turned to look at Kat, leaning up on an elbow. "Calm down," she said, a dark warning look entering her eyes. "I'm as upset as you as to how everything's gone tonight. I mean, for fuck's sake, I just killed a guy. Mr. Rowland is just a pleasant diversion—something to take my mind off the crap that's gone down tonight."

"So what? It's not like you've never killed anyone before. Besides, it looks like you're setting up to screw him."

Summer at first looked like she'd fire back an equally angry retort, then she smiled and preened herself, combing her long blond hair (which reached down to her nipples) with her fingers. "So what if I am?"

"Duh? The obvious . . . as in he's *married* and his wife lives here too and she won't like it?" She smirked at her fellow blonde. "And he might not like you either."

"It didn't look that way to me. He was eating me up with his eyes."

37

"He was looking at your *breasts*. And with his wife there. That's both sleazy and shameful."

Summer grinned like a cat and pushed her huge chest out for Kat's appraisal. "It's called big-tit gravity, sister. It's simple physics: attraction between bodies, like with the moon and the tides. The larger a woman's breasts are—the more stellar her body—the higher her magnetic pull on the opposite sex."

"Summer, one of these days . . . Look, this guy's wife looks tough, she might whip your ass."

"Whip my ass after I just slit someone's neck? Ha ha, that's a good one. For God's sake, girl, stop trying to dissuade me, will you? If Mr. Rowland—Shane—keeps his word and calls me, we're gonna meet up, and that's final. Besides, I do threesomes too. Wifey can join in also if she likes."

"As you frigging like." Summer might be in for a surprise this time, what with her sexual issues. "You're long overdue for an ass-whipping anyway."

"Whatever." She ground her crotch at Kat, which made Kat squirm. "Hey, frigging leave me alone. And look, this is an asinine conversation to be having with Chuck lying dead out in our car anyway. If I wanna ball some guy—"

"Will you two stop your damn yapping?" Lance growled. "I'm trying to listen to the TV."

Summer scowled at Kat, then slid her thumb and forefinger across her mouth in a 'zip it' gesture.

Fuming, Kat turned and saw that Lance indeed had the TV on. He was seated on a couch facing it, channel surfing.

After glaring at Summer (who gave her the finger back) one last time, she walked over to sit by her husband.

"Any news of the robbery?" she asked.

He shook his head. "No, but then it's still too early anyway. As long as no one heard the gunshot, Thomas's body likely won't be found till morning when he doesn't open his shop." He pulled her close and hugged her. "Don't worry, darling, we'll make it. You'll see."

Kat was grateful for his strong arms around her. His touch and words gave her an injection of fresh confidence that she definitely needed right now.

Still, after a while she pulled back from him. "But, baby, I still don't understand why in the world the old man came home early."

Lance nodded grimly. "Me neither. Even stranger is how none of us noticed him arrive back at the house. I didn't see him from upstairs, you neither from down in the street. And his car wasn't downstairs either.

"He must've come in by a back entrance. That's the only explanation that makes sense to me. His missing car would seem to support that. Maybe he had a breakdown and walked the rest of the way."

"Have you called Ms. Novak yet?" Summer called airily from behind them.

Kat wished she'd shut up. *Chuck's dead and she's already working up to her next fuck. Shit!* Summer was great at being tactless.

"Not yet," Lance replied, looking back at her. "I'm thinking to wait till I've gotten rid of Chuck's body."

"Better do it now, just in case she's at a party. It'll take her a while to get here anyway. Didn't she say they'll be driving over from Springfield?"

"We're in no hurry, we've got all night. And I don't think she'll be partying on a night like this—"

"Just call her *now*. You've no idea how much socialites value their drunken revelry. It's us who're doing the hard work and taking all the risk here. To Bella, this is just a game; she can party all she wants until we call in with our success report. You heard them last week, didn't you?"

Lance nodded. "Yeah. If we fuck up, it's *our* asses that the cops are gonna be delivering to the stone motel, not theirs."

He looked hard at Summer, who nodded emphatically. "Trust me, man, call her *now*."

He looked at Kat for confirmation. Kat nodded too. It wasn't so much that she agreed with Summer, as that she felt a phone call to their present employer would serve to anchor them all a little bit more in reality, would make this moment seem just that little bit more solid to her. And also, contact with Bella Novak would reassure Kat that tonight hadn't yet fallen totally out of hand. Sitting here in this luxurious motel room, they all seemed to her adrift in a current they couldn't control, still very liable to be swept away by a sudden unexpected storm. And to Kat, who still had her gut feeling of impending disaster, that was worse that being chased and shot at by the police, because it meant that just about everything bad in the world could right now be headed their way.

On Kat's nod of assent, Lance got out his phone and dialed. When the call connected he put the phone on 'speakerphone' so the others could listen in on the conversation:

"Hello, Lance."

"Hi, Bella, we've got the diamonds." (Kat listened hard over the phone for the sound of background revelry, but could hear none. It seemed Summer was wrong about Bella partying tonight. That was a good sign.)

"Good, very good," Bella Novak replied in her cool clipped tones. "But you don't sound happy, Lance. Did something go wrong?"

"My man Chuck is dead. Thomas too. It was unavoidable. He came home early and shot Chuck."

A pregnant pause, then: "Oh, pig poop! Thomas should just have sold the gems to us in the first place, then we'd all have avoided this waste of his damn life."

Next, her voice grew warmer, softer, more human: "I'm really sorry to hear about your friend's death though. I liked him a lot and was really looking forward to getting to know him much better after this was all over." A loud (though it sounded contrived to Kat) sigh followed. "Still, life goes on, I guess. We must lay the dead to rest and conclude our brazen business. So tell me, what is our situation now? I mean, where are you?"

Lance shrugged at the others. "We're at the Sunflower as agreed."

"Okay, let's see—at the moment it's half past eleven. Give me an hour and a half. Rafael and I will be right over."

"With our money?"

Bella laughed. "Of course. Two hundred grand as agreed. You've no idea how pleased I'll be to finally have those stupid diamonds in my hands. The boss has been breathing down our necks for a month now, demanding that we buy or steal them for him. Okay, Lance, I've got to take a shower and get dressed. See you all shortly."

She hung up.

The three of them were silent for awhile.

"Well, that's taken care of then," Kat said finally. "Lance, you forgot to ask her where *she is* at the moment."

"Yeah," Summer said. "She might have meant it'll take her an hour and a half to get here *after* getting dressed, which might take an hour of its own to accomplish."

"She sounds like she's at home. Look, ladies—it doesn't bloody matter. Like I said earlier, we've got all night to do this."

Kat nodded. Now the familiar feeling of excitement over their getting paid, and paid a lot, was running through her veins. Fifty grand apiece . . . no—she did some quick arithmetic—it was sixty-five thousand each now that Chuck was dead (a tear formed in her left eye, but she blinked it away) and they were splitting three ways instead of four. No, she'd still gotten her calculations wrong: there was also that other fifty-five thousand which they'd found in Thomas's safe. That made two-fifty-five thousand dollars in all—all untraceable raw cash—for the three of them to split. Eighty-five grand each. Her lips spread in a smile. Now how was that for a single night's work?

Then Lance pulled something from his jacket and handed it over to her. She saw it was the small wooden box that contained the diamonds. As she gripped the box, an intense fear—a horrible bastard premonition—spread over her, like spilled gasoline with the Devil holding a lit match nearby.

In her horror, she almost dropped the box. Then she steadied herself and looked enquiringly at her husband. "Why are you giving this to me?"

"Hold on to it till I get back, just in case Bella arrives before then."

"Where are you going?"

He pointed out through their motel room window. "I need to hide Chuck's body somewhere before morning. We don't want any cops stopping us on a routine check and finding him in our trunk."

Kat nodded. "Yes, that's right. But where?"

Lance got up, a cold smile spreading over his unhandsome face. "What Summer said earlier gave me an idea of where to put our dead buddy."

"Which of the several smart things I said earlier are you referring to?" Summer called lazily from the bed. She'd now ditched her jacket and pants and was lying there in T-shirt and panties.

Lance waved his cellphone at her. "When you said, 'Chuck needs a bed in a graveyard, not in a hospital.' Where better to hide a corpse than in a graveyard?"

"Dude, are you serious?"

He swiped the surface of his phone and called up Google Maps. "Of course I'm serious. Can you think of somewhere better?"

And at that exact moment, Kat felt a cold, cold, shiver rush through her, and this time not just because she'd been entrusted with the stolen jewel box. Maybe it had been triggered by her husband's words, or by her dislike of funerals, with the miserable faces of the mourners and depressing 'return to ashes and dust' sermons, or by her fear that Lance might get intercepted by the police on the way and not return, but she again had that unmistakable, unshakeable feeling of something being about to go horribly wrong for all of them.

She almost leapt out of her skin in fright when Lance, after studying the screen of his phone for a while, announced, "Alright, girls, I believe I've found the right place to bury Chuck: Pleasant Street Cemetery."

And then her husband—her love—was gone, leaving just she and Summer in the motel room.

She stared at the door in confusion for a while, as if she'd rush after him to beg him not to leave her behind, or plead with him to take her along with him; as if by accompanying him she'd somehow destroy whatever hideous jinx they'd stumbled into tonight.

Then she sighed in defeat and turned and stared at Summer Wallace instead.

Summer had just gotten up from the bed and walked into the kitchenette where she was checking out the fridge. "Shit, it's empty. We should have bought beer and eats on the way. Still, it's not all bad—I've got some grass in my—"

Then she noticed how rattled Kat looked. "What's the matter with you now? C'mon, girl, he's only gone to hide Chuck's body somewhere safe."

"A whole lot more is gonna go wrong tonight." Kat held out the wooden box in her hand. "This thing is bringing us bad luck. First it was Chuck, and now—"

Summer took the small box from Kat and opened it up. She regarded the pair of stones with disdain, then shrugged at Kat. "Girl, I don't believe that mumbo-jumbo crap. Look, pull yourself together. If *you're* having"—she made finger quote marks for emphasis—"'blood diamond' tremors, how should *I* be feeling? After all, I'm the one who"—she made a deliberate 'thumb across the throat' gesture—"slit his throat like he was a goat."

Kat gaped at Summer, wondering how she could be so damn insensitive. Then she snatched the jewel box back from her, and went over and sat facing the TV again, staring at some old 30's flick with everyone in pirate garb. The blonde heroine's cleavage was almost as deep as Summer's. And that without implants.

Behind her, Summer giggled about something or other on Instagram and settled back on the bed.

Kat did her best to calm herself down. Okay, no she didn't blame Summer for killing Thomas. That was just business, and like Lance had explained during the drive over from Attleboro, it couldn't be helped anyway. At least this way the old man couldn't testify against them in court now.

Prickles of conscience or not, Kat had no interest in doing jail time. She had no intention of being the cell block bitch and feasting on dyke pussy every night.

But . . . she dropped the box of diamonds on the coffee table and stared at it, her unease unabated.

This thing we've fallen into is a can of poop, maybe a little can, but it's still a can of poop.

"Okay, I don't understand why I'm so edgy tonight," she muttered to herself, "but the sooner Bella Novak gets here and takes her pilfered property off our hands and away to her boss the better for us."

"Hey, you want some pot?" Summer called to her after a while, as a sweet haze filled the room.

"Nope, I don't want any," Kat called back. "I'm paranoid enough at the moment as it is."

CHAPTER 5

Lance

As far as Lance could tell from the online map, the directions to the Pleasant Street Cemetery were simple enough: After leaving the motel on Carver Street, you turned right onto Broadway, then almost immediately, turned left onto Center Street (which, true to its name, led into the heart of Raynham town). Then, at a point, Center Street became North Main Street. And then he just needed to keep his eyes open for the Pleasant Street junction, and turn left there for the cemetery.

He kept Google Maps open in his lap, but had no further need to look at it.

Once he had the Ford rolling down Center Street, he relaxed a little. It was approaching midnight and there was little to see. The road was deserted except for the trees, some of which looked creepily humanish in the yellow streetlights. Most houses he passed were set well back from the road, the warm yellow squares of windows at the end of their driveways comforting markers of human existence.

Otherwise, for all Lance knew, he might be motoring through a patch of desolate forest somewhere.

Despite his need (and hurry) to get the grisly deed of hiding Chuck over with, he drove at a moderate speed. Triggering some police radar now would be a total disaster.

He was glad to be away from the women. Now he could let the tears form in his eyes; show some grief over the loss of his good friend. It was a man thing: one simply didn't cry when there were girls or women about. You had to be strong, to provide the leadership they expected from you, or else they started freaking out on you. If you lost it too, your womenfolk were disappointed in you, they viewed you as less than the man they needed you to be.

Yeah, he mused, reaching up a hand and wiping the tears from his eyes, *damn bitches can weep all they like, and we can't. I mean, they tell us we should cry too, but if we do, they sneer at us!*

The tears didn't last long though. Sure, Lance was sad that Chuck had kicked the bucket, but on the positive side of things, it also meant he no longer had to worry about Kat running off with the dashing son-of-a-bitch.

Lance wasn't anybody's fool. He'd never been and never would be. Sure, he knew that Kat had been lusting after Chuck ever since they'd met. But Chuck had his playboy ethic to live up to, while Lance, who knew he wasn't handsome, was both stable and in love with Kat, and had asked her to marry him.

And Kat too, despite her lust for Chuck, valued herself highly and wasn't about to be just another of his endless bedroom conquests. Lance had respected that about her from the beginning—he liked women with standards.

Still, even though they'd been dating and having fun together, he'd been surprised that Kat had accepted his marriage proposal.

Lance readily admitted that he'd had some luck with that: At the time Kat had joined their gang as their getaway driver, Chuck had just started a dating a nightclub singer named Monique Brannigan. Their relationship didn't last long, but while it lasted, it kept Chuck off Kat. Which was long enough for Lance and Kat to tie the knot. They'd done it last April, down in Vegas following a successful heist job.

(To Lance it seemed like once Chuck had a taste of a woman's pussy, his dick got claustrophobic in there, like the vagina was choking his manhood, and he needed to escape before it squeezed his penis to death.)

But even after they'd been wed, Lance still couldn't rest. He'd kept having a vivid nightmare of waking up one morning and finding that Kat had dumped him and eloped with Chuck. Sometimes the thought put such a scare into Lance that he considered snitching on Chuck to the cops just to be rid of the romantic threat he posed.

Well at least he had, up until Freddie Roxton's Christmas party seven months ago. Despite his intense dread of an affair starting between them, Lance was certain Kat hadn't yet slept with Chuck up till that point, and it was confirmed for him that night.

Kat was correct in her worries—her husband *hadn't* been that drunk at the Christmas party. While on his way to the toilet to empty his bladder of its latest load of beer, Lance had heard a couple smooching in Freddy's bedroom. He'd stopped by the bedroom door and listened. He'd quickly recognized the lovers' voices: it was Kat and Chuck in there.

On discovering that, a numbing pain squeezed Lance's chest, so hard that he couldn't breathe. It felt like he was having a heart attack. He stood there, wanting to rush in and kill them both, but at the same time dreading the sight of what he'd likely see if he entered the bedroom—maybe Kat's legs up in the air while Chuck leaned over her, with her feet on his shoulders and his penis connecting them; or Kat on all fours like an animal, while Chuck knelt behind her and . . .

He wanted to flee past his cuckolding, but his legs felt wooden, like his feet were glued to the maroon hallway rug. So he was forced to listen to their conversation:

"No, Chuck," Kat was saying in a voice thick with wine, "I can't do it. I don't want to hurt Lance."

"So what'cha drag me in here for, if you don't wanna get nailed?"

"I don't want a screw, Chuck. This is a Christmas party, and I want to be kissed and romanced, and my goddam husband is too goddam drunk to kiss and romance me. So you'll have to do for the moment."

"C'mon, baby, stop playing hard to get."

"Chuck, get off me, goddammit! Just kiss me nicely. I already told you, we're not doing the other. I'm not hurting Lance." Her voice slurred. "I just don't want to kiss someone with vomit on his lips tonight."

"How're you gonna hurt him if he don't know? And I ain't tellin'."

"*I'll know*, and it'll hurt *me*—I'll never forgive myself. And Lance loves me, I don't wanna hurt him."

"You serious about this? How 'bout we do it up your ass then? That way you'll still be keeping the real thing clean and pure for Lance."

"No. I really like you, Chuck, I really do; you know that. But I'm not gonna cheat on Lance."

"And if he dumps you for some big-titted slut with nymphomaniac tendencies? What then? I might not be available for you then."

"Look, Chuck, stop trying to tempt me. I made up my mind on this ages ago. We're not screwing—not tonight, not ever—while I'm still married to your best friend. C'mon, dude, let's just kiss a little more then rejoin the party. And then you can either go home with that fat girl—Lynn—who's been giving you the eye all evening, or have a wonderful wank by yourself while thinking about me."

"Aw, Kat . . ."

"C'mon, baby. Kiss, kiss . . ."

A zipper sound. "Hey, look—it wants you! See how swollen it is!"

"Chuck, put your goddam penis back in your pants before I start screaming."

There was a short silence after that, then another zipper sound, then Kat said: "That's much better, baby. Now let's just cuddle and kiss."

And then, there was the sound of the pair smooching again.

Feeling like he'd just won the state lottery, Lance staggered the rest of the way to the bathroom. The pee he let out that night felt like he was having the best orgasm of his life.

After that night, Lance had begun treating Kat a whole lot better. She definitely deserved it. (It wasn't like he'd been mistreating her since their wedding, but now he became very conscious about never taking her for granted.) And oddly, instead of being pissed off at Chuck for trying to fuck his wife, he found that he now liked Chuck (already his closest friend) a whole lot better.

He didn't mind anymore when Chuck flirted with Kat. He'd discovered the incomparable satisfaction of having something that someone else really wanted but couldn't have. And Chuck would never have Kat—Lance had no intention of ever driving her away from him. That would be like putting one's favorite piece of cheese in a starving mouse's mouth.

As Lance figured it, Kat was the real winner in all this. She was saving herself the heartbreak (and guilt) of having Chuck stir up her honey pot with his lightning rod once or twice, then, like the bee he was, buzz off to the next floral-scented female in line.

Lance put his reminiscences on hold. He'd just reached the Pleasant Street intersection. After looking around for squad cars, he turned left.

The cemetery was situated a quarter-mile down the road. Once Lance had the place in view, he turned off his headlights and parked. He waited till the oncoming cars in the opposite lane had rolled past him. Then, keeping his lights off, he drove across the double yellow line and into the residence of the dead.

***

Though it lacked true walls (being surrounded instead by a two-foot-high hedge of piled rocks), Pleasant Street Cemetery had a fair-enough scattering of trees that could serve as concealment. Once inside its boundaries, Lance parked behind a large cedar tree whose branches overlapped one of the cemetery's internal routes.

Then he got out of the car to investigate his surroundings.

The first thing he checked was that he was invisible from the main road. He wasn't quite, but so long as he ducked before the cars announced by any oncoming headlights reached the cemetery, he'd be hidden enough.

Next thing he did was check out the cemetery buildings. He squinted through the darkness till he found them—about halfway deep into the grounds on his right, right at the cemetery border, and almost hidden from view by a right-angled tree formation.

Crossing the lawn like a shadow flitting between the headstones, he walked towards the buildings, then studied them from behind a tree. All their lights were off, though he imagined he heard Beethoven's 9th Symphony playing somewhere in that direction. But the music might have been coming from the houses bordering the cemetery.

He turned back to attend to the business at hand. He needed a grave to put Chuck's body in, and one that no one would be checking out soon.

This posed a clear difficulty. Pleasant Street Cemetery had lots of graves, but the headstones were all out in the open, spread out like misshapen gnomes or concrete mushrooms on a park lawn.

Lit by the moon and a penlight, it took Lance fifteen minutes to find somewhere secluded enough to leave a body and expect it not to be disturbed for a few days at least: Beneath the trees at the farthest end of the cemetery's left border, stood a solitary headstone surrounded by a metal picket fence. The tombstone bore no inscription whatsoever, as if whoever was buried here in this secluded corner of the graveyard was meant to be forgotten. Most important where Lance was concerned, no one seemed to come here—he had no idea why—the rectangle contained within the rusty pickets was full of fallen leaves and branches from the trees overhead.

Lance couldn't believe his luck. He did some quick thinking: Firstly, for some reason (he wondered what that could be—a town superstition perhaps?), no one came near this particular grave, not even the cemetery caretakers. Secondly, this tomb was so well concealed beneath its trees—twin maples with overlapping branches—that (combined with its location deep in a rear corner of the cemetery) it couldn't be detected from the main road.

He smiled for the first time since Chuck had been shot. Then, while pondering how long it took for a corpse to decay in hot weather, and how far a bad smell could travel—but would anyone even question a smell of rotting flesh in this territory of the dead?—Lance made his way back over to the Ford to get Chuck's body.

Ten minutes later, he was done. He'd laid Chuck to rest at the bottom of the pile of leaves and branches, in company of several chipmunk skeletons. The ground here was sunken in almost a foot over the submerged corpse, more proof of neglect. Chuck fit snugly into the depression.

Once done, Lance stood by the picket fence and said a short prayer for his dead buddy while making the sign of the cross several times.

There by the grave, the night felt heavy on him, liquid darkness dripping through the leafy cover. And for a moment, staring at the shroud of vegetation marking his friend's remains, he felt a heavy sadness, and in the wake of this sadness, cold chills on his scalp and down his spine. He forcibly shrugged the morbid feelings off. Chuck's death was bad enough to contend with. There were no ghosts here under the trees, just night winds caressing the corpse of a man who'd lived and loved hard, and had bitten an unexpected bullet tonight.

Then, relieved of his psychic burden, he threaded his way out of the trees and back to his car, started up the engine, and slowly drove out of the cemetery and back to the Sunflower Motel to meet up with Kat and Summer.

Bella Novak should arriving with their money any time soon.

***

What Lance didn't know, and which if he had would have kept him well away from the Pleasant Street Cemetery tonight (he'd have elected instead to chance the drive south to the neighboring town of Taunton to stash Chuck's body in either the Mayflower Hill or St.

Joseph's graveyards), was that the Raynham Police Station was situated on Orchard Street, just round the corner from the Pleasant Street Cemetery. In fact, if Lance had kept on driving instead of making that last turnoff onto Pleasant Street, he'd have driven right up to the cops' front door.

What was relevant about this was the fact that the Raynham police tended to bury bodies in the cemetery too, particularly *unclaimed* ones . . . which in this case, included the corpse on whose grave Chuck had just been left.

Which wouldn't have been too bad either, except that the solitary grave beneath the trees at the far rear corner of the cemetery was situated over there for a very good reason.

What lay under the ground there wasn't a human body. No one was really sure what it was. It was something everyone desired to see the last of, but didn't know what else to do with. The thing had proven impossible to destroy. Fire—the usual last resort in such cases—had proved as powerless to decompose it as acid baths and pulverizing forces. After six futile attempts to reduce the thing to its component atoms in an increasingly hotter furnace, the crematorium staff had given up.

So where safer than a cemetery to dispose of something you didn't want dug up? As well as wanted out of both sight and mind? At least it had seemed to be dead. And up until tonight no one had had any reason to assume otherwise.

But unfortunately, tonight . . .

And what was ironic in this case was that the occupant of the secluded grave wasn't even going to be dug up. The damned thing was going to dig itself out of its confinement . . .

***

Six feet below Chuck's body, the 'thing' stirred. Its long-dormant senses were instantly as sharp again as those of a shark smelling blood across two miles of water.

Galvanized by the pungent odor of Chuck's blood, it slowly unfroze out of its almost three-year-long dormancy. After its last enforced 'death,' it had tried to live again many times, but the conditions had never been right.

50

Once, it had almost awakened. That was when an overhanging branch had snapped in a storm and crashed on its grave, in the process braining a family of chipmunks. The rodents' spilled blood had sung to it deep in its slumberous chapel of undeath, but the lure of brain matter their tiny heads promised had been too minuscule to revive it.

But now . . . now . . .

The smell of the blood over it provided it with sufficient strength to climb up to the source of the life-giving scent. This was phantom-strength—similar to the oxygen-debt human muscles built up during strenuous exercise—an emptiness that would be recharged once the target was reached.

It first burst out of the wooden coffin it had been buried in, then dragged itself up through the hard-packed dirt of its grave.

Finally its hands reached what it sought, the head of the corpse who'd been left on its grave. With a silent howl of triumph, it burst up through the grass that had it covered for two years, up into the night.

And then, with its body still buried in the earth, it spread its massive jaws wide, and with a single bite, bit out the entirety of the dead man's brain.

It chewed the brain and chewed it and swallowed it, feeling its body fill with strength anew. The brain was delicious soft meat in its mouth, sweet like candy was to a child, as addictive a craving as chocolate was to the overweight.

Invigorated, the creature now pulled itself completely out of the ground.

Had anyone been there beneath the thick tree-shadow on this dark night, they would have been appalled by the emerging thing's appearance, just like the police who'd buried it here had been.

The creature—named Brainchew by the Raynham police because of its peculiar diet—looked like a short, muscular man with hide-like gray skin and a massive two-foot-high head. Its head—thrice the size of a man's—gave it an overall height of over six feet.

It had three fingers on each hand and three toes on each foot.

It was completely hairless. It was also sexless—all it had between its legs were folds of warty skin. As far as it knew, it was the only one of its kind. But it felt no need to reproduce: it would live until the stars in Earth's night sky all went dim.

The features of its massive gray head? Brainchew's eyes were red circles buried deep in the folds of its elongated face. Its nose was small, with a single vertical slit of nostril; despite which the creature's olfactory sense was a hundred times keener than any human's. It had very small ears and poor hearing.

The most prominent feature of its HUGE head, however, was its HUGE mouth. Brainchew's mouth was rimmed outside with thick ugly lips. Inside, the yawning maw was ringed with black thorny teeth that bore more resemblance to vulture talons or alligator claws than any known vertebrate dentition. Also, its teeth were all of different sizes, and set with no logical arrangement in its jaw.

Compared to Brainchew, even sharks had neat teeth.

But even the great white sharks, the undisputed kings of the elasmobranch kingdom and feared as they were by all in the sea, never had the power in their jaws that Brainchew did.

***

Brainchew shook itself. As two years of earth dropped off its rough skin, it looked around to determine its current location.

It wasn't smart—its massive head contained only a tiny brain—and memory and cognition came slowly to it. As a general rule, Brainchew found concentration and deep thinking a chore. Better, it felt, to simply 'live'—feed and feel.

Finally though, it understood where it was. It was in a cemetery, a human 'dead place,' where expired humans were kept.

It stepped out of the tree cover and surveyed the moonlit expanse of the graveyard with its tiny eyes, the rows and dots of the headstones. Its nose took in the scent of the freshly mown grass. The occasional wreath of flowers on the more recent graves added an unpleasant sweetness to the night.

Now it could smell the many bodies underground: rows of atrophied and rotted brains, worm-riddled brains, decades-and-centuries-ancient dried brains.

It felt disgust. All the buried brains were corrupted, diseased, time-corroded. Not one of them was worth digging up its corpse for.

Brainchew liked its food fresh and sweet and tender. Brains tasted best of all plucked straight from the human skull. Then they had that slick coating of blood all over them. And after eating the delicious, soft, head-flesh that seemed to dissolve in its mouth, Brainchew loved to slake its thirst with the blood it got from ripping out the fresh corpse's throat and drinking its fill. The red liquid always tasted best fresh from the body too.

It peered back through the leaves, down at the dead man who lay on its recent grave, a huge concave shape bitten out of the back of his head. Too bad the man's blood had all leaked away or clotted in his veins—there was none to drink.

The reborn monster stroked its misshapen jaw with a gnarled gray finger. What should it do now?

At that moment, a southeasterly wind blew through the graveyard.

Brainchew instantly stiffened. It had caught on the wind the smell of the man who'd dropped the corpse here.

It locked on to the scent, keeping it in focus after the wind changed direction.

Even over the distance separating them, it could smell the man clearly, as clearly as if it could see him.

The man had just stopped moving fast and was meeting more people—two women—inside a room that dimmed all their smells.

But there was something else . . . a knowledge even more exciting and interesting to Brainchew than the wonderful promise of living food and drink. It realized that it knew the place where the man was now. A single word formed in its mind: *Sunflower*. Yes, it knew that place. It had been there before. It had even 'lived' there (a strange concept to its primitive mind).

And (its nonhuman heart beat faster with anticipation as it determined this), besides the man who'd been here and the two women, there were many other people at the 'Sunflower' place. More delicious food and drink.

And then, with a combination of rage and dread, it smelt *him*: the human called 'Ambrose.' The hated Ambrose—the one responsible for imprisoning it here in this field of the human dead.

Though it initially trembled and quailed at the thought of being shut away in the darkness again, of being re-imprisoned underground, the monster finally made up its mind—it was going to the 'Sunflower.' It was going there to feed and slake its thirst, and to maim and to kill.

And this time it would kill Ambrose also.

That infernal determination fixed in its little brain, Brainchew looked up from staring at the moonlit graves for a moment to regard the moon itself. The cold light on its face filled the monster with a certain satisfaction—it was a delight to see the moon again, after so, so long.

Finally, Brainchew turned northward and tramped out of the Pleasant Street Cemetery. The 'Sunflower' smell was thick in its nostrils now—that place packed full of juicy feeding—and soon it was running to arrive there quickly, running faster than a terrified fox.

Then it smelt water. A moment later, it was plunging into Johnson Pond and swimming across to its far side. A blur of gray motion as fast as a speedboat running on hell-fuel.

And then, barely two minutes later, it was up on land again and once more running, dashing through the woods between King's Pond and North Main Street, racing harder than before towards the Sunflower Motel's unsuspecting guests.

And when, a short while later, it reached Center Street, and the man-scent it had been tracking, previously a thin trail, now thickened sweetly like spilled blood clotting, Brainchew raised its head and laughed its noiseless laugh.

Yes, it was going to feed tonight, for sure.

CHAPTER 6

Dusty & Shane

"You know, I think we're being hasty here," Dusty Rowland told her husband. "And that could be financially detrimental to us."

He leaned forward. "What d'you mean?"

The time was 00:26. Husband and wife were both seated behind the reception desk in the motel lobby. Shane kept turning the bloodstained hundred dollar bill over in his palm. (A few moments earlier, the gray Ford belonging to the guests in Room 8 had just returned to the motel after leaving for about thirty minutes.) On any regular night, they'd have both have been planning on retiring by now.

Dusty explained: "What I'm trying to say is, I think there's more to this than first met the eye. You know that old expression 'being unable to see the wood for the trees?' Trying to hustle more money out of Bella Novak may be the wrong way to go about this."

Shane considered the bill in his hand. "I don't follow you."

Dusty controlled her impatience. "Shane, what we need to find out, is *why* Bella hired those four in the first place. Think about it for a moment: they're clearly lowlifes, and she's high-society. They're meeting here and she pays us to forget the meeting. So, they've clearly done something *illegal* for her." Her brown eyes gleaming with excitement, Dusty leaned forward and pointed to the bank note in Shane's hand. "And it likely involves *a lot* of money. Rich folk tend to be stingy as hell except when they're gonna get something out of you."

Shane scratched his head. "Hmm, you got a point there, darling." He scrutinized the note again, his handsome face creasing up. "Okay, so what can you tell us, blood money?" Then he frowned at Dusty, who was rearranging her hair.

She stared back at him, her expression expectant. "What are you thinking?"

"It's a robbery," Shane said. "Has to be." He stared at the hundred dollars again. "I'm confused tho'—Bella Novak looked way too rich for money to be *her* motive . . ."

"Jewelry then," Dusty said, feeling a sudden pleasant thrill rush through her at the thought.

Shane nodded. "Very likely. But how does that help . . . ?" Then his expression turned worried. "There's also the possibility that she simply hired them to kill someone—maybe her husband's mistress." He gave an involuntary shudder. "In that case, trying to strong-arm Bella may backfire on us. She could have them murder us too."

Dusty considered that option: "No, Shane, *no*. Yes, she might have sent them to kill someone, but if she did, it was because she wanted something that person had."

He drummed nervous fingers on the desktop. "What makes you so sure of that?"

"Think, baby, think! Those four . . . I mean, three now, are here tonight to meet her again, right? Why would that be? You figure it out."

Shane mused a bit on that. "Hmmm, you mean she's coming to collect what she sent them to get?"

Dusty nodded. "Exactly. Meaning they still have whatever it is on them." Her gaze turned predatory. "We need to find out what it is they've got, and if it'll be worth our while to steal it from them."

"If we steal it, we can't fence it—if they killed someone to get it, it'll be too hot. The law will be on to us in a minute."

"If so, we'll put the squeeze on Bella instead. She'll just pay us instead of them. And, believe me, baby, she'll happily pay us extra not to tell the police she ordered it stolen in the first place."

Dusty carefully regarded her husband's face now, trying to gauge his reaction to what she was suggesting. While Shane wasn't exactly a coward (and anyway, how did one test that quality in a man in modern times anyway?), he wasn't by nature a violent, 'macho' sort of man. (To her bedroom delight—and endless angst outside of it—he was the kind of man often referred to as 'a lover not a fighter.') She could clearly see that she'd piqued his interest—just like herself, Shane wanted more money for the motel. (And maybe to wine and dine his mistresses too?) But would he do what needed doing when push came to shove?

She shoved anyway. He already looked nervous; if she gave his negative train of thought sufficient time to work up a head of steam, she might as well forget about robbing the robbers.

She pointed to the pump-action shotgun lying on the middle of the shelves built into the rear of the reception desk. It was loaded in case of a robbery or break-in. "One shot each if necessary."

"This is getting really dangerous," Shane said. "They'll have guns too."

"It's less dangerous than you think. And"—the realization had just come to her—"they've got money in there with them too. And I think it's a lot."

He stiffened momentarily and she knew she'd hooked him. (That was something Dusty had discovered since being married: if a woman was observant enough, after a while she knew exactly what button to push to get the desired effect out of her man. Some things merely required taking off one's panties [or putting on silk stockings and high heels *and then* taking off one's panties]; others required a blowjob or letting the guy have your anus. In tough cases like this though, you couldn't buy your husband's cooperation with your body. And then you needed to know what to *say*. Sometimes you prodded his ego, at other times his conscience or sense of ethics. In this case, she was prodding his greed.) Jewelry that they couldn't offload might not interest Shane, but the prospect of getting their hands on some cold hard cash did.

But . . . he still looked a little unconvinced. Dusty hid her irritation with her man. She wished he'd just grow a damn pair already!

"We don't know for sure that they've money in there," Shane said.

"No, we don't know that, baby."

She pointed to the banknote on the desktop with its smearing of dry red. "Do you remember *how* Summer gave you the money?"

"How'd you mean: *how?*"

"I mean, do you recall where she took the cash from to pay you?"

He thought a moment. "Sure, she pulled it from her right pants pocket."

"Shane, hon, reason with me. Ask yourself this question: how many times in your life have you ever seen a woman take money out of her *pocket?*" She waited until his eyes widened with understanding, then added: "Yes, baby. "*Men* keep money in their pockets. We women keep our money in our purses, or in our bras. The strange placement of that hundred dollars means Summer picked it up off the floor, likely in a rush after they'd killed whoever they did. I suspect the cash spilled from a bundle of bills and it was a rush to pick them all up. And I don't think lady robbers take their handbags along on jobs, so into her pocket they went. D'you get it?"

He nodded slowly, his lips trapped between a grin and a frown. "Okay, so they've got money in there with them then." Then he scowled. "So yeah, alright, baby, this is all great as theory, but if we're doin' it, we need a workable plan."

She nodded, then after a quick glance outside through the glass door, said, "I've got one in mind."

"Okay, let's hear it."

"First thing we need to do is find out exactly where they went, what they've done, and how much they've got on them."

Shane winced. "And how do we do that? Dusty, this is just getting more and more complicated."

Dusty smiled. "Don't worry, darling, that part's easy. You're gonna call Summer as promised and romance her like crazy till she tells you everything."

"*What?*"

Dusty grinned. "Shane, I know sluts like that. She's dying to fuck you. And you're dying to fuck her too." She pointed to the lobby phone. "Alright, call the top-heavy bimbo up and put the make on her."

"Hell no."

"Do it . . . do it. Do it!"

Shane picked up the phone and dialed. "Hello, this is Mr. Rowland from the Sunflower reception. Is this Room 8? . . . Yes? . . . Please can I speak to Summer? . . . No, nothing important. . . . Hi, Summer, yeah it's Shane. So, how're you guys settling in? . . . Nah, baby, nothing's wrong. I just remembered that we'd planned to meet up and finish that story I was telling you earlier. . . . Dusty? Oh she's gone off to bed; I'm free now. . . . Okay, I'll meet you by the passageway. . . . Yeah, the split in the front block. . . . Kiss you too, sweets."

He hung up and stared guiltily at Dusty. "She said . . ."

"Don't worry," she replied, "I can imagine what she said. At the moment you could likely squeeze two liters of pussy juice out of her panties." Then she smiled coldly at her husband, who seemed suddenly nervous. "You know, Shane, you were really good at that.

Too good, in fact. I wonder how many times you've actually made similar calls like this behind my back?"

His face turned stony. "For God's sake, don't start with your damn jealousy trip again! This was your idea!"

"Yes, it was!" Her eyes flashing, she nodded fiercely back. Shane grimaced, it looked like another fight was about breaking out between them.

But then Dusty said calmly, "But yes, not tonight—we haven't the time. Bella Novak could arrive at any moment now."

Now that she was sending her husband out into the warm July night to seduce another woman, Dusty felt incredibly conflicted. This went completely against the grain of everything she believed in where marital fidelity was concerned. She winced internally, but kept a straight face. *Am I actually doing this crap? Willingly letting another woman have my husband?* Okay, it was just once, and for thirty minutes at most. *But what if he likes her more than me, and goes back later for second and third helpings?*

She couldn't get the blonde's huge breasts out of her mind, the way they swung tauntingly left and right as she walked, like they each had secret seductive lives of their own separate from their owner.

But, Dusty conceded to her unvoiced shame, for a comfortable and richer life ahead for herself and her husband, the disgusting price had to be paid.

She sighed deeply, which made Shane look worriedly at her. "No, I'm fine, go on," she answered his look, then forced a laugh out between her lips. "You go and do what needs to be done. Go pump Summer for information. Pump her exquisitely hard."

Watching Shane's ass muscles shift in his jeans as he strode towards the front door (and knowing that they'd soon be pushing his manhood deep between Summer's legs), she once again had misgivings. *Maybe I should have sucked him off first? That way, there'd be nothing left for . . . oh, shit, what am I thinking? We need him to do her and do her real good, so she gasps out everything she knows.*

(Most women Dusty knew were experts at gushing out confidences after having an orgasm, as if the sexual release had in turn untied the cord of secrets binding their tongues. It seemed a universal truth: satisfy a woman properly in bed and she'd tell you everything she knew. [Men were reputedly better at keeping their brains and sex organs separate. But history argued otherwise: or else how had Mata

Hari and the Russian 'flame-haired beauty' Anna Chapman been so successful?] Dusty was basing her opinion on personal experience too: once Shane had made her come, she always felt an intense need to talk to him, to share herself with him, to make the moment more than just a communion of their flesh. And so she yapped happily away, and if a shared confidence somehow got tangled up in her net of self-exposure, so be it.

And from what she'd heard, the lesbians were even worse—two satisfied and tingling-in-afterglow vaginas meant twice as many secrets being revealed.

Maybe the only women safe from damning afterglow-tattling were nuns, hookers, and those middle-aged society sluts—the ex-model celebrity whores with their own reality TV shows—the type that were so cold in person that you imagined they didn't own freezers at home, they just sipped some water and bingo—instant ice cubes. [Dusty had met lots of the type during her modeling days, and had always regretted being introduced to them.])

Shane vanished out the reception door. Dusty watched it swing to. Okay, the die was cast now; their plan was in action. She stared grimly down at the pump-action shotgun for a moment, then picked it up and double-checked that it was fully loaded.

CHAPTER 7

The Monster

As it neared the Sunflower Motel, Brainchew slowed its run to a walk.

During the course of its endless resurrections into the human world it had learnt the value of caution. Most of all, like an animal in the wild—the mighty lion or tiger—it had learnt to fear man. True, humans were weak, puny things, easy to kill and feed on, but—for some reason beyond the scope of Brainchew's limited mental powers—humans were also the most dangerous creature of all.

It couldn't count the number of times that some man or woman had sent it back to sleep in the darkness.

Brainchew had no true concept of time. It wasn't intelligent enough to count passing days or years. It slept, it woke, it fed until it slept again. All its sleeps were forced on it, and some had lasted longer than others; that was as much as it knew. This last sleep had been particularly short.

It had no desire to sleep again. No, not ever again. So, although it wasn't an animal, it acted with the instinctive cunning of the predator beast.

It had arrived at the start of the short motel drive. It stood there, in the border of trees, smelling its intended victims. Yes! In addition to the sweet mingled scents of the others, there was a woman in the first building (from which a man was just exiting). And behind the front block it could smell *Ambrose*.

AMBROSE!!! Oh, how it *hated* Ambrose!

Brainchew considered its options. It was currently too hungry for revenge, the run up from the 'dead place' had sapped its strength. It must feed quickly. Should it kill the woman in the building with the air-like windows, or the man who'd just left there and was walking right-to-left away from it?

Then it smelt something else, something smaller and close-at-hand, coming up along the road.

It turned and stared down at the creature.

***

The dog stared back up at Brainchew. It was a brown mongrel, attracted this way by the creature's strange smell.

It walked a few paces further towards Brainchew. Brainchew stretched out a hand to grab its head. The dog waited till the hand was close, then it bit it hard and deep and turned around and dashed off yelping, its tail between its legs. It had no idea that it had just escaped its death, but it could tell from smell alone that this was a horrible nasty creature it wanted nothing to do with.

The mongrel didn't stop running till it was three miles away. Then it fell exhausted into a patch of grass and lay panting with its tongue lolling from its mouth.

***

Brainchew stared regretfully after the fleeing canine. Dog brains were nutritious too—salty and sweet—just not as large and filling as the human kind. It took more of them to satisfy its craving.

It looked back towards the motel. The woman still sat inside the nearby building, holding a metal tube it recognized as the type that ejected those painful metal pellets.

The man who'd been walking away from it was now out of sight. Brainchew located him by smell: he was in the space between the two halves of the front building. Should it attack him or the woman?

Then its concentration was broken again. Another smell was approaching it, human this time. Once more it turned from regarding the motel to study the road.

Yes, its eyes confirmed, there *was* someone coming. A human who smelt incredibly old and dirty.

***

The old wino stared at the monster blocking his path without a flicker of fear. He was way too drunk to be afraid of some short, naked man, even if the guy had the largest head he'd ever seen.

"Hey, stop blocking my damn way!" he croaked with a drunken wave of his arms. "I gotta gets me down to Rudy's Truck Stop 'fore they close." While speaking, he lurched left and right. "Get the damn fuck outa my way, ya long-headed gray asshole—I gotta buy me some J.D.! And puts some goddam clothes on, goddam you—no one wants to see yer damn weiner!" Then the expression in the old drunk's bloodshot eyes turned puzzled. "Hey, where's yer damn weiner anyway? And if you'se a girlie, where's your damn tits? Or is you one of those trannys?"

Then, as the 'long-headed gray asshole' still didn't grant him passage, but kept coming at him regardless and blocking the way even more, the wino's eyes flashed with a sudden spark of recognition.

"Hey, don't a know you?" he asked with a fevered expression on his sweaty face, his voice a garbled croak like he'd expire from lack-of-alcohol poisoning if he didn't have his next drink quick.

Then a big smile spread over his cracked lips. "Yeah, *I do* know you! WWE! You'se that famous masked wrestler, Rey Mysterio Jnr. Damn pleased to meet ya, buddy, I'se a big fan of yers! Sorry I didn't recognize ya with yer new mask—looks like Kamala's." He extended grimy fingers for a handshake. "Hey, what'cha think? Let's both of us get down to Rudy's an' have us some drinks. Man, I'se tickled. Fancy meeting ya out here tonight. I'se got—"

Then 'Rey Mysterio Jnr.' grabbed hold of his head.

The old wino had no idea what happened next, just that suddenly he felt a horrible pain in his neck and his head seemed to have been twisted round behind his back so he could now see the road back the way he'd been coming.

Hey, Rey, what'cha doing, buddy? Let go a me—this ain't no wrestling match! The wino thought the words, but with the air passages in his neck twisted shut, there was no way for him to vocalize them.

And then there was a sharp pain in the back of his head and his drunken thoughts cut out for good.

***

63

The first thing Brainchew did after killing the wino was to drag his corpse off the road and under the cover of the trees.

Then it took its time eating the wino's brain, savoring the soft meat's taste as it first crumbled on its tongue, then slid unhindered down its throat. Somehow, the old man's dirtiness added a unique flavor to the brain. And Brainchew, even though it didn't know what alcohol was, got a distinct unfamiliar buzz from the substance, both from that which had spread through the old drunk's brain and gotten him inebriated, and also from the booze in his bloodstream.

Yes, the wino tasted good. It was good to eat fresh brains again after so, so long. And there were many more brains waiting for it in the Sunflower. And it was going to eat them all tonight.

CHAPTER 8

Dusty

At her desk in the motel lobby, Dusty finished inspecting the shotgun and replaced it on the shelf. Then she sank back into dour consideration of what she'd just sent her husband off to do.

A sudden sharp sound sliced through her black mood. Had she just heard someone yelp in pain at a distance? Or had it been a dog?

She listened hard, instinctively leaning forward on the reception desk and angling her ears towards the door. Her hand inched slowly forward till it rested on the stock of the shotgun. Tension increased in her by leaps and bounds.

Dusty remained poised like that for a full minute, then, when the noise didn't repeat, she decided she'd just heard a branch fall from one of the trees bordering the lot. Her tenseness uncoiled and she went back to brooding on how she'd just traded her husband's penis to some big-breasted slut for money.

Being a madam sucks, she thought.

CHAPTER 9

The Gang

"So, guys, I'm off to get lay-aid," Summer sang enthusiastically, her eyes agleam.

"Hey, look," Lance protested, though he knew he was wasting his time. "How about waiting till *after* Bella's been here?"

Summer pouted and squeezed her massive breasts at him, which made Kat wince. "C'mon, man, how long does it take to ball a guy? Fifteen minutes tops. I'll be back before you remember I'm gone. Besides, we've been waiting for Bella and Rafael to show up for a full hour now—an hour she's likely been spending bathing and choosing which set of pantyhose to wear."

"Yeah, but she's the client—"

The ring of his phone cut him off. "It's her," he mouthed at the two women, then accepted the call.

"Hello? . . . Yes, Bella, we're still waiting. . . . What? . . . Aw, c'mon, woman . . . Alright, how soon? . . . Yeah, sure, we'll *still* be here when you get here."

He hung up looking pissed off. "I don't frigging believe it: Bella Novak, who sent us on this fool's errand, says she's been delayed. She apologized, then said something unavoidable came up that she just had to attend to before leaving home and as a result they set out late. We've possibly another half-hour to spend waiting for her. We're looking at at least a two o'clock ETA now."

Summer smirked. "I told you so. You don't know these executive chicks like I do. Sure, it's her boss's cash she's spending, but one major perk of a PA job is power tripping and burning through a monthly expense account that most people wished was their yearly salary. Something unavoidable came up? Ha ha ha—that's just a cute way of telling us that her boyfriend Rafael got an erection and she had to suck

66

him dry first." She grinned at them. "And if the bitch can fuck on our time, so can I."

While Lance was on the phone, Summer had been getting dressed, pulling on her previously discarded denim pants. Now she zipped them up, slipped her pretty feet into her flip-flops, and headed out the door.

As it swung shut behind her, Lance remembered something. "Hey, Summer, wait!"

Too late. The door had already shut, and Summer Wallace, her eyes glimmering with lust, had vanished like a sexual whirlwind.

"Summer!" Lance called at the window.

"Hey, let her go," Kat snapped angrily. "At least we don't have to listen to her whine about how horny she is anymore." Then she sobered thoughtfully. "You know, one of these days, she's gonna pick the wrong guy and she's gonna wind up with her throat slit."

Lance grimaced at the image. "All I was gonna ask her is if she had any smokes in her purse. I'm all out."

"You know Summer—all she ever has is pot."

"They may have cigarettes in reception. I'll walk down there and see if the wife is awake."

"Don't bother. They only had magazines, potato chips, toothbrushes and shaving kits; and his wife won't be there to serve you anyway. You heard Summer: According to the randy Mr. Rowland, his missus has retired to bed; which is why he's free to philander." She winced in disgust. "And right under his wife's nose too. My god, you men are just dogs."

Then, her expression turning grim, she pointed to the wall clock. "Lance, can't you just wait till morning? It's almost one o'clock."

Lance shook his head. "Nicotine is a harsh mistress, baby." Then he grinned. "Brighten up, Kat, at least I'm not cheating on you with another *woman*." Then he correctly read her expression and asked, "What's eating you, baby?"

She pointed to the little brown jewel box on the coffee table. "*That's* what's eating me, darling. I really don't want to be left alone with it. Alright, I know I'm being silly and irrational, but now, with the 20/20 vision of hindsight, accepting this job looks to have been a bad idea from the beginning. Something we should never have taken on."

Lance thought awhile. He was tempted to snap at her to get a grip on herself, but . . . yeah, she was right: it felt odd to him also; this *had* been a rather weird night so far. He too felt jumpy from having to go hide Chuck in that graveyard, and also from Bella Novak delaying her arrival. They should have made the exchange by now, should already have the cash in hand.

And now, he had no cigarettes either. A smoke would cool him down, but . . . aw, shit!

A surge of anger rushed through him. All these damn unforseens were almost becoming a trend tonight! If there was another one, he'd . . . !

Looking at his wife's seriously sober face though, Lance clamped down on his own unease. The last thing he needed now was Kat freaking out.

"Alright," he told her. "I'll stay with you till Summer gets back in."

CHAPTER 10

Rafael

1:03 a.m.

The black Cadillac Escalade rolled through the darkness, its yellow headlights the eyes of a mechanical panther prowling the night.

Rafael Marquez, the luxury SUV's driver, glanced into the rearview. Front and back the road was deserted, he was just looking at Bella. She lay back restfully on the right rear seat, luxuriating in the vehicle's warmth. Her eyes were shut, her bosom rising and falling slightly as she catnapped.

(They'd set out thirty minutes late from the mansion because their billionaire boss Ellis—who had chronic wanderlust and never remained long in the USA—had suddenly called in from Monaco to give Bella the details of some ancient occult scrolls he wanted bought *immediately* from an antique dealer down in Buenos Aires. And then Bella had had to call him back to confirm that she'd ordered the items. This wouldn't normally have caused a delay—Bella Novak was an efficient woman and could have handled everything in the car on their way—but . . . she'd been painting her fingernails when he'd called, and making bank payments on a Stuart Hughes' iPad 2 Gold History Edition with wet nail paint on her hands had proved very complicated. Afterwards, while cursing Ellis, she'd wiped her ruined hands clean— the pink paint had smeared all over her fingers and even gotten on the tablet screen—and gotten in the car.

Rafael, who was very used to her, had simply laughed as they drove off.

The black car sped past the streetlight at an intersection, and for a moment Rafael's rear view of Bella was crystal clear. As if the slumbering woman felt his eyes on her, she smiled.

He returned his attention to the road, immediately needing to nurse the Escalade through a sharp turn.

He wished he could sleep like Bella did. She really didn't seem to care too much about whatever it was that their employer demanded of them.

Rafael, though, kept feeling the prick of his conscience, like someone was sticking pins into his soul. *The boss really needs to stop pulling stunts like this. One of these days one of them is going to backfire big-time again.*

But Rafael knew this was mere wishful thinking. It would never happen. Ellis Drake was addicted to acquiring occult objects, the stranger and more forbidden the better. He bought magical relics the way kids bought candy. He shipped them in from around the globe and kept them at home in his Drake Mansion. And when they caused trouble, as they invariably did, he was never at hand to deal with the problem—that miserable lot fell to Rafael and Bella.

And this case was even odder than usual. What they were on their way to collect now wasn't even magical. Mrs. Drake had merely seen the diamonds in a magazine somewhere and commented that she liked them. And Ellis had told Bella to get them for her—whatever they cost. As always, money was no object here.

Which had led to . . .

Rafael winced. Sure, he respected Mr. Drake—he was a swell guy to work for—but he couldn't understand how the boss could approve of their hiring those four lowlifes to rob harmless Mr. Thomas. That was going from merely reckless behavior to the criminal.

And from what Bella had told him, the crooks had killed the poor old guy.

Just the thought of that made Rafael Marquez cringe. *Shit, I practically predicted to Mr. Drake that this would happen. That Lance chap is a textbook psycho if I ever saw one. At first glance, I just knew the guy was a loose cannon.*

So now, Thomas was a dead fish, and the police would be asking questions. And all for what? Some crappy gemstones that Louise Drake had taken a fancy to?

Rafael was uncertain which was darker—the night outside the car or the inside of his soul. Thomas's death was a burden on him that he didn't need; the sort of emotional drain that made him question if the money he got paid—and it was a whole damn lot—was worth the psychic leeching he kept having to endure.

Sure, neither he nor Bella would ever dare rat to the cops. That would be suicidal. *Oh yeah—we hired those hoodlums in the first place, and if the police find that out, we're both facing some serious jail time.*

To calm himself, Rafael took a hand off the wheel and touched the dashboard to turn on the radio. Then, remembering that Bella was asleep behind him and that the noise would likely wake her up, he changed his mind.

He sped on through the night towards the Sunflower Motel, their destination. The others would be settled in Room 8 now, having gotten the key from the motel owners.

The motel owners . . . hmmm. Rafael's thoughts wavered on memory lane for a few moments:

While paying for Room 8 the first time, Rafael had thought he recognized the lady owner, Mrs. Rowland, from down in NYC.

She looked like the super-hot runway model who'd once slapped him in the face for pinching her tight ass. It had happened five years ago, at a party to which he'd chauffeured the boss and his (then) fiancée Louise Chung.

"C'mon, baby, you're just a damn driver, and I *never* fuck the hired help," she'd sniped nastily while he rubbed his smarting cheek. "Go pick up one of the maids."

Rafael had been mortified, and rightly so, he conceded. This girl was so, so, so far out of his league she could have been an airplane and he a skateboard. Both were means of locomotion for sure, but the difference between them couldn't be disputed. He didn't know what had gotten into him to act like he did. It had to be the Devil. But her buttocks were so inviting in her spandex leggings that he couldn't help but have a feel of them.

Even after she'd slapped and insulted him, he'd kept gaping at her through the crowd, amazed that any woman could be that breathtakingly gorgeous.

Later, that same model had gotten drunker than a fish sautéed in 100% proof moonshine.

Then, at about 2 a.m., when Mr. Drake was ready to go home, he'd sent Rafael upstairs to find Louise, who'd earlier complained of a headache and was resting in one of their host's bedrooms.

Rafael had climbed up to the second floor then checked the doors on either side of the corridor. He'd knock politely on each door, then enter the room to see.

The first four bedrooms were empty. However, even before reaching the fifth door, he could hear that it was occupied. Loud carnal grunts spilled through a crack where it had been left slightly ajar.

Still, he'd knocked before peeking—it would be embarrassing if he'd stumbled on his boss's fiancée in bed with another woman.

No answer came from inside the room, so he looked in, and . . . WOW!

Rafael could only gape. It was the same incredibly beautiful model who'd snubbed him downstairs. She was naked except for her white high heels, and was getting screwed by two beefy guys at once. Her legs were up in the air, her delicate feet up on the shoulders of the guy pounding away in her ass and . . . her nose was powdered as white as the peaks of the Alps with cocaine.

She was rubbing more of the white powder on the head of the other guy's penis.

Then Rafael had leaned a little too heavily on the door and it had swung inward so the trio had seen him.

She'd giggled on recognizing him. "Hey, guys, look—it's Ralfie, my favorite driver." Then she'd crooked a finger at him. "Come on in and join my party, baby. I've got enough holes in my body for everyone."

Rafael had almost hurried off instead. Ellis was ready to leave and would have a fit if he dallied. But then he'd reconsidered: Why not? Even the errand boy needed his fun sometimes. Besides, any man who turned down a woman of such high grade as this didn't deserve to be called a man. Such a betrayer of the male sexual cause should simply hand in his hetero card and turn gay immediately.

The boss and his girlfriend can wait, he'd decided.

Rafael had entered the bedroom. He'd stripped off in a flash and climbed onto the bed with the other two men. The beautiful woman instantly put her hand on his member and guided it into her mouth. Then, once his penis felt harder than steel, she'd spat it out and began sprinkling cocaine on its tip. Then she'd pushed away the man sweating between her legs, and shoved Rafael down there to replace him, slotting him smoothly into her honey box.

Ooooh! Even now the memory hit Rafael like a freight train. Entering her body had felt like entering Paradise. The orgasm that he'd had with her had been . . . oh my sweet God!

And next, he remembered her grabbing his balls in a vise-like grip when he got up to leave. "Uh uh, Ralfie. You gotta fuck my ass too first!"

She'd sucked him to erection again then rolled over onto her belly. One of the other two men (who were both stoned out of their minds) pulled the cheeks of her buttocks apart to grant Rafael easy access to her anus. "Just park your limo in my rear garage, Ralfie," she'd called back, giggling. "You'll find it's very spacious and accommodating."

Rafael had parked his 'limo' in her 'rear garage.' He'd discovered she hadn't been lying either about how 'spacious and accommodating' it was. And again, when he'd come, it had felt like she was killing him. The pleasure had been that intense, like she was pulling two fat strings of licorice out of his testicles.

He'd staggered out of there almost too drained to resume looking for Louise. Damn, what a woman that one was!

And so, staring at Mrs. Rowland behind the motel desk a week ago, he'd wondered: was this the same woman?

He'd doubted it. What would an awesome, super-hot, testicle-expanding bitch like that—Dusty something-or-other her name was, if his memory served him right—be doing in a nothing town like this, and running *a motel*, of all things? And putting on bags of weight? No, he had the wrong woman. *That* Dusty was likely over on a Japanese or Hong Kong catwalk now, wowing everyone and breaking hearts—if she wasn't long dead of a drug overdose. Those supermodels certainly partied hard.

But she had been super-hot. For real. (Way, way, way hotter in Rafael's opinion than the retired supermodel currently asleep on the Escalade's rear seat.) Just the memory of her was giving him an erection.

They'd reached the outskirts of Charlton. Rafael's thoughts returned to the present. The night sky was heavy with clouds. The cold but damp breeze blowing in through the car window made him think it was raining up ahead.

Well, he consoled himself, for he and Bella, tonight was just another job. They did what the boss paid them to do and did it well. (True, they'd hired the crooks, but they'd not killed anyone themselves.) He didn't foresee any further complications. With any luck, they should be done and back home soon enough.

CHAPTER 11

Crystal

Riding him like she was, the penis felt like it was penetrating her heart.

Crystal was in the reverse cowgirl position—squatted over Ambrose facing his feet and ramming herself down on him as hard as she could, chasing a third orgasm like an ornithologist hunting a rare sparrow. Under her, Ambrose grunted and squeezed her ass, and tried to slot his manhood even deeper into her body than he already was.

The orgasm that Crystal sought hit her then. Like an angry sea buffeting an ancient schooner, the waves of sexual pleasure threatened to capsize her. Her legs gave out and she collapsed down on Ambrose, her only motions now the tensing of her thigh muscles as the delicious sensation ravaged her. Kneeling on him, she held on to his thighs, and, her eyes closed, shuddered desperately for all she was worth. Then just as her own pleasure subsided, she heard Ambrose's breath quicken and felt his sweaty body tense under hers. She quickly turned herself around on him, and, gripping his shoulders hard, ground her buttocks on his groin till his eyes rolled up in his head and his body went as slack as if he'd just had his brains blown out. She watched his chest rise and fall as his breathing gradually slowed, felt his satisfying penis softening inside her in its latex sheath.

With Ambrose, sex was always a great feeling, the closest Crystal had come to feeling 'in love' with anyone for a long time. She was a prostitute and excellent at her job, and she both liked making money from sex and having sex. But most of those couplings were meaningless, mainly because the men came and went too frequently for her to form any lasting emotional connection with them. Even her regulars (those of her clients who lived in Raynham) hired her mainly when they were hard up—the wife was out of town or having her period or pregnant, or they'd broken up or fought with their girlfriend—but once normalcy was restored in their lives, whatever post-coital feeling they'd shared with Crystal soon dissolved in the tender moistness of their permanent woman's vagina.

Crystal lay flat on Ambrose, her arms limp by his side. With Ambrose, she'd found something: maybe not love, but satisfyingly close. True, if viewed coldly, Ambrose Duggan could be considered just another trick of hers—he paid her after all—but she believed there was more to their relationship than just a series of pleasant business transactions.

While their alcohol-infused breathing mingled (they were both quite drunk now), and his chest rose and fell under her breasts, in this moment of afterglow lucidity, Crystal Parr tried to get a clear hold on emotional concepts which, even when she was sober, were hard for her to concretize.

The best she could make of the special attraction she felt for Ambrose Duggan was that he understood her pain. That seemed to be it—she had no need to explain anything to Ambrose—their separate histories of suffering made them close to soul mates, perfect for one another.

One point in all this was tricky though: the fact that they'd only become friends after Ambrose had lost both Nina and Mike, and had embarked on his endless 'lost weekend.' What would happen if he ever sobered up? Would he still understand her like he did now? Would he still *like* her? Or would she have lost him for good? Would she be back on her daily grind, only this time with no one to unburden her dark emotions to?

The latter scenario would be a disaster for her. Because, though she did enjoy her job, Crystal would be the first to admit that prostitution was as hard on a woman's soul as it was on her body. (Stripped of her profession's glamor tag, she understood that a sex worker was primarily meat, meat that accepted other, more urgent meat into itself. And she understood too that life was more than that, a whole lot more that just being endlessly used for the pleasure of others. She knew she was definitely more than just flesh that rubbed against other flesh for material benefits.)

But for the moment, she had Ambrose and it was enough, at least for tonight. She relaxed back into her pleasant drunk haze.

Ambrose stirred under her. He'd slipped out of her body now. She leaned up on her elbows and kissed him.

He kissed her back boozily, then rolled her off him and stood up. The condom dangled off the end of his penis like an overstretched foreskin. He lurched naked into the toilet. She listened to him piss. The piss took ages, a relentless liquid trill of water into water.

Finally, Ambrose emerged from the bathroom. He staggered over to the fridge and opened it.

"Hey, babe, care for another beer? Or you prefer scotch?"

"Beer's fine, lover man." Her body tingled sweetly at him.

He got out a couple of cans and crossed back over to her. Halfway to her side, he banged his leg against the coffee table and dropped one of the cans. Cursing, he dropped to his knees and picked it up. Then he crawled over to the bed and climbed aboard again. She grinned down at him as he rose completely over the foot of the bed with his member swinging between his legs.

"Here you are, babe." He handed Crystal her beer, then sat beside her, their legs touching.

She popped the can open and sipped. Outside, the night simmered, hot and bothered. Inside, her heart fluttered with intoxicated pleasure. She could hang out here with Ambrose forever, getting drunk and screwing. Too bad she was gonna have to leave him behind again soon.

That last thought, occurring as it did at this particularly sensitive point in her night, suddenly had Crystal maudlin. A deep sadness filled her and she began crying.

Ambrose gaped at her. "Hey, what's the matter?"

"You wouldn't understand!" she wept back. "It's a woman thing!"

"C'mon, Crystal," he drawled drunkenly, "tell me . . . I'm listenin'. Y-you know I'm your best friend."

She shook her head at him. The tears just wouldn't stop coming.

He looked like he'd say a lot more to her, and she wanted him to. It would make tonight perfect, if he'd just say he . . . he loved her? That they could run away together from this life, escape together into a bright Disney happily-ever-after?

He opened his mouth to say more . . .

Then, just like that, Ambrose gave a massive burp and threw up all over her. The puke splattered her chest, coating her breasts in a thick, stinky, chunky layer.

Ambrose looked confused for a moment, then he stumbled off into the toilet again, where she could hear him retching.

Shit! Crystal thought glumly. *This really ain't what I need right now.*

For a moment she considered following Ambrose into the bathroom and breaking something over his shaggy head, or pulling his straggly beard off his chin hair by bloody hair.

Then she looked down at herself again—all covered with vomit— and suddenly all she felt was horrible. Really horrible. *C'mon, God, what kind of a bullshit life is this that you've given me?*

Ignoring a splatter of puke on the rim of her beer can, she raised it to her lips and took a long swallow. Then she got down to finishing the beer.

She was still weeping while she drank, but at that moment both actions seemed to be one and the same thing.

CHAPTER 12

Rosie

In Room 3 of the Sunflower, Rosie Bellamy blew a kiss at the fat naked man in the motel bed.

"Next Wednesday, hon? Same place, same time?"

Hands folded over his rotund belly, Mr. Jacobs gave her a delighted grin. He was middle-aged with thinning black hair, and even if he hadn't been overweight wouldn't have been good-looking. "Oh, hell yeah, girl. I ain't been blown like that in three years." His face scrunched up in sad reminiscence. "My wife Mabel used to give the best blow jobs in this whole damn Bay State, and then all of a sudden, right after she had our third kid Anthony, she just quit on sex. I mean, she quit on *everything*—she don't even want to spread her legs anymore. And she ain't regained her interest since. Our doctor says she has LSD—Low Sex Drive syndrome."

Rosie nodded with fake sympathy though she could honestly care less, she just wanted to be gone from here already. "I'm so sorry to hear that, honey. It might get better with time." Then she favored Mr. Jacobs with more fake gaiety and cocked her hip. "But I sure hope it don't. Her loss is my benefit, ain't it?"

He laughed. "It's *our* benefit, Mandy. If Mabel was still dishing out first-rate fellatio, how would we ever meet?"

Rosie had told Mr. Jacobs her name was Mandy Richards. She didn't want him telling anyone her real name. She wasn't at all proud that she was hooking to make ends meet. If even a hint of a rumor of this news got back to Walmart (where she worked as a cashier), she was screwed—out of a job. But that was the irony of her goddam life, wasn't it? If her day job paid her enough to afford Tommy's daycare expenses ($200 a week? How the hell was she supposed to afford that on her $9.45 an hour salary?) she wouldn't be here with Mr. Jacobs now, would she?

Shit! I'm screwed if I screw, and screwed if I don't.

Mr. Jacobs meanwhile—he was a manager with the Bridgewater Savings Bank—misread Rosie's conflicted expression. "Are you okay, Mandy?" Then his eyes turned worried. "Are you sure I paid you enough?"

She nodded quickly. "Yes, yes, honey, more than enough. I just need to get home in a hurry."

"I dunno why you won't just let me drop you off at home like I offered to. It's past one already, much too late to be alone on the streets. A pretty girl like you shouldn't take your chances at night like this." He made to pull his bulk out of bed, his member wobbling in his crotch like a snake about to bite her again. "C'mon, lemme drop you off. It's just ten minutes drive there and back."

She shook her head vehemently. Now that their dirty business was concluded, she wanted nothing to do with Mr. Jacobs anymore. She wanted to be as far from him as was humanly possible. Even being here in the same room with him now threatened to make her sick.

Then, scared that he might see the revulsion she felt for him in her eyes and cancel next week's rendezvous and find another girl to fuck, she forced a tired smile.

"Hon, I've already explained how I don't want my neighbors seeing any strange man bringing me home. Miss Potts who lives opposite is an insomniac, and she gossips like crazy. You've no idea what she's like once she gets started. Before you know it, the whole town'll know about us."

To her relief, he settled back down in the bed. "Yeah, I guess you're right, discretion *is* the better part of valor. He who fucks and runs away, lives to fuck another day." He grinned broadly. "Okay, girl, run along then. I'll see you next Wednesday."

She hurried across and kissed him on the cheek, ducking out of the reach of his bear-like arms in case he suddenly felt amorous again. Oh no, not again tonight! She could still taste his come on her tongue. He ejaculated a lot and it was revolting.

"Damn, Mandy, you're some hot piece of ass. If we lived in Utah, I'd marry you tomorrow."

It was with intense relief that Rosie shut the door to Room 3 behind her.

For a moment, she stood there on the walkway bordering the parking lot. Mr. Jacobs's car sat in front of her, a large green Toyota SUV that felt great to ride in.

The summer night was too warm, the moon high. She imagined she heard voices to her right. She looked that way. The voices seemed to be coming from a dark space about three rooms away, either a corridor or the mouth of a stairway.

Suddenly she felt less confident. *Maybe I really should let Mr. Jacobs drive me home.*

But no. Now that she had his money, money she desperately needed, she no longer wanted his company. He'd been nice to her—nicer than she'd expected—but she intended to keep their relationship on a strictly business level. That was how it was done. And that was why she'd refused to let him kiss her, even though he'd offered to pay extra for that. He'd found it weird that she would suck his penis but not his tongue.

A small 'skinny but pretty' redhead, Rosie Bellamy was prostituting herself simply because she needed extra money to cover the costs of her son's daycare. A single mother since she and Billy Bellamy had gotten divorced two years ago, Rosie had to work, and someone had to look after four-year-old Tommy while she did so. Originally, her ex had contributed his share to the kid's expenses—she'd seen to it that he'd paid child support regularly—and he'd even been trying to take Tommy away from her through the courts. But then Billy, who had a violent temper—the primary reason they'd gotten divorced—had broken some guy's arm in three places with a hammer for sassing his new girlfriend, been convicted of aggravated assault, and had been sent to the Old Colony Correctional Center in Bridgewater for a two year vacation from well-behaved society.

(A friend of hers, Crystal, had previously tried to get Rosie to hawk herself for money, but she'd been so scared of Billy's using it as evidence in court against her that she'd refused. Now though, with Billy doing time in the slammer, she'd figured 'why not?' To Rosie, it was almost a party joke: a hooker or an ex-con, who made the more unfit parent?)

While Rosie appreciated Billy's defending a woman's honor even if it wasn't hers anymore, him being sent to prison meant that she was now left without the child support money he'd been paying. And so . .

And so here I am now, selling my precious ass for cash.

For a enraged moment, Rosie decided she hated all men. They were all alike assholes: Billy for not being able to control his temper; and men like fat Mr. Jacobs in the room behind her, who simply used women like herself who found themselves fallen on hard times.

It was only when she found herself starting to hate her son Tommy for his father's stupidity, that she got a hold on her emotions again. *No, all men aren't shits and exploiters. Even if they are, Tommy won't be one of them. I'm gonna raise my little boy right, and he's gonna be a good man in future, a loving husband and a great father, and—*

"Ooh!" came a sudden erotic gasp from the shadowy rectangle on her right. Then there were loud sucking sounds like two people kissing.

Rosie gave a start. Horrified, she realized she'd gotten sucked into her angry thoughts. *Oops, I really need to get a move on if I plan on getting home tonight.*

Feeling increasingly uneasy while uncertain as to why, she ducked around Mr. Jacobs's green Toyota and stepped quickly out onto the parking lot.

Rosie didn't head left, towards the motel reception and driveway. Instead she walked straight ahead across the lot, to in turn cut across the bordering lawn and join the main road. She was headed right, to her mother's house on Cal's Court (a half-mile down Carver Street), and the short cut would shave a hundred yards off her journey.

With her sense of unease still high, her shoes clopped fast across the gravel until she reached the grass and the shadow of the lawn trees.

Calm down, she told herself. *I'm just edgy 'cos of this whole hooker scene. Sure it's a shit vocation, but I made good money tonight and Mr. Jacobs wants a weekly session. With him as a regular client, I may not need too many others.*

She strode briskly over the short grass. Insects buzzed around her; crickets chirped everywhere. The road, bright with streetlights, was ten yards off now.

Then her foot struck something and she stumbled.

She caught herself before she fell, balancing against a tree and breathing fast and hard. Then, curious as to what had tripped her, she looked back. This close to Carver Street, the streetlights let her see quite clearly.

She was horrified when she saw what she'd stumbled over—a human leg sticking out by the base of a oak trunk, the rest of the body hidden by the tree's bulk.

Her first impulse was to flee screaming. But . . . what if this person on the ground was hurt and needed her help? Her lips trembling, Rosie stepped around the oak to see who was laid out on the floor there.

Then she froze with a hand to her mouth.

She recognized the old wino on the grass—he was always pestering shoppers for change on lower Broadway and buying booze from the liquor store opposite the Broadway post office. He was old and dirty as they came, and with several front teeth missing.

But . . . he was dead. She could tell that at a glance—the way his head was wrenched all the way around so it faced the main road while his body lay facing the motel . . . and his dirty gray hair was matted with blood, likewise his dirty coat.

When Rosie stepped even closer, she saw that the entire rear of the old man's head was missing—like someone had taken a massive ice-cream scoop out of it. And there was no brain left inside there.

I've gotta call 911! Rosie instantly began fumbling in her handbag for her cellphone. Her heart was thumping furiously in her chest and she found it impossible to make her hands do what she wanted. She swore to herself as condoms, a pack of breath mints, and a tube of KY Jelly fell out of the bag. *Where the hell is my goddamn phone!? Whoever killed this guy may still be around!*

She found the phone. *Okay, now let me . . . !*

Two things stopped Rosie from dialing the police. The first was her sudden realization that they'd want to know what she was doing here at this time of the night. She was screwed if she told them the truth—she'd lose her job and her house. She might even lose her son: even though Billy didn't qualify as a model parent anymore, she doubted that the DCF social workers would want Tommy living with a prostitute. (Worse still, her mother—who was presently babysitting the kid while Rosie had a well-deserved 'night-on-the-town with the girls'—would be scandalized.)

The second reason Rosie didn't call the police was because she'd just both smelt and noticed something odd. The smell was disgusting. Not semen-on-tongue-when-you-didn't-swallow disgusting. It was much worse than that, a fetid reek akin to how a buried cat would stink after two weeks in the ground.

But she couldn't even gag to the horrible smell, because another thing she'd just noticed, was that something was separating itself from the tree next to her. She now realized that the 'thing' had been standing there watching her for a while. She'd just not noticed it because, shadowed by the motel-facing side of its tree, it had blended perfectly with the dark bark.

Now it disconnected from its hiding place and came at her across the grass.

Rosie stood paralyzed, staring at it. The creature was horrible: an elongated head that was three times too large—like an African tribal mask—on a squat, muscular body. Eyes that were just dots in the upper half of its head. Its shoulders were level with hers (she was 5'4"), but its HUGE head made it much taller than her.

Its mouth and chest were covered with the dead man's blood.

As it came at her, its mouth yawned open. The mouth was a toothy chasm, its tongue a red spade about to fork her into those endless depths.

Rosie's paralysis broke. Gripping her cellphone like a gun, she spun around and ran for the road. She was too terrified to scream, too terrified to do anything but run, though she knew it was hopeless.

It caught her as her feet reached the Carver Street sidewalk, its smell of wet sand and rotting meat wrapping around her like a cloak. She felt she could scream then, but its hands had covered her mouth, so that what escaped her lips wasn't even a muffled gasp.

And then, to Rosie's horror, the nightmare creature was dragging her back in among the trees to where she'd discovered the old man's body, and she could hear it gurgling happily to itself as it pulled her along.

And then, it turned her around and she felt its breath hot on the back of her head . . .

And then, the inconceivable was happening to Rosie: She was dangling in the monster's grasp, unable to get free. Unable to do anything, while her head was . . .

***

Brainchew bit deep into the woman's head. Its huge teeth crunched through her skull as easily as a child's teeth would through a cracker.

Then it was inside her head, savoring the taste of her brain while her blood flowed out around its lips.

It expertly swallowed the skullcap in a single gulp, then licked her exposed brain with its tongue, while she trembled at the contact.

It took its time with eating this one—her red hair had a nice perfumed smell to it that added an unusual sweet and tangy spice to Brainchew's palate. So for several minutes it stood there with her in its arms, just nibbling gently on the contents of her head, letting that perfume smell into its nostrils and down its throat.

It knew she was still alive and scared out of her wits and hurting bad with its teeth sunk deep in her brain, just not so deep that they killed her—it liked the stink of her fear. It held her close, while her blood ran down her face and her body and . . .

And then, Brainchew smelt another smell.

She was pissing herself!

Immediately it smelt that, Brainchew stopped nibbling on her head and quickly turned her upside down so that her exposed brain swept across the grass, while her terrified eyes stared at its feet, and her mouth gibbered her otherwise inexpressible terror. It spread her legs wide, then clamped its misshapen gray lips tightly over her crotch and sucked on her panties and vagina, drinking down all the sweet warm urine till it was finished.

Yes, that had really tasted good. It had a real liking for human urine. For Brainchew, humans never made enough of that glorious liquid while dying.

But then it remembered it still had other people to kill inside the Sunflower tonight. So it turned the redheaded woman right-side-up again, and with a single bite cut the brain out of her skull and sucked it down whole.

It never noticed the relief in her eyes as the light went out of them. (Rosie Bellamy had long gotten past the stage of worrying what would become of her son Tommy after she died—either his father or his grandma could look after him; for the past five minutes she'd simply been praying to expire quickly.)

Then it ripped her neck open with a claw and drank its fill of her blood.

CHAPTER 13

Shane & Summer

Rosie had been right about the kissing noises from the passageway. No sooner had Shane and Summer met than they were locked together at the lips.

It was in fact Rosie's emergence from Room 3 that made them duck into the stone aisle, behind a stack of crates. From there they'd watched her cross the parking lot and vanish between the trees.

But not with any serious interest, because, to his delight, Shane was discovering that Ms. Summer Wallace was way hotter even than he'd imagined.

Shane was slightly conflicted. While still angry that Dusty was actually pimping him out to this lady, he wasn't so dumb as to pass up a good thing.

In fact, Shane never passed up any chance he could get to have some extra sex. How he looked at it? *Well, it ain't my fault that I'm so damn handsome and the ladies can't keep their hands off me. Maybe if they kept their tits to themselves . . .*

And Dusty? Well, sure Dusty was great and . . . *Yeah, she should be enough for me.* But it was hard to control himself when he kept having pussy shoved in his face at every turn. He'd almost been relieved when Dusty had insisted that he stop driving his taxi. If she had any idea what had gone on in the back of that cab sometimes, she'd very likely bite his dick off.

The way Shane reasoned it was, so long as he went back to Dusty each time (and made love to her on demand) and most important, always used a condom with the women so he didn't pick up any STDs or (worse still to the female mind as he'd discovered) get one of his casual lays *pregnant*, no real harm was done. Hell, he'd suspected for some time that Dusty actually enjoyed the drama of crying about how unfaithful he was. Then, the next thing, she was again dragging him off to one of her divorced girlfriends' houses for dinner, and scowling while the lady made cow's-eyes at him.

But back to now. With Summer all over him like glue, and her huge breasts (hot damn, I'd forgotten they made implants this large!) pressing against his chest, he was finding it hard to concentrate on the task at hand, which was pumping Summer for information. *Well, I'm definitely up for the pumping bit . . .*

Summer bit his lip gently, then pulled her face back slightly and grinned. With her long blonde hair slightly scattered, and her big blue eyes bright and clear as a morning sky, and her large pink lips all wet from mingling with his, she looked absolutely breathtaking. (Up close, the artificial perfection of Summer's features—the tight smoothness of her cheeks, her flawless nose, and particularly the size and shape of her mouth—screamed plastic surgery in Shane's head. But just like with porno actresses, the singular effect of him considering Summer's enhancements was to pump more blood into his already turgid manhood.) Then, to Shane's delight, she pulled off her T-shirt so her breasts spilled free. Oh God, what succulent breasts they were. Large and white and . . .

Then Shane remembered that they were standing outside. The piled crates—*When the hell is that lush Ambrose gonna get rid of these damn things?*—blocked off view from the front, but the rear . . . Even this late at night, someone in the middle block might get out of bed for a drink of water, open their drapes for a peek at the moon, and spot them making out.

He nodded towards the front lot. "Hey, she's gone now. How about we get nice and cozy inside Room 5 like I suggested."

Summer shook her head. "Nah, baby, let's do it out here. I dig the thrill of it."

Shane nodded. Lots of women liked to fuck outside. "Alright, yeah, okay . . ."

But he was clearly talking too much for her. She was already pushing him hard against the wall, then kneeling down and unzipping his pants.

When she took his penis in her mouth, Shane sagged against the wall. And after that he found himself on a sexual endurance course. As he watched her blonde head bobbing up and down, it was all he could do not to come. It had been ages since he'd last had to exercise this much willpower against ejaculating.

Her lips moved back and forth along the shaft of his erection. Her tongue flicked deftly over his glans, then, when she had him fully in her mouth, it licked his scrotum. Summer continued sucking him off with an expertise that was scary.

Where did this girl learn to eat dick like this? Was she once a hooker? Or in porn? Yeah, with her Barbie-doll looks, I'll just bet she's made some adult flicks.

And she was really patient with her fellatio too. She didn't rush the act like many women did (like even Dusty did sometimes), as if while they'd initially been interested in fellating him, they'd suddenly decided they had better things in life to do than sucking dick and could he please hurry up and come already?

In fact, Summer was if anything too patient with pleasuring him. *If she doesn't stop right now . . .*

He felt himself about to explode in her mouth. But he wanted to ejaculate into the depths of her. He was certain that her sex would be as perfect—as surgically adjusted for pleasure—as the rest of her.

He halfheartedly pulled her off his phallus and back up to her feet.

"You don't like it?" Summer asked, running her tongue over her lips.

"Are you fucking kidding me?" he gasped at her. "I utterly *love* it! But, c'mon, don't make come yet, baby. I gotta taste the rest of you too."

She smiled and he almost shot his load just from that. The lust in her eyes mirrored his.

He spun her around against the wall. "Alright, your turn, baby. Let me have at that sweet pussy. Oh, girl, I'm gonna eat you so good, you'll be singing hallelujah."

Summer giggled. "Oh, I just love choirs." Then grinning, she kicked off her flip-flops, unzipped her pants, and stepped out of them. Shane hastily got down on his knees before her and dragged her panties down to her ankles. He was desperate to reach her promised land.

Then he froze.

"Like what you see, baby?" Summer asked from above him, intense amusement in her voice.

Shane still couldn't move. He was staring at the stiff penis which had just flipped forward between Summer's legs. Behind the erection, also uncoiling like a rattler that had accidentally knotted itself, a large set of testicles slowly fell under the pull of gravity.

"Oh shit!" Shane gasped, looking up at her. "You're a tranny?"

She smirked down at him. "Oops, sorry, forgot to mention it; but yes, I am."

Then, before Shane could get up again, Summer produced a switchblade, flicked it open and pressed the blade against his neck. "But don't let that little detail bother you, darling," she gasped throatily. "We're still gonna fuck. The only thing that's changed is that you're not gonna be fucking me—*I'm* gonna be the one fucking *you*. Yeah, better believe it, sweetheart—this time you're gonna be on the receiving end of the dick."

Shane tried to get to his feet. She kept him down on his knees with a firm hand on his head. "No, baby, the rules just changed. I just sucked you off and you're gonna repay the favor. And if you don't, or if you make a crap job of it"—she shrugged—"I've already killed one person tonight. One more murder won't really make much difference to me, will it? You'll just be a handsome corpse."

Staring up at her, Shane was horrified. Oh, he definitely believed her, that she had already killed one person, and that she'd kill him too if he tried to run. Her eyes still flickered with lust, but her smile had altered into a darker shade of itself, as if her lips had somehow been infected with viciousness.

Now Summer looked as cruel as the Devil. Evil incarnate, but no less beautiful.

"Alright, get to work on me, lover boy. My cock ain't gonna suck itself."

He nodded hastily. The deadly knife was pressed so tightly to his throat that he could feel his skin split and the blood trickle.

He regarded the penis facing him. It looked exactly how he imagined his own penis looked up close to Dusty—fat and swollen, and covered with ugly veins like worms glued onto its side. The sight added to his horror. His own erection, previously so strong and woman-threatening, was now completely deflated.

"Open your damn mouth," Summer ordered.

With no choice, Shane obeyed. The next moment his mouth was full of her penis. Stinky with sweat, and with a deodorant oversmell of roses. Then she was holding on to his hair and thrusting back and forth between his lips. Some infernal instinct made him shut his mouth so it could be properly raped.

Shit! Shane thought with realization as the sweaty penis slid and out of his face, *Dusty was right—MEN keep money in their pockets!*

CHAPTER 14

Kat

In Room 8, Kat lay flat on her belly, being screwed from behind by her husband while she made a pretense of watching TV.

After Summer had left for her tryst, they'd sat together for awhile, drinking from a half-pint bottle of Smirnoff that Lance had unearthed in the Ford's glove compartment on his way back from the cemetery.

Then, to her dismay, he'd gotten a randy look in his eyes and begun grabbing at her breasts and pinching her nipples, which hurt.

She felt disgusted with him, she wasn't even vaguely in the mood for sex—not with Chuck just dying (and the old man too) and the knowledge that at any moment now Bella Novak might knock on their door.

But Lance either didn't read the disgust in her eyes or didn't care. Next moment, he'd unzipped his fly, grabbed her hair, and started pushing her head down towards his boxers.

"Alright, but give me a minute first, I need to pee," she'd told him, then dashed off into the toilet. She sat in there for five minutes. Hopefully, Lance would have jerked off onto the carpet before she got out.

However, on returning to the front room, she found instead that her husband had gotten undressed in the interim. Lance was standing buck naked by the bed with a hard-on, stroking himself, and clearly waiting for her. He'd grabbed her and steered her towards the bed. Her protests fell on deaf ears, so she stopped making them. What else was a wife to do in these sort of situation?

In moments, she was naked too and flat on her belly and was having penis shoved up her.

She felt like crying while they did it, but bravely held back the tears. The threatened tears weren't from pain—at the moment she was so emotionally anaesthetized that she hardly felt the penis in her vagina—but from her feeling that having sex like this, getting naked and sweaty on the sheets tonight was grossly disrespectful to Chuck.

Oh wow, this really sucks! His body's hardly cold yet and this is the kind of wake he gets? We're all having sex—humping in his memory? Summer and Lance and me? Like we don't give a shit about him? How can Summer and Lance both feel horny tonight?

Most of Lance's weight lay on her. It felt comforting, being pressed into the mattress with each thrust like this, like she was being smothered inside a cloud. For the moment she was merely a desired object being used; something other than herself, without will or choice in her sexual destiny, a willing captive unable to flee, unable to prevent herself being taken and exploited. Which added to her feeling of detachment from everything. Except for her sense of outrage at the wrongness of their actions, this fuck was a wonderful waste of time.

Positioned as they were on the bed, the rear of a couch blocked the coffee table and hated jewel box from view. *Oh, how I want that thing gone away from us already!* All she could see was the rectangular eye of the television as it fed the world into the motel room.

She wasn't paying any real attention to what she was watching. She had no idea what channel the TV was tuned to, maybe the local Raynham station. First it showed a perfectly groomed lady newscaster, then it cut to a lot of people running about looking agitated—someone had apparently jumped from the top of a high-rise and smeared himself all over the sidewalk.

She couldn't connect to the onscreen man's death, or, for that matter, to any death in the rest of the world. *People are dying everywhere tonight—so frigging what? Welcome to the club, folks.*

Lance gave a really deep thrust into her sex. She *felt* that one push her cervix. It almost stirred her to reach a hand between her legs and help the hard penis, to finger her clitoris so she climaxed also. She decided against it. She preferred what she had now—using this fuck to reinforce her dead emotions. So instead of helping her own pleasure, she reached back with both hands and gripped and stroked her husband's buttocks as he pushed deeper and deeper into her body.

"Yeah, baby, give me that hard rod," she moaned.

"Oh yeah, baby! You've got the sweetest pussy ever!" her husband groaned back. Then, pausing a moment, he spread her legs and slid a pillow under her crotch so her buttocks were raised higher in the air. Then he thrust himself home extra-deep again.

"Yeeesss!" she moaned. "Deeper!"

He was totally unaware that her pleasure was made up. *His* pleasure wasn't though. And feeling him getting there, his pulse drumming on her through their shared skins, threatened to make her feel something.

She resisted the instinctive impulse to indulge her flesh. No matter how sweetly her body sung its promise of erotic delights to her tonight, she utterly would not break her concentration and allow herself to come. This was her private wake for Chuck. He deserved at least that much from her.

Lance was really close now; she could tell. His breath was shortening and his thrusts were growing violent.

She didn't look back at him. She knew she'd laugh if she did. Lance most likely looked utterly enraged now. He always looked that way when nearing orgasm. His neck muscles would get all bunched up like gym ropes and his eyes would bulge out like his head was going to explode. Ah, men had no idea what they looked like while ejaculating.

While Lance's hands gripped her buttocks and spread them wide, permitting him unrestricted access to her center, Kat cast her mind outward from herself, remembering the first time that she, Lance, and Chuck met Summer Wallace:

***

The three of them had been hanging out in an apartment in Grand Rapids, Michigan.

They were celebrating a successful heist job: they'd gotten in, gotten the dough from the safe, and gotten out cleanly. But they were a woman short to go out on the town partying it up, so Chuck had hired an escort named Sam from an agency.

Kat, Lance, and Chuck had been waiting forty-five minutes by then for Sam to show up.

Then the buzzer sounded and Kat had let this tall blonde in. Summer's breasts weren't as huge back then, but they were clearly enhanced, and she had a beautiful face, and her short blue dress cradled an exceptional figure.

What was most important/misleading, though, was that she looked like a professional slut.

"Hello," Kat said, "we'd almost given up on you showing."

"I'm Summer Wallace," the blonde said, "I'm here for the—"

"Yeah, yeah, Sam, we know," Chuck said. "Get over here and suck my dick, girl!"

Summer's face crinkled up. "You must have me mixed up with someone else. I'm here about the job, not the blowjob."

Chuck smirked. "The blowjob *is* the fucking job, girl. Now get over here to my penis and talk sex to it."

Kat had meanwhile wandered back to Lance's side and was rolling a joint.

"Alright," she heard Summer say finally, "I'll take the blowjob too, and it won't cost you extra. But not out here with everyone watching." She pointed to the bedroom door. "Inside."

Chuck growled, "What is this? A modest prostitute?" But he got up and followed her into the bedroom.

The door had shut behind them and Kat had gotten down to smoking her marijuana and fending off Lance's grabs at her breasts. She wasn't about screwing him now: she'd taken almost thirty minutes putting her makeup on, and she didn't want Lance kissing it all off her face.

But then, both she and Lance had become aware of a loud altercation from the bedroom. When they'd leapt up and opened the door, they saw Chuck down on the floor on the far side of the room. There was blood on his neck and he was pointing his gun at Summer. She in turn was holding a knife and her blue dress was pulled up over her crotch, revealing . . .

"What the hell's going on in here?" Lance asked.

Chuck's eyes were wide with alarm. "Keep that bitch away from me or I'll shoot her. She's a *he!*"

"What the hell are you—?" Lance began saying, then along with Kat, he looked down at Summer's crotch, where a softening erection hung. "Aw, shit! You're a . . ."

Chuck got to his feet. "The bitch put a knife to my throat and tried to force me to suck her dick." His eyes turned cold now. "I'm gonna beat the crap out of the gay slut."

Summer wasn't saying anything. She was smiling, and licking her lips like the air in the bedroom was delicious.

Kat finally took her eyes off the blonde's penis. It definitely was shocking to look at. She couldn't imagine how Chuck had felt having *that* shoved in his face.

"So . . . who are you?" she asked Summer.

"She's a rapist bitch, that's who!"

"Calm down, Chuck," Lance said. "There's clearly been some mistake. And for heaven's sake, put your gun away before you shoot someone."

"I'm going to kill—"

Lance shook his head. "No you're not. Man, put the damn gun away. We can't have you bringing down the cops on us now."

Once Chuck had holstered his pistol, Lance gave their visitor his full attention. "Hey, that goes for you too, ladyboy. Stick your goddam knife back in your goddamn purse before I castrate you with it."

Summer smirked. For a moment she looked like she'd call Lance's bluff, but he was staring at her with eyes colder than cans of Bud Light left in the freezer, and Kat saw a visible change come over her face. She knew that look—Lance got it a lot: Summer had clearly realized that Lance wasn't someone she could screw with and walk away unscathed. True, she had balls, but she didn't have the balls to fuck with *him*.

Summer clicked her switchblade shut again.

"And pack away your dick too. Shit!"

"Yeah, stuff that goddam thing away!" Chuck angrily agreed while swabbing blood off his neck with a handkerchief. "Shit—my life's a goddam freak show tonight."

"And once that's done," Lance added, with an unmistakable threat in his voice, "you'd better have a sensible explanation for what you're doing here in place of the party girl we called for."

"Look, man," Summer began, "I don't know who you're talking about. I just came . . ."

The front door buzzer sounded then. Kat left them talking and went to answer it.

It was Sam the call girl. Curvy, slutty, and eager to fuck for bucks. No mistake this time; exactly what Dr. Chuck had ordered.

"I'm sorry I'm late," she said brightly. "My cab broke down and I had to wait for a replacement."

"Damn. You could just have phoned over that you'd been delayed."

"Sorry, I was chatting with the cabbie. I didn't know time was flying."

Her words had the air of a skillful liar's to them. Kat doubted that the prostitute's taxi had broken down. More likely she'd been screwing the cabbie for extra earnings. "Yeah, sure, no problem," she said, stepping aside. "Come on in."

"Who the hell is it this time?" Lance called from the bedroom.

"It's Chuck's hooker."

Lance peered out of the bedroom door. "Yeah, it is." Then he grinned that wolfish grin he always got when he had an evil idea in his mind. "You know, you two," he called back into the bedroom, "since you both have dicks and both wanna get laid, how 'bout if you both share Sam here?"

Kat didn't hear either Chuck or Summer's reply to the idea, but the just-arrived Sam shook her head. "Oh no. On the phone you only said *one* guy."

Lance scowled at her. "Like you give a goddam how many dicks you suck. Shut up, toots, okay? Your not getting here on time just caused me a little trouble that I'm smoothing out. So, now that *you are* here, you'll do everything damn thing I tell you to and you'll fucking *enjoy* doing it."

Sam tried to stare him down, but his eyes were too cold for her. She trembled violently before his predatory gaze and nodded.

Lance vanished back into the bedroom again and shut the door behind him.

Kat tried to set the prostitute at ease. "Look, Sam, don't sweat it. We'll pay you double, and there's not gonna be any rough stuff involved, alright?"

Sam calmed down at little. "No rough stuff, for real?"

"Seriously. They don't like themselves enough to try any double-penetration in the same hole. And besides"—she laughed—"the second guy isn't actually a guy anyway."

In the end, after everything had been resolved, Chuck and Summer did share Sam in bed. The sex, however, proved to be anticlimactic. Summer couldn't get an erection with Sam. She was only interested in men—penises and anuses turned her on, not vagina. (They of course didn't yet know about her rape fetish.) Once faced with a woman's sex, Summer went limp as a noodle. So, while Chuck enjoyed Sam, Summer watched while fantasizing about how lovely his rectum would feel wrapped around her erection. Then, after he came, she fingered Chuck's semen out of Sam's vagina and used it as lubricant to masturbate with.

Summer's being there that night was just a misunderstanding. It turned out that the previous week, she'd had been contracted to do a bodyguard job by the last guy who'd lived in the apartment, but then his phone had gone dead, so she'd come over then to see if the deal was still on. (As they later discovered, her should-have-been-client was at that moment freezing in a mortuary drawer, after having his throat slit by his girlfriend's angry brother after he'd beaten the shit out of her.)

Summer lived on the wrong side of the tracks herself. Mostly she did bodyguard work. She was very handy with a knife.

Lance, who for a while had been saying they needed a fourth member in their gang, asked Summer to join them.

So she did.

***

Above Kat, Lance grunted once then ejaculated deep into her body.

Steering her thoughts out of Reminiscence Avenue, which had at least put a smile on her face—she got the giggles whenever she remembered Chuck's mistake that first time with Summer—she rolled her hips under Lance and shoved her buttocks up at him. Maybe the semen would hit her cervix just right tonight and she'd get a baby out of this. That would be one positive thing to come out of tonight's mess. If she did get pregnant, she'd insist that they name the kid Chuck.

Lance collapsed on her and began kissing her neck while gasping huskily.

"Damn, Kat," he gasped. "How the hell do you do it so good? I've had lots of pussy in my life—slack, tight, black, white, fat lips, no lips, bare and with hair, you name it—but no woman, and I mean *no* fucking woman, ever made me feel in bed the way you do. Oh, shit, baby, you're the absolute tops!"

She grinned to herself, flattered, though she knew she'd not put in anywhere near as much effort to please him as she normally did. "It's the feeling that counts, darling." She twisted around to face him. "It's because we love each other. The depth of emotion that we share sparks between us when we make love. That's why the sex is always so great."

His eyes were full of need for her and he kissed her hungrily, and feeling his lips smother hers and suck on them, she was surprised by how good she suddenly felt. It was odd; she felt satisfied with his satisfaction.

At that moment, while feeling Lance's deeply-shot liquid love for her seeping from her womanhood into the bed sheets, she was struck by the feeling that she'd been right all along in choosing Lance over Chuck, and of never cheating on Lance with Chuck, even though she'd have *loved* to. This is what love really is, she understood, being one with each other and for each other, no one else inclusive.

Kat found this train of thought almost as satisfying as an orgasm would have been. In a way, it was more satisfying than a sexual climax, because, while an orgasm faded, she could relive her new understanding/interpretation of the dynamics of sexual love whenever she chose to.

Lance rolled off her, onto his back. He draped a proprietorial hand over Kat's thigh. "Shit, honey, I really need a smoke now, even if it's a joint. Where the hell is Summer?" Then he laughed. "I wonder how that punk Rowland is getting on now that he's discovered Summer's sausage surprise?"

Kat winced with distaste. Damn, trust her bullish husband to shatter a sweet romantic mood.

"Please, darling," she pleaded with him. "Not now. At the moment, I'd rather think about our coming happy autumn years than about that horrible Summer."

CHAPTER 15

Shane & Summer

Shane still couldn't believe his present straits. Summer had now tired of ramming her penis into his throat. With her knife held to that same throat, she'd forced him to remove his pants and underwear and bend over. He was bent over now, trembling with fear, while she prepared to rape him anally.

"Now hold on good, baby, the dick is thick. Alright, here comes an ass-full for you!"

"Please, don't!" He was mortified. She wasn't even putting on a condom first.

"C'mon, man, I *need* to have your virgin ass."

He heard her spit twice, then . . . contact. A stiff penis-head pressed against Shane's anus for the first time in his life. And then, she was forcing it in. He instinctively clenched his ass as tight as he could. It didn't seem to work though. As if his anus imagined the invading erection was an exiting piece of excrement, it seemed to be doing its best to cooperate with Summer. Shane clenched tighter but still felt the penis entering, a hard and painful intrusion into the sanctity of his rectum.

"I'm warning you," Summer growled from deep in her throat, "relax it or it's gonna tear." To compel him to obey her, she jabbed him in the back of his neck with the knife. Not deeply, just enough to take his mind off resisting her.

With a soft groan of pain, Shane relaxed his ass. He couldn't tell the difference—it still felt like it was tearing.

And then Summer's 'womanhood' was fully inside his body—he felt her scrotum smack against his—and he was filled with horror and shame, and worst of all, *fear*. Fear of being discovered. Fear that someone would come upon them like this and see him being sodomized. (At the moment, Shane wasn't even scared that he might contract AIDS from Summer. He was just terrified of being caught by someone in this horribly compromised position, bent over and with a penis stuck between his buttocks.)

No one would believe he was being forced into this, they'd all think he was enjoying it, that he was *gay*.

Summer groaned. "And yes, baby, your ass is now open for business!"

He considered pushing her off and running, but the switchblade was expertly placed at his throat, positioned neither too far forward or back. Even without Summer exerting additional pressure on the knife, any sudden movement of his would likely slice his blood vessels open.

Shane realized he had to bear it. *She can't go on all night, can't she? Sooner or later she'll ejaculate and I'll be able to escape her.*

But the important thing now was to keep as quiet as possible, quieter than the proverbial mouse, so that no one found out what was being done to him. And outside, of all places! Damn the nasty bitch! Knowing that she intended doing this, couldn't she at least have let them take a room, where no one would see? Or was the public humiliation of others also part of how she got her dirty kicks?

He grunted with pain. Maybe she couldn't last all night, but Summer was definitely taking her time with screwing him. Just like when she'd been sucking his penis, she clearly wasn't in any hurry to get this rape over with. She was pumping him hard and slow, and with a regular, relentless rhythm. She was doing it so contentedly that Shane could almost hear her purr.

"Yeah," she said with a satisfied groan as she thrust deep into him, "I knew it. You're just like every other macho guy I've ever known."

"What the hell are you talking about?" he gasped through his rectal nightmare.

She laughed. "Well, you aren't screaming for help, are you? No you're not, and I'll tell you *why* you're not—you're too ashamed. You know that if you start yelling for help now, everyone will come running, including your sweet little wife. And you don't want *her* to see you with a cock up your ass, do you?"

"Why?" Oh, God, the tearing agony! It felt like he was having his hemorrhoids removed without anesthetic. "Why are you doing this to me?"

She leaned forward and grabbed his hair and pulled him back up to a standing position, then pushed him forward against the wall. With her knife now held directly below his Adam's apple to forestall any resistance, she kicked his legs further apart and speared him deeply with herself. Her entering his body at this angle felt like a knife slicing his buttocks apart.

"Why? Because it's fun." She gave him several violent thrusts, then added in a voice full of lust, "And it's the best way that I've found to get all of you hunky hetero studs who'd never give me the time of day if you knew I was a transsexual." She leaned forward and bit his shoulder, then whispered throatily into his ear. "And this is *payback*, payback for all those sexy, beefy football players who bullied me in high school, while all the while I was just dying to fuck them—I mean, I'd have given anything, I mean fucking *anything*, to have been able to suck those stud's sweaty cocks in the locker room, or have them gangbang me in the showers, but instead, all I got were threats that they'd kick the crap out of me if I so much as looked at them with desire."

She caressed him roughly under his shirt. As her fingers pinched his unresponsive nipples, his mind reverberated with her damning confession, those smiled words that still held him in thrall here: 'I've already murdered one man tonight. One more murder won't really make much difference, will it?' Shit. *And Dusty wants us to rob her and her friends? Is she nuts?*

Well his wife couldn't be any nuttier than this transsexual bitch trying to bust a nut up his backside.

"But . . . okay, baby," Summer was still saying, "and I'm telling you this in the strictest confidence, so don't you dare share this with anyone—since perfecting my looks, I've had more than my fair share of tight football-player-ass." She smirked. "I fucked them all. I knew they'd never dare tell their wives and friends . . . or the police . . . oh, man, your ass feels so fucking good, so incredibly nice . . . All those studs? They never told anyone what I did to them . . . just like you, fag!" She laughed softly and ran fingers through his dark hair. "I remember one famous guy who I did like I'm doing you now. Afterwards he was crying like a baby and threatening to commit suicide. Ha ha ha!"

"You're sick, you need psychiatric help!" This was just horrible. Shane was terrified now that she'd murder him afterwards.

"No, I do not need a shrink. It's just like what men said about feminists back in the stone age—I haven't got anything that a good screw won't fix." She laughed. "The great thing about punks like you is that you're always to scared to report it afterwards—oh, this *girl* fucked my ass—how's that for bullshit! *I'd* scream it happily to the heavens if *you* fucked my ass."

She gave a few more thrusts into his hurting body, then reached forward and grabbed his limp penis. "C'mon, at least try to enjoy it!" Her hand felt below his penis and grabbed his testicles and squeezed. "Wow, your balls feel super-full. Look, baby, you might as well come, 'cos I'm damn sure as hell gonna fill your ass with my love milk. I'm having the time of my life here. You've no idea what virgin male pussy feels like to deflower. You're so damn tiiiiiigght."

Her hands returned to fondling his penis. Her huge breasts were soft on his back, her nipples rock-hard against his skin, her knife deadly at his throat. Shane just grunted at each additional stab of agony in his rear and prayed that it would be over quickly. He was grateful that for all her braggadocio, Summer wasn't being loud enough to draw attention to them. Either from passion or caution, her voice was an abominable husky whisper:

"Take that, asshole . . . and that!" she gasped. "Oh, baby, you make my cock hard as a rock, and I'll make you tingle like an electric shock."

YEOW!!! It felt like she was shoving a rock inside him.

(Had Shane been able to peer into Summer's mind, he'd have been appalled by how fragile her grip on her self-worth was. He'd have wept for her, understood her, and maybe even forgiven her for her current ill-treatment of him.

Unknown to Shane, Summer was screwing him with every ounce of frustration she'd ever felt in her life: all the discrimination she'd suffered from family and supposed friends; all the disapproving grimaces when she'd cast off her born-into masculine identity and taken to wearing dresses and lipstick; and especially, all the rejection from the hunks she'd wanted to date but who were all romancing the cis-gender girls.

Everything—all the pressure and disgrace and rejection and frustrated desire—had finally heated to boiling point in her soul and corrupted it. Summer almost couldn't control her own actions anymore; her sexual bad behavior had become a compulsion. Every so often, her repressed rage against straight men peaked, and she had to take it out on one of their anuses.

Unable to have what she craved most of all—to simply be loved for herself as a transgender woman by a nice man of her own— Summer Wallace had made a career out of becoming the most desirable female around and instead taking her men by force. Each man she seduced away from the straight girls was to her a victory over oppression.)

Finally, it was over. Shane tensed at the ultimate disgrace— Summer ejaculating what felt like a bucketload of come up his ass. It felt like she was trying to impregnate him.

Then she sagged against him and gripped him hard.

"That was frigging great; you were simply incredible," she gasped, with what to Shane's horror sounded like sincere affection in her voice.

What the hell is wrong with this crazy bitch? he wondered.

She pulled out of him and the semen drained from his hurting ass hole. She ground her crotch against his buttocks, running the dread switchblade down his right side, caressing him with it, grabbing his tight abs under his shirt. Her spilling ejaculate ran down his legs into his socks and some of it fell straight from his ass and splattered on the floor and on her bare feet.

"You've a frigging great butt," she groaned, still grinding herself against him. Then she kissed his right shoulder. "I think I'd like to fist it."

"No!" Shane gasped. "Fist my ass? With those big hands of yours? Are you out of your mind?" Then, realizing that he'd unconsciously raised his voice, he quickly lowered it again to a hoarse whisper. "For fuck's sake, just let me go! Please!"

The knife was instantly back at his throat again. "You only go when I say so, baby. We're not done until then."

She caressed his cheek from behind, then spun him around to face her. Her face was still flushed with her evil and wanton desire for him. Her beautifully huge breasts were rising and falling fast with each breath she took. Shane gulped at the knowledge that he'd been suckered by her breasts, those incredible tits—excruciatingly LARGE like she'd mugged Eva Karera for her implants—as swollen as if she'd just given birth, and covered with the most beautiful and delicate tracery of blue veins ever.

The blade pressing painfully into his neck, he glanced down at Summer's penis and was horrified to see it was filling with blood again.

She laughed at his horror. "I told you that *I like* you, baby. Damn, my balls feel so weighty, it's like I didn't give you anything at all first time around. Maybe I'll just screw your ass again instead of . . ." Then her voice turned perplexed. "What's that godawful smell?"

Shane had smelt it too: like wet earth mixed with rotting meat.

Then, before Summer could turn around to see what had caused the sudden reek, *it* was there with them.

Looking over Summer's shoulder, Shane instantly recognized the creature, with its rough gray skin and three-fingered hands and that monstrous head—a head at least three times the human norm in size.

Shit, it's Brainchew!

And Brainchew's huge mouth was open and it was rushing at them around the stacked crates.

"Noooo!" Shane gasped, his eyes widening in horror.

Summer was turning towards the monster when it grabbed her from behind. It yanked her back towards the crates. Her eyes suddenly bugging out with terror, Summer kicked and flailed wildly to free herself. She was trying to scream too, but the monster had a hand clamped tight over her mouth.

Summer was tough though, Shane had to gave her that credit. She fought it, fought the unseen thing trying get its mouth around her head. She'd kept a hold of her knife when it had grabbed her, and now she began stabbing hard at Brainchew with it. But even though she ripped deep holes in its body, the wounds had no effect whatsoever on the creature.

Shane knew that he should flee for his life, but he didn't. It wasn't that he was paralyzed with fear either. He was just so surprised, so completely shocked to see this monster again, that he stood there gaping at it.

How the . . . ? How in the . . . ?

While bravely fighting the creature, Summer's eyes were pleading with Shane for help. But Shane, even if she'd not just gotten through violating his butthole, wasn't going anywhere near Brainchew. *Oh no, lady, not me!* Keeping an eye on their fight, he was struggling his legs back into his pants as fast as he could, then buckling up his belt and pulling on his shoes, while wondering: *How the damn hell did this damn thing get out again?*

And all the while there was that rancid stink everywhere.

And then it was all over for Summer. Brainchew finally got its mouth in the right position around her head. Then, with a soft crunch that almost made Shane piss himself, its teeth went through Summer's hair and skull to rendezvous with each other in the center of her head.

Summer's fear-bugged-out eyes widened to their fright-filled limits, then instantly went blank. She went rag-doll-limp in its grasp.

Her hands dropped, leaving her knife stuck deep in the creature's belly.

When the monster pulled its head away from hers, it had her blood all over its jaws and Summer had nothing but a scooped hole behind her face—the entire rear half of her head was missing.

Then Brainchew shook her corpse violently, flinging thick gobs of blood across to splatter Shane.

Aw, fuck, he thought as the blood splashed over his head and shoulders. He quickly wiped the red mess out of his eyes, while at the same time backing off towards the rear of the passageway, in case it was done with Summer and was coming at him.

But it wasn't. Like a lion or wolf that had caught a prey, it was concentrating on consuming what it had. (It was greedy like that—like a monkey unwilling to let go of a handful of nuts in a jar to free itself, it was unwilling to give up what it had in exchange for something else before it had eaten its fill.) Its jaws grinding slowly, the creature regarded Shane with eyes like cherries planted deep in rancid dough.

It stopped chewing for a moment to pluck Summer's switchblade from its belly and cast it aside. The knife left a deep but bloodless incision in its gray flesh.

Then, while still gripping Summer's corpse like they were lovers, Brainchew opened its mouth wide so Shane saw the crushed mess of her pinkish brains and hair and blood inside the ring of its uneven teeth.

The sight made Shane sick. It also brought home to him with resounding clarity the fact that his curiosity had long outlived its 'sell by' date.

He turned and fled, running faster than he ever had before in his life for the safety of the reception building.

He stopped for a moment at the end of the front block to catch his breath. The reception building was just twenty yards off now, separated from his current position by a lawn and some rose bushes, and a fish-shaped fountain. A slight wind was moving and a few orphan raindrops were coming down here and there.

While panting hard, he warily looked back at the wan rectangle which marked the just-departed passageway.

Brainchew was still back there. He could see the monster's shadow, cast by the corridor light onto the parking lot. The shadow was moving, but within the same general area.

Here at his temporarily safe vantage point, Shane's horror at what he'd just witnessed reduced slightly and he did some quick thinking.

There was no mistaking his primary emotion: he was *relieved.*

Yes, he was glad that he'd escaped the monster, and also that Summer hadn't murdered him after screwing him, but his primary relief now stemmed from knowing that Summer Wallace was stone dead and couldn't tell anyone that she'd raped him.

Thank God! Thank God! Oh, thank you, God!

It was an intense, ass-felt relief that made him (but only in the safe haven of his thoughts) want to go back and thank the monster that had killed her, and even hug the damn thing. For a moment, his heart beat with gratitude to Brainchew. Shane wasn't even bitter or angry at Summer anymore, because, now that she was dead, there was no chance of anyone ever finding out that she'd been in his ass.

He wasn't telling, and corpses certainly told no secrets.

So now, he figured all he had to do was pretend that nothing had happened back there—and to accept that in reality, no actual harm had been done to him other than a little tearing of his rectal tissue. Sure, his ego had been punctured along with his anus, but not much. The way he clinically viewed it, what was most important here was that he hadn't been aroused by the evil shemale penis! That was the vital thing here—he'd preserved his manhood intact without succumbing to the fruity lure of Summer's queerness.

All he needed now was a double dose of Dusty's super-sweet sex, and he'd be right as rain again.

And then, once Shane had resolved the knotty issue of his rape, and found that sweet mental space where his masculinity remained unthreatened, he was properly scared shitless again and ran for safety to the reception building.

CHAPTER 16

Kat

The shower water streamed hot over Kat's body, cleansing her of the sweat of sex. Soaping herself as the liquid jets beat on her skin, she now felt much calmer than before. That was one of the things she loved about sex—the violent tenderness of someone else moving inside her generally set her at her ease. Even tonight, when she'd not had an orgasm.

She shut her eyes and let the water soothe her further. Her ears fed the outside world to her: the hiss of the shower, the splatter of water in the bathtub, and its swirling gurgle as it ran from between her toes and drained away . . . and inside her human shell, she heard the soft thumping of her own heart.

She was alive.

For a while Kat luxuriated in being herself, in being female, in being free as the air. She felt particularly free now. $85,000 each! The most important purchase money bought you was freedom. Money was the key that unlocked the doors to the twin houses of pleasure and delight, where you forgot your plebeian upbringing and reigned as queen of all you surveyed.

Ten years ago, she'd hitchhiked south to Boston from Kingfield, Maine with nothing except her ability to handle a car. She'd been running away from an everywoman future of husband, kids, and perpetual boredom. And now it looked like life was about handing her a good break for once.

Kat grinned beneath the rushing water. Ah, memories. The past—both the good and bad parts of it—was totally behind her now. She and Lance had made sufficient money tonight (and tax-free at that) to invest in something worthwhile.

Yes, what she'd nudge him towards was owning a shoe shop. She loved shoes and Lance was very picky about his footwear too. So a shoe shop it was then; maybe in some seaside resort town where the beach was a stone's throw away. Or, maybe even (though she knew it'd be the devil's work convincing Lance to go along with her on this), maybe they could both emigrate outside the USA, say to Italy or France. She'd always loved French cuisine and could even manage a few words of their lingo. Yes, a shoe shop in France—in romantic Paris if possible—would be just perfect for them. Of course, Lance hadn't ever shown any gift for languages, so that might prove problematic for him.

The water flowed over her; her pleasant thoughts flowed with it. In her liquid cocoon she refused to conceive that the water's end and that of her dreams might be one and the same—flushed down the drain. Yes, tonight would work out all right for her.

She was uncertain how long she remained like that, enjoying her simple innocent pleasure. It was with regret that she finally opened her eyes again and turned the water off. Loath to exit her emotional oasis, she got out of the bath and reached for the towel with a sad smile on her face.

While drying her hair, she heard Lance moving about outside.

A moment later, he opened the bathroom door. He already had his pants and shoes on, and was busy pulling on his shirt. He had a preoccupied look on his face.

"I can't get Summer on the phone," he grumbled before she could ask anything.

Kat refused to be bothered by that; she chose to remain in her peaceful place. "She most likely enjoyed the guy's ass so much that she's having a third helping."

Lance shook his head. "No, if that was the case, she'd at least answer the damn phone." He glanced at his wrist. "Damn! Bella Novak should be here any second now."

Kat placed cool fingers on his arm. "Relax, the two of us can handle it."

Lance shook his head again. "Sorry, baby, but I can't relax. I'm more jumpy than a Mexican bean. Maybe it's just tonight, but until we hand Bella her boss's gems and get our cash, I'm going to keep feeling jumpy." He winced. "And you know what, sweetheart? I don't even know why the hell I feel so damn uneasy. Like you rightly pointed out, it's a done deal."

He scratched his chin. "At least, let me go have a look around. I'll just walk down to reception and back—"

"Lance, she might have him bent over a chair there with her knife to his neck, and her . . . up his . . ."

Kat couldn't say the damning words because she found the mental image so remarkably horrible. Over and over she chastised herself, feeling guilty for even knowing Summer: *Hell no, I DO NOT support her nasty behavior! What if it was Lance she assaulted?* But she knew that Lance could never be one of Summer's victims. *Is that why I still tolerate her— turn a blind eye, or a merely disapproving one, to her catalogue of serial rapes?* Kat knew that Lance would rather let Summer slit his throat than agree to fellate her or be sodomized. And then he'd choke her to death while dying.

Lance grinned back. "If she is smearing Mr. Shane Rowland's brand of rectal chocolate on her female sausage, then I'll simply tell her to hurry up and hurry back here."

He leaned forward and kissed Kat. Once again, his lips were hungry against hers, which, after her warm shower and in her current 'good feeling zone,' made her tingle erotically.

She reluctantly pulled away from him. If she didn't, she might insist that they make love again, for herself this time. "Alright, darling, run along. I'll be fine for at least ten minutes."

He nodded grimly and left.

Kat resumed drying her blonde hair, then she spent a little while appraising her figure in the bathroom mirror: No she wasn't fat yet. She *was* putting on weight though, but at her age—thirty-two—that was only to be expected.

Yes, for certain, I needed to reduce my drinking. All the booze we regularly consume ain't doing my body any favors.

It was when Kat came out of the bathroom, and realized that she was now all alone with the little wooden box containing the diamonds, that her good humor cracked.

She forced her brain back to thinking logically. *No,* she told herself firmly, *I'm not going to lose it tonight because of an irrational feeling. I didn't kill Thomas, and even if I did, I'm not hexed.*

She felt a sudden strong impulse to confront the hated cause of her worries. Lashing her bathrobe tight around her, she hurried over to the jewel box and flipped it open.

Sitting opposite the TV, she stared at the two diamonds on their velvet cushion. She glared hard at them, daring them to hurt her in some way. The diamonds glinted back at her like crumpled butterfly wings. Her lips trembling, her heart beating faster each second with a dread anticipation, Kat stroked the twin stones, then resolutely shut the case again. She felt even more rattled than before, and still without knowing why.

It's just me, she decided finally. *My conscience is working overtime from guilt that we caused Mr. Thomas's death.* She got up from facing the TV and used the remote to turn it off. Then she made her way over to the bed and sat on it.

She closed her eyes and concentrated and tried to recover the delicious sense of freedom that she'd—oh, so recently—felt in the bathroom. She couldn't. Opening her eyes again, she considered going back under the shower to see if it would return, then decided against it.

That would be just silly. Argh! Why am I being such a scaredy-cat tonight?

Her eyes fell on a hundred dollar bill that Summer had dropped in her rush to go meet Shane Rowland. She picked it up, then quickly dropped it again when she saw the wide bloodstain on it. Was that Chuck's blood, or Mr. Thomas's?

She looked away from the note, her gaze shifting instead to a strip of discarded condoms that Summer had to have also dropped. She grimaced. *Oops, someone's gone bareback riding tonight.*

She realized she was growing increasingly nervous, coming close to freaking out over nothing. Desperately, she looked around for something to occupy her mind until Lance returned. *Oh, why the hell did I ever agree to let him out of here?* (Yes, she was a strong, capable woman, but some atmospheres defied strength: in this case, it felt like the motel room was full of ghosts she couldn't see.) She considered turning the TV back on and watching a soap, but then realized that doing so would necessitate her moving back beside the creepy jewel box to get the remote control from the coffee table.

She finally found a satisfactory distraction. As bravely as she could, Kat sat in bed flipping through Summer's recently purchased copy of

Vogue magazine, checking out the latest in haute couture, and waiting for her husband to get back from his reconnaissance trip.

CHAPTER 17

The Monster

Outside in the passageway, Brainchew sucked and sucked on the dead woman's penis for a while to see if it could get some urine out of her. There was none of the sweet yellow liquid though. All that came out of the meaty pink tube was some white stuff that tasted disgusting, so it spat it all out and decided to drink her blood instead.

But then it had a idea. Thinking wasn't its strong point—it lacked the brains for intricate ideas—but this one . . .

It thrilled with the joy of its unfamiliar brainwave. Still holding Summer's corpse upside down, Brainchew dug a razor-sharp claw into her groin, a little bit above the root of the penis, then it ripped up through her skin a little. Almost immediately it let out a chuckle of delight. Yes, it could smell the sweet urine now, her bladder was *full* of the yellow liquid. It ripped her body open further and grinned broadly at the exposed purple sac.

But, oh no!—it saw that it had slit her bladder—her sweet water was trickling away and wasting! *NO!!!*

Without further delay, Brainchew clamped its rough gray lips over the dead woman's punctured bladder and sucked all the urine out of her.

CHAPTER 18

Dusty, mostly

Dusty was flipping nervously though a copy of *Vanity Fair*. Every now and then, at the suggestion of footsteps, she looked up quickly at both lobby doors, first outside into the front lot, then into the hallway behind her.

She'd been nervous since sending Shane off to seduce Summer, though she didn't expect anything to go wrong with that phase of their plan. Shane was a good lover and it was never hard to satisfy a woman who was already aroused. And to Dusty's mind, Summer Wallace had been way too aroused for her own good.

Dusty's real worry was time. That was the crux of the matter here. They were running out of time to get the stolen money away from the crooks. Once Bella and Rafael arrived, the plan was off. They'd been short of time from the get-go. Like a crooked pendulum in a grandfather clock, their scheme had hinged on an uncertain window of opportunity to start with, one that shortened with each ticking second. They had no idea when Bella was supposed get here.

Hopefully, Shane should have fucked the info out of Summer's slutty throat by now, and then . . .

And then she heard a rush of frantic footsteps in the hallway behind her. She spun round just as Shane burst into the lobby.

Dusty's heart instantly fell. No one had to tell her that everything had gone awry—the amount of blood covering her husband's head and shoulders was witness enough.

Shane collapsed over the reception desk gasping.

Dusty couldn't wait for him to get his breath back. "Shane, what the hell happened? What did you do to her?"

He pulled himself off the desktop and stared at her. She was scared to see how terrified he was. "I didn't do it, I didn't kill her . . ."

"She's *dead?*"

"Brainchew killed her. It's back!"

Dusty immediately felt faint. She grabbed the desk to steady herself. Around her, the lobby's walls seemed to be spinning. *What?* "Brainchew?"

Shane nodded. "Yeah, baby, the goddam monster's back."

With a huge effort, Dusty managed to stop the room whirling about her. She grabbed Shane's arm fiercely. "What happened out there? Shane, tell me exactly what happened to you. How did Summer die?"

"I told you. Brainch . . ." Then he stopped and grabbed his left buttock and winced in pain. "Shit! The damn thing almost broke my back . . ."

"Shane . . ."

He looked at her. "I'm not lyin', Dusty. Brainchew *is* back."

"Where'd you see it?"

He wiped sweat from his brow and somehow looked guilty, though she had no idea why. She'd been the one who'd sent him on the errand, right?

"We were fucking in the passageway between Rooms 5 and 6—"

Dusty was shocked. "You were screwing the bitch outside? In the goddam open where anyone could see you?"

He raised his hands to pacify her. "Not my fault, baby, honest. I suggested we get a room, but Summer was too horny to wait, and she began sucking my dick, so I pulled off her pants and she bent over and touched her toes and I fucked her from behind like that."

Dusty wasn't interested in the carnal details. "Yeah, yeah, so you did her doggy-style . . . like it's a new thing for a bitch like her. Then what happened?"

"Okay, so after we'd done it like that for five minutes—after a while we changed position, with me banging her hard from behind while she hugged the wall—then Summer said she wanted to ride me. You know, woman on top?" He looked at her questioningly, as if asking if she understood what he meant.

Wondering why he didn't just get on with it, she nodded. She had bigger concerns that his latest orgasm. Shit, if that goddam Brainchew was back, it threw a massive wrench in their monetary gears and they needed to get her brother Ambrose the Drunk in here as quickly as possible.

"So I lay down on the floor and Summer climbed on top of me and was going up and down, rubbing her clit all the while, and . . ." Again he grabbed his ass and winced. "The important thing is, with her fat breasts swinging in my face, I couldn't see a thing, and then she said she wanted me to fuck her in the ass, and so . . ."

"Spare me the goddam recital, will you?" Dusty had had enough of Shane's dallying. Trust a man to boast of his latest sexual conquest to his humiliated wife when their lives were probably in danger. Shit, it sounded like he'd been doing the whole Kama Sutra with that top-heavy bitch Summer. Listening to how much he'd enjoyed having sex with Summer, Dusty felt so bad that she could have cried. But, no, she wasn't going to give Shane the satisfaction of seeing her in tears. Oh no, she wasn't going to cry. She wouldn't give him the pleasure of knowing how much he was hurting her.

"And then, when I was deep in her ass and ramming it to her like a steam engine, she was rubbing her clit like crazy, and she began coming; and she fell on my chest and was kissing me hard and telling me how great I was—that very few guys she'd ever slept with had ever known the right way to please a hot chick like her . . . and I figured this might be the right time to ask her about the money, and . . ."

Dusty grabbed her husband by his balls and squeezed hard. "Listen to me, mister! I don't give a goddam fuck how you fucked that goddam bitch. For all the goddam damns I give you could have fucked her to death and it'd be good riddance to her bad rubbish ass." He was grimacing in pain, but she held on tight. "All I wanna know, you selfish goddam philandering prick, is how she fucking died!! And I'm not letting go of your goddamn nuts until you goddam tell me! So goddam tell me!"

Wincing, Shane nodded. Dusty released her testicle-crushing grip, but not by much.

"Alright," he wheezed, "I was just gonna say, that it was because Summer was riding me and coming that I didn't see Brainchew approach. But then I smelt it, and next thing I knew, it had pulled Summer off of my dick and bitten out her brain, and her blood flew all over me."

Dusty let go of his testicles and sagged back onto her stool, all the anger already drained from her. "You're joking, right? Baby, that thing is buried down in the Pleasant Street Cemetery. We both know it is. How can it be here now?"

"Dusty, I've no idea. We'd better get Ambrose."

"Shane, are you a hundred percent sure it was Brainchew?"

He nodded grimly, his handsome face strained. "You need to have seen the hole in the back of her head."

Dusty was suddenly scared. Extremely frightened. And her fright was reflected in her husband's eyes, even though he was still massaging his ass like it hurt badly, particularly in his butt-crack. The monster must have hit him really hard while he was fleeing.

"Shane, what are we going to—?"

"Shush!" he said suddenly. Her eyes widened in horror as she caught the look of alarm on his face. At first she though it was the monster, but when she turned around she saw Lance Somerset pushing open the lobby door.

Which, considering that Shane was currently covered in Summer's blood, was almost as bad.

"Hey," Lance said, stepping towards them, "I'm looking for—"

Then he clearly got his first good look at Shane. His eyes first widened in shock, then they narrowed to cold snakelike slits.

"Hey, man," Lance growled, stepping quickly up to the reception desk with his face unfriendly as hell. "Why are you all covered in blood? What the fuck have you done to Summer?"

Shane just stared back miserably. Dusty saw that he'd begun shaking, which just made things look worse. And Lance? Yes, her first 'rabid canine' assessment of him had been correct. He did have a very short fuse. His face was already clouding with anger; he looked like a Rottweiler pumping itself up to murder an old woman.

He was glaring at Shane, who looked more guilty than Judas Iscariot right after he'd sent the Son of God to the cross, his good looks all crumpled up into a weasel-like mess. "Answer me, man! Where'd all that goddam blood on you come from? What the fuck have you done to Summer?"

"It isn't what you think, Mr. Somerset," Dusty said quickly to cover up. Shit—this guy Lance looked like he'd explode at any moment; if he'd looked mean to start with, now he looked MEAN. "Oh, you mean why he's covered in blood? It's nothing serious. Summer's just having her period at the moment. And—ugh! How dirty can some men be?—Shane decided to give her head."

"Don't you get fucking cute with me!" Lance snapped at her. "Summer ain't like that. She's a—"

"Brainchew killed her!" Shane blurted out quickly before Lance completed the sentence.

The sudden look of intense panic on her husband's face right before his interruption made no sense to Dusty. *Wow, he's more freaked out than I thought.*

"Brainchew killed Summer," Shane repeated, hanging his head down. "It killed her. Then I fled."

Lance looked coldly at Shane. "What? Summer's dead? Shit!" With Dusty and Shane watching him nervously, he began pacing fast back and forth across the lobby with his hands bunched up into fists. "Damn, damn, damn!" he muttered just loud enough that they could hear him. "Not a-fucking-gain tonight!"

And . . . here comes the explosion, Dusty thought. Her eyes caught Shane's then flickered down towards the shotgun on the desk shelf.

Shane nodded.

Lance stopped his pacing then and turned back to them. Dusty winced. *Dammit, we waited too long.* It was too late to go for the shotgun now. Lance had a revolver out and was pointing it at them.

"Okay, now I want some goddam answers," he said. "And you'd better have them for me, or else . . ."

He let the threat hang. It was a needless warning: Dusty and Shane were both more than willing to talk.

"Put the gun away, man," Shane said. "You don't need it. Look— just ask. We'll tell you whatever you want to know."

Lance kept the weapon trained on them. "I'll be the judge of that. Now, for a start: what the hell were you saying just now? Who or what killed Summer?"

"It's called Brainchew," Dusty said. It was taking her an effort not to grab up the shotgun and let Lance have it right in the face. It was taking her almost as much effort to not look down at the weapon, which might be a giveaway that it was there, which Lance surely hadn't yet cottoned on to. She hoped her husband was using his smarts and thinking in the same direction as she.

Lance asked, "What in God's holy name is a fucking *Brainchew?*"

Shane sighed. "Look, man, you won't believe me if I just tell you, alright?" He lifted his hands in a gesture of peace. "So, come with me back to the passageway, and I'll show you Summer's body."

"No!" Dusty immediately protested. "Hell no! Shane, Brainchew might still be out there!"

"Shut up, Mrs. Rowland," Lance told her with deadly patience. "I like your husband's suggestion. I want to see Summer's body for myself, to be sure that he didn't murder her."

"Why the hell would Shane murder her? They just went off to screw." Dusty had already blurted out the latter statement before realizing its implications. *Oops, me and my big mouth!* she thought a moment later, when Lance's expression turned all quizzical.

"Yes, they did," he said slowly. "But how would *you* happen to know that, Mrs. Rowland? Weren't you supposed to be asleep when your husband called Summer? I thought—"

"We're wasting time here," Shane interrupted him. "If we wanna see the body, we'd better go now, before—"

"Yeah, yeah," Lance agreed. "Alright, let's get out there."

"No!" Dusty yelped.

"Mrs. Rowland, I already warned you to shut the fuck up. Keep your yap closed before I break all your teeth in like they're windows in a house I wanna rob. Me and your husband, we're going and that's that." She shivered as his already cold face turned several degrees colder. "And you better start praying to Jesus Almighty on His glorious throne above that I find everything back there just as your husband said, or else . . . you're gonna need all His angels to put you two back together again. Humpty Dumpty don't even come close to describing what I'll do to both of you."

He looked at her coldly till he felt she understood him, then turned to Shane and inclined his head toward the lobby door. "Come on."

Dusty was trembling as they exited the lobby. She considered grabbing up the shotgun and . . . but Lance's gun was stuck in Shane's back and she knew he wouldn't hesitate to blow her husband away.

CHAPTER 19

Shane / Lance

Outside, a light rain had just started up, altering the colors of darkness in slanting streams of liquid-crystal spears.

The familiar almost hypnotic patter of water on gravel soothed Shane's thoughts a bit. Ever conscious of the gun sticking into his back, and with the rain beating lightly on them, he led Lance across the space separating the reception building from the front block. And his ass hurt like hell with each step.

"So, did you enjoy sucking and riding tranny dick?" Lance asked as they reached the shelter of the adjacent building's walkway. "Tell me, how deep in did she go? To the balls?"

Shane's heart sank; was this asshole going to rub it in? He knew he'd convinced Dusty with his earlier show of macho bluster back in the lobby. He hadn't liked doing it though—at a point Dusty had looked really hurt, like she was going to cry. And next thing, this short jerk who looked like a Rottweiler trying to become a man had come in and almost ruined his cover-up. He'd been about blurting out that Summer was a transsexual? Shit!

But I was thinking fast and clear enough to cover that up too.

The gun poked him in the back. "I asked you a question: how deep in your ass did Summer go? You gonna have her babies?"

Shane cringed. *Oh, hell on a maypole! Is this guy such a frigging Neanderthal that he's not gonna give it a rest!?*

He looked over his shoulder at Lance and smirked. "Dude, you got it all twisted. Sure, I saw she was a tranny, but I worked *her* butt, not the other way around. She put a knife to my throat, but I convinced her to let me go first. It was while she was insisting that turnabout's fair play—you know how chicks can be so unreasonable once you've made them come—that the monster got her."

Lance snorted his disbelief. "So if she didn't fuck you, why are you walking all crooked now like your ass is on fire?"

"It was that goddam monster. It hit—"

"Forget it," Lance said gruffly. "I don't give a shit who was in who's ass—and I won't enlighten your wife as to your gay excursion either. Just think up a better, more sensible excuse for her. That 'period' explanation sucks donkey balls."

Right then it occurred to Shane that Dusty was going to find out anyway—when the cops collected the corpse. Oops.

They were now passing Room 3 and could hear loud snores, which, mingled with the rhythm of the rain, formed a strange music. Then the rain increased and blew in over the walkway, so they quickened their steps.

"There's your proof," Shane said, pointing to several red three-toed footprints on the edge of the walk, right beside the passage entrance.

Lance stared at them in shock, then hurried into the passage.

They stood together in silence, staring at Summer's corpse: at the gaping brainless hole that was now the back of her head (with the splash of bloodied blonde hair rimming it like a sun's corona); and then, after Lance knelt and rolled her over, at her staring blue eyes and the yawning gash in her neck. Summer still looked beautiful, just frozen in an unpleasant moment.

(For a surreal instant Shane again found himself distracted by Summer's incredible breasts, and a vision flashed through his mind, of himself as a plastic surgeon cutting them off her chest and transplanting them onto Dusty's.)

And there was something else wrong with Summer's corpse . . .

"What the hell is that?" Lance asked, pointing his gun at a gaping wound in the lower half of her abdomen, just above her pubic bone.

Shane winced at the sight. Summer's belly was ripped open there and her bladder (that was her bladder, wasn't it?) had been pulled out through the hole. (Doing so had also shrunken her penis, pulling the sexual organ up almost all the way into her crotch, so that it now looked like she had no manhood but three testicles between her legs.)

There was a single red puncture in the middle of Summer's extracted bladder.

"What is this shit?" Lance repeated, utter disbelief in his voice now.

"I think I know," Shane replied dully. "Brainchew has a taste for pee. It might just have worked out how to get the stuff direct from the source."

Shaking his head, Lance gently closed Summer's eyes then stood up. Now he looked horrified behind his toughness. To Shane's surprise, he looked like he might start crying; as sad as he had when he, his wife, and Summer walked into the lobby earlier in the night.

"Believe me now?" Shane asked gently.

Lance rubbed his eyes then scowled. "Do you really need to ask that stupid question?"

Then he reached overhead and smashed the single bulb illuminating the corridor with the grip of his gun. "We'll put her body in my car later," he said as darkness covered them both. "Until then, we don't need anyone looking in here and seeing her."

Next, he dragged Summer's body closer to the crates, wedging it in close by the wall, where in this new passageway of darkness and shadows it was practically invisible. Such ruthless efficiency scared Shane, who'd never been near a corpse before tonight.

Lance glanced both ways out of the passage, then he set off towards the front lot.

"Come on," he snapped over his shoulder at Shane, "let's get back to reception. Then you're gonna tell me exactly what this is about."

He turned the corner, pistol held ready to shoot any attacker. Shane hurried after him. He'd been lucky once tonight, he had no guarantee of a second narrow escape.

(To Shane's delight, he'd just realized that if Lance intended on carting Summer's body away from here before the cops came, there was no chance whatsoever of Dusty discovering that she'd been a transsexual! Ha ha ha! His secret was safe, the shame of his anal rape completely concealed. All he had to do now was insist that Dusty remain behind when they returned to move Summer's corpse into Lance's car. And knowing Dusty, that would be easy—she'd never go near a stiff.)

It didn't escape his notice either that the rain, which had now increased in ferocity, had already erased from existence the set of red footprints they'd first noticed on reaching the passage.

As they made their way to the end of the block, Shane's eyes scoured the trees bordering the lot. *Shit, that damn thing is out there and it's hungry again? If it's killed Summer, who's gonna be next?*

Shivering, he ducked into the rain after Lance, jogging across the space separating them from the reception building.

CHAPTER 20

Dusty, mostly

Back in the lobby, Dusty got out a bottle of Jim Beam Black and three glasses and poured them each a shot. Both men were wet. Shane was busy toweling his hair dry, while Lance looked like a mongrel about to shake itself.

Lance pulled up a tall stool to the front desk and sat down.

"Okay, goddammit, I believe you," he said after throwing his drink back in a single gulp. "I still don't want to believe my damn eyes, but I know what I saw back there. Tell me—what kind of frigging animal did that to Summer?"

He shook his glass at Dusty for a refill. She poured him more whiskey. She was relieved that he'd put his gun away again. There was no immediate need for them to start shooting themselves. She was upset though. The monster's reappearance was a major obstacle in the way of her getting rich tonight.

"It's not an animal," she explained after a deep sigh. "At least we think it isn't. But, that said, we don't really know *what* it is. There's every kind of theory to explain it that you can imagine. Some folks say it's a mutated man; others, that it's an alien that crashed to earth in a spaceship centuries ago and now can't get home again. My brother thinks it's a demon. He may be right. No one knows for certain."

"What *do* you know?" Lance demanded gruffly. "C'mon, don't play dumb with me, woman. You two must know *something*—you know it's goddam name after all!"

"Okay," Shane said wearily. "We'd better just tell you everything from the beginning."

Lance sipped his whiskey and nodded. "Yeah. So get on with it."

"Alright. You've surely noticed that the front block of this motel is different in design from the back two?"

"Yeah, me and Kat were wondering about that." Then he got a 'harried husband' look on his face and pulled out his cellphone. "Shit, Kat's gonna be worried stiff that I'm not back yet."

They waited while he dialed her number and spoke to her. "Hey, darling, it's me. . . . I found Summer. . . . she's—listen, sweetheart, something's come up in reception that I gotta sort out. . . . No, don't worry, just stay in the room. . . . No, don't bother about it. . . . No, I don't need any money—I'll have everything sorted out in a jiffy and be right back. I'll explain then. . . . Yeah, Summer's here . . ."

Even though she still disliked and distrusted Lance, Dusty appreciated this level of concern of a husband for his wife. (Not like her Shane, who would change his schedule on a whim and not remember to call her to say he'd be late in getting in. And then, when he wasn't home at the agreed time, she'd get all worked up that he was seeing another woman and cheating on her even when he wasn't. Oh, her aching heart. Dusty knew she'd be so much less suspicious of Shane if he'd just bother to show some consideration for her feelings at times.)

Lance hung up and put his phone away. "She'll keep for ten minutes or so." He looked darkly at Shane. "Okay, now where were we? Yeah, you were saying the front building is different from the others."

Then his face twisted up like he'd just remembered something else. "Hey, either of you got a cigarette?"

Shane found him a pack of Marlboros that someone had forgotten in their room. Dusty fished out a pack of matches from behind the pump-action shotgun.

"Thanks." Lance lit up, then puffed out a circle of blue smoke. "Yeah, alright, go on with the story."

Shane nodded. Then, picking his words carefully, he said, "The reason the front block looks different is because it had to be rebuilt. It originally looked like the others, but then it got knocked down. Something invisible—we don't know what the hell it was—hit it at 3 o'clock one Tuesday afternoon in August and leveled the whole block."

Lance made a face of disbelief. "How's that possible?"

Dusty raised her hands at him. "Don't ask us. It happened three years ago; we were both living in New York then. But as well as my dad, Tina Kravitz, the Raynham chief of police, was also here that afternoon, and she and several of her officers watched it happen."

"They weren't the only ones either," Shane added. "Old Clint Duggan—my late father-in-law—had to file an insurance claim, and so that the company would believe him, he provided page after page after page of sworn affidavits—from Chief Kravitz and the other cops, from guests staying here at the time, from the firemen who'd initially responded to his call for help . . . there'd initially been some kind of explosion, but it was completely separate from the building collapse. And, two guests recorded the building's self-demolition on their cellphones. You needed to have seen that. It was absolutely crazy—like someone was dropping invisible wrecking balls on the Sunflower from overhead."

Lance nodded through a haze of smoke, then tapped ash into a blue ashtray that Dusty shoved at him. "Alright, so the damn building fell down. What's that got to do with the monster that killed Summer?" Then he looked worried for a moment. "Say, Kat's safe in our room, right? That thing can't get in to her?"

Dusty nodded. "As long as she doesn't open the door—Brainchew doesn't really understand locks. If it's very hungry it might try to shatter the windows though, but since it's recently eaten . . ."

She left the sentence unfinished. A 'Plan-B' was suddenly forming in her mind. This new plan hinged on the rain though. Outside the lobby, the falling water seemed to have slackened off a bit, was now blowing east-to-west in crystal sheets like brush strokes from the Divine Artist. If the rain got heavier again . . . and *if* Bella Novak postponed her showing, maybe *even because* the downpour meant Rafael had to drive slower . . . Too many 'ifs' to bet on (she had to figure the monster into the equation also) . . . but her plan might work . . . *if* Aunt Luck was on their side.

And they had to keep Lance here in the lobby with them and hope the rain became a massive downpour, or even preferably, a thunderstorm.

She poured him more whiskey, a double-double this time (so much the better if they could get him drunk), then looked him straight in the eyes. "Why the building's collapse is so important to what we're telling you, is because Brainchew was discovered in the ruins afterwards."

"Not in the exact ruins," Shane corrected. "The cops discovered a stone room under the foundations. Whatever knocked the building down also drove several holes ten or so feet deep into the ground. One of those holes smashed through the ceiling of this stone room in the middle of the earth." He looked perplexed with the memory. "It was just the oddest thing, realizing that the original front block had been built over it and no one had had the slightest inkling of its existence down there."

"It was probably just an old burial chamber," Lance said, knocking his whiskey back. "Maybe some top-secret Native American sepulcher."

"But ten feet underground, and without any access steps or doors?" Shane shook his head. "Nah, this wasn't any burial place. The markings on the stone walls were later examined by several archeologists from Bridgewater Uni. All were unequivocal in their rejection of any Indian connection. Look, man, what's important is that Brainchew was also in that chamber—a short humanoid statue with a massive, massive head. Dude, you ain't never seen a head that big. It was like one of those Easter Island Moai heads, just scaled down a bit."

Dusty took over again. "Well, at least everyone assumed it was a statue that they'd found down there. Shane and I had just moved back here from the Big Apple then, so we were around when the cops found it. We both walked over from reception to have a look. The police had dug this huge pit in the middle of the ruins and we stood around it, watching them descend into the underground room on ladders. And when they all came up, we got a good clear look at what was inside. It was as eerie as seeing your great grandmother's ghost on your wedding night.

"Brainchew was lying on a stone table in the middle of the room and itself seemed made of stone. There was also a stone knife in there beside it, wrapped up in a leather scroll covered in writing which no one could decipher . . . they still can't make heads or tails of what it says."

She poured herself more whiskey and glanced out at the rain again. Yeah, it was getting heavier. Just a little bit more and then . . .

She continued her narrative: "So they brought it out of its hole and later the construction crew filled the whole chamber in."

Lance nodded. "Too dangerous to build the new foundation over a hole, right?"

They nodded and he went back to drinking and blowing smoke. Dusty regarded him cautiously. He seemed calmer, but his eyes still flickered left and right in an endless search for danger.

She knew his type: he'd kill on instinct once provoked. So they had to *not* provoke him, and wait for the rain to get heavier still.

She looked up over Lance. The wall clock opposite said 01:42 a.m. They still had at least four hours before America began waking up. More than enough time.

"But remember," she went on, "it wasn't any kind of criminal case. What I mean is, finding the chamber and the statue had nothing to do with the police investigation of the cause of the building's collapse, so they left the statue with us until the relevant state agency claimed it."

Dusty sighed with the burden of memory. "My daddy had died a week after the building collapsed—he heard some really bad news that gave him a heart attack. And so me and my older brother Ambrose were left running the motel."

Lance looked at Shane. He nodded, then grimaced. "Yeah, it's like Dusty says. The statue and knife weren't criminal evidence, so the police left them with us to look after till someone came for them."

"I wasn't having that thing in my house," Dusty said emphatically. "I'd hated it on sight with a passion. And if we kept it here in reception, someone might break in and steal it for its antique value."

Shane shrugged. "So Ambrose took it home with him and kept it in his basement."

"And then?" Lance prompted impatiently.

"And then . . . the shit hit the goddam fan." Shane grimaced again. "She-it, man, we'll try to tell you how it happened, but it really all began at Ambrose's house . . ."

Outside, the rain had just ramped up a notch. It made Dusty sad. And also, Lance wasn't getting drunk fast enough for her liking. In fact, he didn't seem to be getting drunk at all.

She said, "Ambrose and Nina and their son Michael were living two houses down from here. My dad owned that house too, but we planned to extend this reception building so both our families could live over it. But then, on that evil day, Ambrose, who was a builder, was working on someone's broken roof—I think it was Chief of Police Kravitz's—and young Michael, who was eight then, wandered downstairs alone into their basement. And while looking around for something or other, Michael decided to whittle away at a piece of wood. Only, see, he'd forgotten his penknife upstairs. So after ransacking the basement awhile for a substitute blade, he decided to use the stone knife beside the statue from the ruins instead. Both were propped up in a corner of the basement where the damp wouldn't get to them."

"And then," Shane added, "just like in the movies, the kid went and cut himself. Gashed his palm wide open with the stone knife. And then . . ."

"And then Hell came to Earth to play," Dusty finished. "Or maybe—if the thing really is an alien—outer space came down to play. Something came to have bloody fun here anyway."

CHAPTER 21

Ambrose

In Room 26, Ambrose Duggan lay in bed beside Crystal Parr. He had one arm draped over her breasts, which still had his vomit on them.

Ambrose was sweating and tossing and turning though, in the grip of a vivid nightmare, so much so that Crystal woke up and watched him. Even drunk as she was, seeing Ambrose like this scared her.

Ambrose had this nightmare often—a vivid DVD-clear replay of the events of a three-years-dead day:

***

He was down on Johnson Street, up on Chief of Police Tina Kravitz's roof. Some of the roof shingles had come loose in last night's storm, and water had leaked into the Chief's bedroom.

Ambrose paused for a moment. A slim and handsome, well-muscled man, he enjoyed his work. It was late September, with the air chilly, and the wind whipping a kaleidoscope of leaves off the trees. The sun had earlier warmed the world, but now it was windy and cold again. Still, his plaid work shirt had patches of perspiration on it.

He ran a hand through his dark hair, checked his balance on the ladder, then regarded the trees surrounding the Kravitz's cottage with a smile. The air was alive with nature's orchestra, with birds loudly tweeting the solo parts.

Yeah, so maybe Raynham wasn't Big City—lights and glitter and all—but it was home-sweet-home town and he was ready to settle down here for good now.

He'd built enough houses for people in Boston and out-of-state, mostly down in West Virginia, where he'd also met, dated, and married

Nina Price (on one skyscraper construction job she'd been his foreman Jack Price's daughter), and where their pride and joy Michael had been born. But now he was back home again and it was time to work on building his own future.

The wind blew through the trees; their leaves fell in a multicolored rain. He brushed away a fresh scattering of leaves within arm's reach, then checked the alignment of the so-far replaced shingles to confirm that another storm wouldn't dislodge them again. Yeah, these were all fine, but Mr. Kravitz and the Chief definitely needed to trim this old silver maple here of branches overhanging the house. It had been one such branch that had snapped off the tree and knocked in part of their roof.

Ambrose reflected some more on his present circumstances. Ever since his elder brother Clint Jnr. had died in that boating accident a year ago, he'd suspected that their old man would leave the motel to him when he passed on. By then Dusty, their father's favorite child, who'd defiantly run off from home to become a fashion model, had wound up working instead as a stripper in the Big Apple. That was something he'd never told their dad. It would have given the old man his fatal coronary years ahead of time.

Ambrose had been as surprised as Dusty to learn of their father's death, and even more so to discover that the old man's will made them joint owners of the Sunflower.

As an added surprise for Ambrose, Dusty, the family wild child, seemed to have finally been tamed, either by love or by an extended dose of failure. Whichever the reason, she'd said she was willing to relocate to Raynham and run the place with him. And once she was back home again, she'd gotten married.

No problem, he thought, *the more the merrier.* He and Dusty would handle the motel. Their spouses both seemed happy enough with the arrangement. Shane was already occupied driving a taxi, while Nina was scheduled to start teaching kindergarteners at Lillie B. Merrill Elementary School once the new school year began in September.

And the motel business looked good. A belated connection being made between the Sunflower and a trio of female serial killers who'd passed through Raynham during the previous month was ensuring the motel had lots of customers nowadays.

Also, a lot of their visitors wanted to see the ruins left behind when the front block had mysteriously collapsed. He mused on that for a moment—unnatural disaster as tourist attraction. Dusty, for one, kept telling him how scared-stiff she was that someone was going to climb over the barricades around the holes in the ground that the collapse had left behind, and fall in there and break their neck. He laughed: women and their endless catalogue of worries. Thankfully, rebuilding was due to start in three weeks. The delay was mostly due to the architects having to fine-tune the deluxe design they'd previously agreed on for the new front block: Dusty was insisting that the new building be split in two with a corridor between the halves.

His phone rang. He pulled it out, saw Nina's lovely face on the screen—short black hair, twinkling blue eyes, and that sunshine smile he couldn't resist even now—and accepted the call with a broad smile on his face. "Hi, honey, love ya! What's up?"

"Ambrose, you gotta come home right now! I mean *right now!*"

The smile wiped off his lips. "Calm down, hon, what's the matter?"

The fright in Nina's voice was palpable. "The statue down in the basement, it's waking up!"

"What?" Like winter winds, frost-laden chills blew down Ambrose's spine. The shock of what she'd just said was so great, he almost slipped off the ladder. "It's *what?* How?"

"Mike went down there to play—"

"Aw, Nina, I told ya not to let him . . ."

"I was washing my hair, I didn't know." The words were spilling out of her now in a jumbled rush. "Then I heard him yelling something and I ran down there to see and . . ."

"And . . . is Mike okay?" Ambrose waited with baited breath for her reply. If anything had happened to the kid . . .

"Yes, yes he is. He'd just cut his hand with that stone knife that came with the statue, and the blood had spilled on the statue."

Ambrose heaved out a sigh of relief.

"But that wasn't why he'd been yelling, darling," Nina went on. "The statue was waking up. We both got out of there fast and I called you."

Fuck, Ambrose thought. "Where's Mike now?"

"We're both in the living room. He's sitting opposite me holding his cut hand. It's the left one. It's still bleeding a little and I need to put some antiseptic cream and a Band-Aid on it. I don't know if it'll require stitches or not."

"Good, good. I'll have a look once I get back. Give Mike the phone, I wanna ask him how it happened."

"Please, Ambrose, just come home, alright? I'm scared. You can ask him when you get here."

"Yeah, yeah, I'm on my way. I'm halfway down the ladder as we speak." He packed his hammer away in his toolbox and left it up there on the edge of the roof, then hurried down the ladder. "Okay, what did Mike tell you happened?"

"You're not joking? You're coming home?"

"Yeah, right now. I'll come back here and finish this later." He walked round to the front of the Kravitz's house, where his white Nissan Frontier pickup truck was parked. "So, how'd it happen?"

"All he says is that he wanted to whittle some wood but that he'd forgotten his penknife upstairs, so he used that weird stone one with the runes, then he cut himself . . . When I got down there, the statue had its eyes open—they're small and sunken and red like cherries— and it was moving its arms, but weakly. Then it yawned. Ambrose, you need to see the thing's teeth. They're really big, like a wolf's or a shark's, but it has a lot more of them." Her voice wavered for a moment, then she added nervously, "Hold on a sec, darling, I think I hear something moving down there."

Ambrose was opening the truck door. Suddenly sensing danger, he asked, "Nina, did you lock the basement door?"

"Shit, no, we forgot!"

At that, Ambrose's heart sank. "Nina, wait! Don't go down there unarmed—take dad's shotgun with you! No, no! Better still, you and Mike get out of the house! Get out right now!"

But she'd already left to investigate whatever sound she'd heard, and she'd apparently also lowered the hand clutching the phone to her side.

With his cellphone pressed to his ear, Ambrose leapt up into the front of his truck, slammed the door shut, and fired up the engine.

"Nina? Nina?"

She never replied. The next thing he heard was her screaming, "Oh, my God! Oh my God! NOOOO!!! Run, Michael, Run!"

Then a loud howl erupted from the phone, a howl that just as abruptly ended.

Ambrose flung his phone down on the passenger seat. Then, in a screech of tires burning rubber, he spun the Nissan out of the Kravitz's yard and sped home.

***

Ambrose's nightmare now became a segued blur of road, vehicles, pedestrians, and greenery replicating his mad drive up to Carver Street.

***

Once home, Ambrose Duggan charged in through his front door.

Michael wasn't in the living room. Nina was, only her body was draped belly-down over the coffee table, and there was something weird about her head . . .

God, no, there's a hole . . . !

Ambrose ran over to Nina, then stopped dead in disbelief. "What the . . . ?"

It took him a full ten seconds to accept what he was seeing, that, yes, the entire rear of his wife's head was missing, and that she had no brain anymore—he was staring into a basin of red bone fringed by bloody black curls.

Once that understanding hit him, he quit staring at Nina and ran upstairs for his late father's shotgun.

"Mike!" he yelled at the top of his voice as he took the stairs two and three at a time. "Mike! Where are you!?"

His single thought was to find and save his son. From Nina's description of the creature's teeth, however, and from seeing what it had done to her, he realized he needed a weapon to counter it.

For the next three years, Ambrose would regret every day that he'd not looked in the kitchen first.

***

In the Duggan's kitchen, eight-year-old Michael was in a world of trouble. He'd seen the creature grab his mom and she'd screamed at him to run, but he hadn't at first. He'd waited, wanting to help her but uncertain how to. The monster—it was uglier than the Devil in those Sunday School pictures, all gray and wrinkled and smelly—moved very fast. It had his mom in a chokehold like the wrestlers used and was trying to get its teeth around the back of her head. But she was fighting it with all her might, flailing and kicking and screaming, and it was having difficulty doing so. The pair of them were crashing about the living room and knocking furniture over as they struggled.

"Run, Michael, run!" his mother howled with tears running down her face, "Get out! Your dad's on his way home!"

But Michael couldn't abandon her in her danger. Instead of fleeing through the front door, he ran into the kitchen to get a knife. He pulled the biggest carving knife they had from the rack and dashed back out to attack the creature.

But he was too late. He stood shock-still in the doorway as, with an audible 'crack' like those gunshots on TV, the gray monster—wow, its head was so godawfully big—bit off the top of his mom's head. Not the whole top, just the back half. And then it seemed to be sucking something out of her head.

Michael dropped this knife. The cut in his left palm simultaneously reopened. The hand really hurt him, and the blood from it was spilling on the floor.

When he'd run out of the kitchen, his mom's eyes had had a pleading look in them, like she'd been staring down the entrance to Hell; she'd had tears in them and all. But then, immediately after the monster had bitten off the back half of her head, her eyes just went kind of blank and . . .

Though both horrified and confused, eight-year-old Michael Duggan was suddenly embarrassed as well. *Mom! You're peeing yourself!*

It was true—as the monster sucked on her head, a wet patch was spreading across the crotch of his mom's faded pink shorts.

Michael watched in horrified fascination as the monster suddenly turned his mom upside down and began sucking on the pee-pee patch.

Ugh, that's gross! If any of the kids at school hear about this . . .

But while it sucked up his mother's urine, the horrible gray monster's eyes never left Michael's face. Like it was telling him, "Hey, kid, you're next. Just you wait, and when I'm done with your mom, I'll come eat your head and suck up your own pee too."

And now that it had her upside-down, he could see that there was now a BIG, red-dripping hole in the back of her head with nothing inside.

Michael's fear now forcefully returned to the forefront of his mind. He had to hide himself from the creature.

The little boy thought hurriedly on what to do. His previous best option of escape—to flee by the front door—was no long available to him. In the interim when he'd been in the kitchen, his mother and the creature's struggles had moved them into a position where they now blocked off the route to the front door.

If he went that way, all it needed to do was drop her and grab him instead.

He looked desperately around. To his young mind, it would be bad to flee and hide down in the basement, since that was where the monster had come from. Who knew, there might even be more of them down there.

He turned and started towards the stairs, then stopped in fear. Upstairs might also be bad: if he locked himself in his bedroom, there were those other monsters under the bed and in the closets too; they might be friends with this one. No matter what his parents said, he'd often seen the monsters in the closets, moving like shadows once the lights were off. It was only by pulling up the covers over his head that he'd kept them at bay.

"Dad! Help me!" he yelled at his mom's discarded phone, then turned and ducked back into the kitchen.

Once inside there, Michael now found that he'd made a mistake. He couldn't lock the door behind him—the kitchen door had no key. And it would be dangerous to go back outside. He didn't bother trying the side door that led out into the yard: the big red security lock his dad had fixed on it was too stiff for his young fingers to work even when he wasn't injured.

Instead, he began desperately looking around the kitchen for somewhere to hide himself, before the creature—which must have seen him enter here—came in to eat him too.

There wasn't enough space under the sink, and the cupboards were full . . .

Finally, he decided on the freezer. He pulled it open, climbed in, and shut the lid over himself again.

There, now he was safe. Even though it was darker in here than at night in winter with the lights off, and definitely darker than inside the closets in his bedroom where the monsters lived, at least he knew that all that was ever here inside the freezer was food. Packages of cold meat and vegetables and other things that were dead and couldn't harm any one.

Ouch! His hand *really* hurt now; and it was so dark in here that he couldn't be sure he wasn't getting germs on it from the food. And germs might make it get all swollen so that he'd have to get shots again at the clinic. And he hated shots.

It's really cold in here though, Michael thought. *I really mustn't stay inside here too long, or I'll get frostbite. So, I'll wait just a little, like when me and Sally May Jenkins and her brother Jake played hide and seek. I'll count to thirty, VERY slowly, and then once the monster has looked in the kitchen and found that I'm not in here, I'll come out of the freezer and leave the house, and go and wait by the road, right at the bottom of the driveway, where mom said I'm not supposed to play because of drunk drivers.*

And then, remembering that the monster had killed mommy and that they'd now have to bury her too like they'd just buried nice-but-grumpy old grandpa, Michael began crying inside the freezer, his tears becoming ice the moment they touched the metal box's sides.

Mom said dad will be home soon. Mom said dad will be home soon. Mom said dad will be home soon.

***

The gray monster stood confused in the midst of the kitchen. Where had the little boy gone? It had watched him run inside here, and his smell was still in here, but it had no idea where he was now.

A trail of blood—the boy had had a wound, the wound that had woken it up from its ageless slumber in its underground tomb—led across the kitchen to a large white box that hummed unpleasantly. It disliked the white box on sight—its humming spoke of unfamiliar arcane forces, of an immense but unfathomable sort of power. The white box scared it. It decided it would not go near the thing to investigate further.

It turned to leave the kitchen. It had just heard someone else enter the house.

The demonic creature listened and smelt. Its sense of smell delineated the new arrival as both adult and male. It could hear him moving about upstairs, running frantically from room to room, shouting desperately for the little boy.

It decided to eat the man's brains instead.

Only, as it turned towards the kitchen door, it heard a creaking sound behind it that made it pause. And then, just as if a chef had lifted the lid off of a pot of steaming meat broth to stir it, suddenly the kitchen was full of the little boy's delicious smell again.

The monster grinned its ugly grin of bloodstained teeth and turned back around to face the white box again.

***

Little Michael had suddenly found that he was suffocating inside the freezer. He couldn't breathe and it was oh so cold, so cold that the tears seemed to be freezing in his eyes before he cried them. And worst of all, he was feeling really sleepy, and if he slept, the monster might come back in and open the freezer and . . .

Okay, he decided, the monster must be gone by now. He'd counted up to thirty and started again, just to make certain.

So he pushed open the top of the freezer. It was horribly hard work to get it up, so hard that he was glad he'd not waited too long to do so, or he'd have been much too tired to do it. Even now, as he exerted himself, the gash in his left palm opened up again and began trickling blood.

The freezer open, Michael leapt upright and gulped in air in thirsty breaths.

The change in temperature from below-zero to normal, and the transition from absolute darkness to light, were both so abrupt that for a moment the little boy didn't recognize the grinning gray thing right in front of him as the monster he'd been hiding from.

Then he did, and he gulped in more air, this time for screaming in terror:

"Dad! Dad! It's got me! Help! Help!"

And then the monster grabbed him and hauled him out of the freezer.

***

Shotgun clenched tightly in hand, Ambrose was just starting down the stairs again, on his way to check the basement for Michael, when he heard him screaming.

"Dad, it's got me! Heeeelllppppp!!!"

Ambrose leapt the rest of the distance to the floor, and, charging like a bull, burst into the kitchen.

Then he sagged in the doorway.

God! Noooooo!

Right as he entered, the monster—that goddamn stone statue that had somehow come to life—was just ripping its head away from Michael's own, and amidst the spray of blood everywhere there was something large and familiarly ridged and obscenely white between its jaws . . . and Michael was slumped lifeless . . .

And then, keeping its eyes on Ambrose, it began chewing on his son's brain.

NOOOOOO!!!!!!

Half-crazed by the sight, Ambrose raised the shotgun and fired.

The blast flung the creature across the kitchen.

Michael's corpse fell on one side, the monster on the other. But then it was up off the floor and coming at him. It had a hole in the right side of its head now, a curved, jagged wound under its right eye, but it wasn't bleeding at all.

And worst of all, it was still chewing—relentlessly chewing his son Michael's brain.

With a howl of rage, Ambrose cocked the shotgun and fired again. This blast slammed the monster back against the kitchen counter, from where it toppled onto its back on the floor.

But again, it got up. It now had a hole the size of a football through its middle, through which Ambrose could clearly see the kitchen sink, but it was still coming at him.

And now that he could see inside it, he worked out the basic problem with stopping/killing it: unlike a human or animal, it didn't appear to have any organs inside its body that one could damage—it seemed to be all one solid mass. The gray of its skin continued inside its body, a featureless waxy compound that ran through it from front to back.

Ambrose fired again, this time at its head. Again the monster went down and got up again. This time, though, when it got up, it didn't attack him. Instead, it leapt over the counter and smashed its way out of the kitchen window.

Shit! It's gettin' away! Ambrose quickly unbolted the side kitchen door and chased it outside, but it had vanished.

Shotgun raised at the shoulder like an extension of his body, he made a full circuit around the house looking for it, but the gray monster was nowhere to be found.

Shit! Now that he'd been thwarted, his anger seeped from him, to be replaced by a deadly sense of loss. His emotions felt like they were organizing a bulk shutdown.

The shotgun still poised ready to shoot (though he was practically on autopilot now) Ambrose reentered the house by the kitchen door. There he dropped the shotgun on the countertop. Then he gathered up Michael's brainless body in his arms, and carried the boy's corpse out of the kitchen to place it beside his mother's.

Then, he somehow managed to dial the police. Then Ambrose collapsed to his knees and wept and wept and wept.

***

The next two weeks of Ambrose's life passed him by as a sequence of frozen 'occurrences' with blankness in-between. Afterwards, he considered it his 'lost fortnight.' He remembered it as being in a waking coma. Everything happened, but he, the central focus of those occurrences, couldn't focus on any of them:

The coroner collecting the bodies . . . sitting in the police station telling the officers what had happened . . . his shocked sister and her husband . . . Dusty organizing the funeral because he couldn't even organize himself . . .

Nina and Michael's funeral mass was like one of those movie effects where the faces in a crowd were smeared across the screen. Ambrose went through the motions, nodding and smiling on demand. He pretended to recognize those who offered their condolences; pretended to hear what they said.

But really, he was totally disconnected: Sitting there in the front pew of St. Ann's Church on North Main Street while the priest's words flitted through his brain like angry ravens. Staring at the closed coffins at the front, particularly the smaller one. Wishing with all his heart that he'd decided to look in the kitchen first before rushing upstairs for his gun.

That was what he found impossible to forgive himself for: *If I'd just opened the damn kitchen door . . . Mike would still be alive now . . .*

And afterwards, at the Pleasant Street Cemetery: "Ashes to ashes, dust to dust . . ." Sprinkling earth on the coffins . . .

And then suddenly, all the fuss and hullabaloo was over. And everyone else's lives went back to normal.

It was then, without the wall of sympathetic noise filling his head and smothering his horror, that Ambrose began drinking. The booze drowned his recollections, and though everyone else disagreed, helped Ambrose face himself in the mirror.

(With great foresight, his sister Dusty had removed their father's shotgun away to the motel, lest Ambrose one night stick its barrel in his mouth and blow his head off.)

In the meantime, an exhaustive police investigation had turned up nothing. The cops had pictures of the statue from when it was first found, and of the bloody footprints it had left in the Duggan's kitchen, and even several chunks of its flesh blown off by Ambrose's shotgun, but they couldn't find it. Ground searches with dogs, overhead helicopter searches, even diving teams in the Bristol and Plymouth county rivers and lakes were unable to find Ambrose's reanimated statue.

The only thing preventing the State Police from declaring a hoax and arraigning Ambrose in court for the murder of his family was the fact that other brainless bodies kept turning up.

By a month after Nina and Michael's deaths, there had been sixteen more corpses found with their heads empty and their blood drunk. Eleven of the victims were from Raynham. The other five were from Bridgewater, the town bordering Raynham on the northeast.

But of the monster doing the killing—by now everyone was calling it Brainchew—there was no sign. It was still in Raynham, that was for sure. By this time all the townsfolk were sleeping with one eye open, and some with bike helmets on.

Ironically, it was Ambrose himself, who, during one of his shortening periods of sobriety, solved the mystery of the missing monster's whereabouts.

At the time, Ambrose, though well on his way to arriving there, wasn't yet the total lush he'd soon become. One reason he still stayed partly sober was because, so long as his family's killer still roamed the countryside, he had a strong sense of unfinished business.

If I can just get my hands on that damn demon-thing. I'll kill it . . .

This wasn't some idle mental threat or boast either. Ambrose *had* already worked out how to kill it. Entirely by accident.

Once, while getting himself a sandwich in the middle of the night, he'd tripped and fallen against the kitchen counter. He'd wound up flat on the floor with his head angled just right to see a strip of the monster's skin that was wedged under the fridge. The police had missed that little bit.

After retrieving the chunk of rubbery skin, Ambrose had forgotten about eating anything. Instead, he'd had a sudden burst of 'drunk's inspiration,' and decided to 'stab the piece of skin to death.'

So, at two o'clock in the morning, Ambrose staggered down the stairs to his basement, fetched the stone knife that had come along with the statue, and tried to kill the piece of monster that he'd found.

On the first stab, the strip of skin had instantly hardened back to its previous rock-like consistency.

Ambrose was disappointed. The strip of skin wasn't playing fair; he'd expected more of a challenge before it 'died.'

"Shit, this ain't no goddam fun," he'd growled and passed out.

However, when he'd sobered up in the morning, he realized what he'd accomplished, and the implications of it.

The stone knife would petrify Brainchew again. If he could just find Brainchew to stab.

But in this too, fate was on his side. Even if he'd been drunk as a skunk last night, he did remember one thing about that rubbery skin before he'd petrified it:

Its distinctive smell.

Brainchew's strange stink had been haunting Ambrose for a while now. Mainly because it had proved so impossible to track. Like 'rotting earth' was the best he could describe the smell; like wet sand that was somehow also raw meat that had gone off.

As the days of failed police hunts became weeks, and the body count rose, Ambrose had been increasingly perplexed by the riddle of how something that stank that bad could prove so hard to find. Surely anyone walking by the monster's hiding place would smell it ten yards off.

But not so the sniffer dogs.

And now—as his alcoholic mind filtered itself through the sieve of his latest hangover—it hit him as to *why* they couldn't smell it:

The damn monster has to be hiding somewhere that stinks even worse than it does!

And after two hours of fevered thinking, aided by six cans of Bud Light, Ambrose realized that he knew where Brainchew was hiding out. Whether by drunken genius or inspiration, his mind had latched on to one particular location and refused to leave it.

McKinney's Pig Farm—the damn creature has to be there! It's the only place!

The more he thought on it, the more convinced Ambrose was that he'd guessed right. Pig environments stank by nature, with all the mud they needed to keep cool, and the slop they got fed, and all their poop, and mash and . . . and old Ed McKinney had literally hundreds of the damn beasts.

With that kind of almighty reek rising heavenward 24/7, no one was going to notice a little additional smell, no matter how weird it was.

Time to get busy, Ambrose thought, staggering to his feet. He first plodded towards the staircase to the upper floor, then stopped on remembering that Dusty had taken the shotgun away to the motel so he didn't off himself with it.

"Aw well," he slurred, "a bellyful of buckshot didn't kill the asshole the first time around anyway."

He did, however, make a trip back down into the basement to get a hard hat. Once that was firmly in place on his head, he picked up the stone knife. Last of all, he slipped a fresh pint of Jack Daniels into his right pants pocket.

Live or die, a guy needed his liquor nearby.

Finally, holding the knife, he staggered towards the front door. "I'm gonna skin me a demon this afternoon. Hell yeah, for sure I am."

***

Ambrose's white pickup truck screeched to a halt in the mud of McKinney's Pig Farm. He switched off the engine, leapt out of the truck, and walked towards the rows of warehouse-like barns, looking for Ed McKinney.

The old farmer saw him coming and met him at the entrance to the second barn. He knew Ambrose well, had attended his family's funeral. In fact, he was Ambrose's uncle once removed—Ed McKinney and Ambrose's father Clint Duggan were cousins.

Hands stuck in the pockets of his muddy denim overalls, he greeted Ambrose. His smile was sincere and sympathetic, his greeting warm. "Hiya, son, what brings you here today?"

"Ed, I think you've got an intruder on your property."

Ed McKinney could instantly smell that Ambrose had been drinking. And with that hard hat on, he just prayed that Ambrose wasn't about going on any construction jobs—if he did he was a sure bet to fall eight stories and break his neck. And why was he even behind a steering wheel? *I mean, this young man needs to lose his driving license already—that's clearly a whiskey bottle bulging out his trouser pocket.*

On another day Ed might have chosen just to humor Ambrose, invite him over into the farmhouse for a drink and chew the fat about family stuff till he drove off again. But today, Ambrose had the sort of crazy look in his eyes that Ed only ever recalled seeing during the Vietnam War, when one of their platoon felt his number was up and his bucket list resolution was to take as many Viet Cong as possible with him when he died.

And then there was that odd knife Ambrose was holding. It didn't glint like metal, but it sure looked sharp. One thing was sure— Ambrose was here for deadly business, though what sort of business, Ed had no idea. *What the hell does he mean—I got an intruder on my land?*

Ambrose meanwhile, was looking down the line of swine residences like a starving wolf desperate to eat the piglets they contained.

"Son, are you okay?" Ed ventured to ask. "I mean, as in *really* okay?"

After a loud burp, Ambrose asked, "Tell me, Ed, are any of your barns empty at the moment? And which ones are they?"

Ed mused awhile on the question, then, while Ambrose adjusted his headgear, he answered, "No idea why you wanna know, Ambrose, but number eight's vacant at the moment. It's been empty for about a month now. We had to move all the hogs into number six. One of the walls fell in, and three pipes burst and flooded everywhere, so . . ."

But Ambrose wasn't listening any more, he was already running down towards the empty barn.

Ed watched him go for a moment. Then he made his worried way into the farmhouse to call the police. Ambrose sure was acting crazy-like all of a sudden.

***

Inside the eighth pig barn was dim and stinky. The electricity had been turned off to prevent an electrocution accident, but the area of collapsed wall on his right let in enough light to see by.

Ambrose grunted and trudged into the half-light. Then he paused and got out his bottle of Jack Daniels. He took a good long drink, then looked around for the monster.

Damn! That burst pipe Ed mentioned really swamped this place. He was standing in water up to his ankles, water that even now trickled out through the barn door to soak away. Ambrose drunkenly figured the old guy had a well on the farm, or else his water bill would be sky-high. Which would also explain why he hadn't yet bothered with plugging his damn leak.

Ambrose capped his bottle of drink again and put it away. Then, after checking that his hat was still firmly on his head, he unsteadily walked a short distance down into the semi-darkness. He held the stone knife up in front of him, ready to stab anything that moved in here.

The deserted pig sties everywhere commanded his attention. All those empty enclosures stretching out left and right of him hypnotized him with their orderliness. Wet straw was scattered everywhere as though the evacuated pigs had been forcibly prevented from dragging it along with them to their new homes. Most of the straw was either submerged in, or floated on, inches of water.

Then there was the smell that permeated the place, like waterlogged cartons of stuff were rotting away somewhere. And the stink of rancid, moldy pigswill . . . and there was a thick reek of rotting meat too, like Ed McKinney had forgotten some of his hogs in here and they'd died of hunger.

And when Ambrose paused for a moment and sniffed the air, he imagined he could also smell the monster he was after here in the barn. Like the reek of an evil orchid planted among toadstools, Ambrose could just make out that 'rotten earth' smell over the others.

Yeah, the gray demon's in here somewhere.

His first target was the stack of crates piled at the far end of the barn, big crates that had at one time housed machinery. That area would make a great hiding place.

On some primal level—maybe via its layers of overlapping shadows like dissolved gods—the realm of crates magnetized Ambrose. Once he reached them, he stood staring for a while at their wooden towers.

Then he traced the bases of the stacks of boxes, splashing water and tapping each wooden container in turn with the stone knife.

"Hey, stinky, I can smell you, you damn murdering motherfucker. Get your ass out here where I can kill it!"

There was no response. But it was true: he sure as hell *could* smell Brainchew now. The monster was definitely nearby.

Ambrose turned and scanned the barn again. "Now where the hell are you, demon? I'm killin' you today for sure. For my dead family."

This statement was the trigger for a month's worth of suppressed emotions to bubble to the surface of his anguished soul.

For one sober and crystal-clear moment, Ambrose saw his dead wife and son how he loved to remember them: Nina wearing a cream-colored party dress patterned with red flowers, her blue eyes twinkling at him with love, her lips and nails painted a deep red, and with her black hair piled up and pinned back because today was Dusty's thirty-third birthday and they were all having dinner—Italian—at Harry's La Casa Mia down on Broadway. And Michael, who wasn't going with them because it was a Tuesday, sitting on the living room sofa with Cora Watkins, who was babysitting for them. Michael grinning and insisting that they bring a slice of Aunt Dusty's birthday cake home for him or he was boycotting school tomorrow, and Nina walking over and ruffling his already tousled brown hair, and the two of them giggling . . . and Ambrose finally having to walk over and practically carry Nina out of the living room (while 13-year-old Cora hid her eyes in embarrassment). Much like he'd have to carry her back into the house later because she'd gotten drunk on two glasses of red wine again . . . Then making love to Nina, and falling asleep wrapped in her arms, and the next morning, both of them giggling madly because they'd forgotten to bring Michael his slice of birthday cake, and then conspiring to fake it by buying him one from the Cake Diner shop at the corner.

The memories brought hot tears to Ambrose eyes. To steady himself, he got out his pint of whiskey and took a long pull. *Oh, I'm so gonna kill that monster!*

Then he caught a movement out of the corner of his eye and hastily capped the bottle again. *Shit! What the hell just moved over there in the corner?*

He turned to look. He wiped the tears from his eyes to see clearly, then squinted through the shadows. But it was just rats chewing on a swollen hog carcass . . .

So where the hell was the damn thing?

What Ambrose was too drunk to consider, was that the monster was *hiding* from him. After the outcome of their first fight, it was wary (even scared) of him. And so it was waiting, trying to ambush him.

And then suddenly, it was attacking him. He spun around at a sound from behind and overhead to see a dark shape falling at him from the top of the stacked crates.

His instinctive forward leap out of its way slammed him against the wall of crates, which made him drop the stone knife into the water. Before he could either retrieve the knife or spin around to face the monster, it was on his back and trying to bite into his head, its claws digging like spades into his shoulder blades.

Ambrose's reflexes were dulled by all the alcohol in his system, but his desire to kill the 'demon' and avenge his family sliced through his inebriation with the keenness of a hunting knife. The pain of its claws in his flesh also helped to alert him.

Still facing the crates, he heard a loud 'Krak' as Brainchew bit away the back of his hard hat, then his survival instincts kicked in fully and he shook the monster off his shoulders. He felt it fall away from him and splash into the water.

He spun around to face it. It was already back on its feet again, its form more shadow than substance in the semi-dark, its red eyes glittering like LEDs in its oversized head.

He winced. Yeah, just like he'd thought, the damn thing had healed itself—it no longer had that shotgun-blast-hole through its middle. Nor did it have any scars that showed he'd ever wounded it either.

Its mouth was moving. Ambrose saw that it was trying to eat his safety hat. Then, with a disgusted sound, it spat out the chunks of cracked white plastic.

"Hey!" he taunted it. "My head's still intact. Better luck next time, ya slimy motherfucker."

Not taking his eyes off the monster, he felt around with his left foot in the water for the stone knife. The monster wasn't attacking him yet, and he had no idea why, but he needed to be ready when it did—when it had spat out the bits of hard hat he'd gotten a shadowy look at his teeth, and for God's sake, they looked ridiculously big now. Almost like they'd grown larger since that last encounter in the kitchen.

He finally located the knife, only it was at that exact moment that Brainchew launched itself at him.

He ducked right, away from the fallen knife, but he knew where it was now.

The monster bounced off the crates and came at him again, its hands going for his neck like it planned on strangling him. He knocked its fingers away from his throat, and they grappled. He was surprised at how strong it was—much stronger than its short stature would suggest. He also now realized that its elongated head was helping it get its mouth much closer to him than he liked. Its shoulders barely reached the height of his chest, but its goddam head . . .

And now, to his added disadvantage, the alcohol in his body—temporarily dethroned by adrenalin—was regaining the rulership of his nervous system again.

And positioned as they were, Brainchew was between him and the only thing he knew could kill it.

Shit. Now that they'd gotten 'up close and personal,' the thing's horrible smell was suffocating him. It smelt like he was being buried alive under a deluge of wet sand and maggoty meat. He shoved hard against it, with his muscles threatening to quit on him at any moment and betray him into the embrace of his enemy.

Brainchew was forcing itself in real close to him now, trying to clamp its teeth on his throat. And all the while, its two sunken red eyes—those eyes like pits filled with tomato ketchup—gleamed at him with an infernal hunger.

All the alcohol in his head aside, Ambrose now realized that this asshole creature remembered him, and it wanted to eat him as payback for the pain he'd once caused it.

Oh yeah, like you didn't piss me off too?

He kneed the monster in its belly, then, while it fought to close in on him again, he got a foot up between their bodies and booted it off him. It splashed back into the mud again, then got up again.

While it regarded him sullenly, Ambrose figured 'what the hell?', pulled out his bottle of whiskey, and took a long drink. This was purely wino-instinct at work—the fight had got him so thirsty that he needed a nip. At that moment it was crucial to him—way more crucial than saving his skin—that he quenched his liquor craving.

The monster had no idea what Ambrose was up to, but it saw its opportunity to strike. It charged at Ambrose, who, caught off-guard and having no other recourse, simply spat his mouthful of booze in its face.

He was shocked when the creature, flinging up its hands to its eyes, reeled back howling like a whipped dog, the first sounds other than grunts that he'd heard it make.

Still howling and scratching at its eyes, Brainchew collapsed into the water-logged straw and mud on the barn floor, then began splashing water everywhere.

Ambrose stared bemused at it for a moment. "So, I guess then that there's *two* things you don't like, asshole."

He took another swig of whiskey and put the bottle away again.

Then quickly, before Brainchew recovered its wits, he got the stone knife out of the water and slammed it hard into the top of the flailing monster's head, growling, "This one's for Nina and little Mike!"

As before, with the strip of skin at home, the result was immediate. Brainchew instantly stopped thrashing about and froze back into a statue—its arms straightening out by its sides, its legs coming together, its eyes shutting, and its mouth slamming shut into an expressionless seam across the lower half of its elongated face.

The stone knife Ambrose had stabbed it with rolled off its petrified head and splashed into the water.

He retrieved the knife and prodded the 'statue' with it, taking his time to ensure it wouldn't revive itself.

Then he smirked at it. *There! I said I'd get you, and I did!*

Still smirking, he sat down on the frozen monster's ugly head and polished off his whiskey.

***

Ambrose's nightmare recollection always ended at this point, on a high, with him falling asleep in the barn.

Beside him in his motel bed, Crystal had been finding it impossible to get back to sleep, so instead she'd been watching Ambrose do so. The call girl blues had their hooks sunk deep in her tonight, and were refusing to let her go.

Crystal was sipping from a can of cold beer, wondering why the air conditioning didn't seem to be working, and why she felt so goddam depressed tonight.

Maybe it's 'cos I haven't yet washed Ambrose's puke off my boobs?

Now she saw Ambrose grin broadly in his sleep. That puzzled her deeply, and depressed her even more, so she began crying again. *What the hell is he happy about? What does either of us have to be happy about?*

Then she heard Ambrose growl: "Fuck you, you stinky, gray, head-eating motherfucker . . . I win!"

She shuddered.

CHAPTER 22

Dusty / Lance

". . . When the police got there," Dusty concluded, "Ambrose was out cold, lying on his back in the mire. The investigators figured he'd originally been lying on Brainchew but then had slid off it into the water. The only reason he hadn't frigging drowned himself was because he was using the monster's head for a pillow."

She grimaced. "No one knows how long the creature might have gone on killing folks for if Ambrose hadn't worked out its location. The damn thing had been busy. The thing that the rats had been eating—what my brother thought was a rotting pig carcass—was actually the remains of a missing 12-year-old girl, Rosemary Brown, who'd vanished two weeks earlier. Rosemary was missing the back of her head too. There were six or seven or eight more bodies in the barn . . ."

Dusty stopped speaking and stared at Lance. She felt worn out by the horrible emotions the recollection had brought with it; it felt like her sister-in-law and nephew were both freshly dead again and she'd just come home from attending their funeral. "Do you understand what we're up against? I mean, how goddam hard to stop it is?" Then without waiting for his answer, she looked away from him, out at the rain, which was still coming down in thick sheets. Let Shane deal with Lance for the moment.

She heard Lance ask, "But if your brother stopped it, how the hell is it suddenly awake again tonight?"

Shane replied, "That's a puzzle for Marilyn vos Savant to solve. We don't frigging know, man? After the investigations were done, the cops buried the thing in the Pleasant Street Cemetery, which is just round the corner from our police station. Its grave is set in a deep corner of the graveyard, beneath a clump of old trees; the basic idea

149

of separating it being that, so long as no one bled on it again it couldn't wake up."

Then Shane asked, "Hey, man, you okay? Why're you looking so sick all of a sudden?"

Ah, he's just had too much booze, Dusty figured happily. She noted with additional delight that the rain had just got much heavier.

***

Lance was staring at Shane in horror.

Shit, he thought, remembering where he'd left Chuck's corpse and putting two and two together in his mind. *I woke the damn thing up! I did!*

Then he calmed a bit. There was no point in enlightening the motel owners that he'd had anything to do with their monster's resurrection. The sensible thing for him to do now was to hurry back to Room 8 and get Kat and blow this joint, then call Bella Novak and set up their rendezvous elsewhere, for tomorrow night. Or better still, they'd wait till the heat over Thomas's robbery and death blew over—they had Thomas's cash to spend till then . . .

Lance stubbed out his cigarette in the blue ashtray. Leaving his fresh drink untouched, he sat back on the stool, scratching his chin while his mind worked to resolve this latest of tonight's unforeseens.

Okay, he needed to put Summer's body in the trunk of the Ford first. And he'd likely now need to drive back down to the damn cemetery and retrieve Chuck's body too. (Thank God it was still just two in the morning!) His best bet to dispose of their bodies now looked to be to bury the pair out in a cornfield somewhere. Heaven knew there were enough of them around these parts.

Oh yeah, and for the moment they'd best remain in the state: Lance didn't want the goddam Feds looking for them too.

He looked from Shane Rowland to his wife, who for some reason now had her attention focused outside the lobby. She was a pretty woman, this Mrs. Rowland, and she had a good figure too, though her face showed evidence of major hard living in her past, like she'd had a bad drug habit during her twenties. Lance saw them all the time: small-town girls who, in a fit of rebellion, ran off to their Big City of choice—Boston or Philly, or the Big Apple. The really desperate to get away crossed the country to Las Vegas or L.A. Once there, they played the Hot Mess Game till they were thirty-two or thirty-five and their looks were starting to give out, and they were tired of waitressing because they couldn't be models or movie stars, and then they ran back home again to daddy and mommy, who told them all was forgiven, and could darling returnee daughter now please settle down and marry Robert Redneck who lived down the street and who'd been in love with her since fifth grade? The answer to which was invariably yes.

Then Mrs. Rowland turned away from staring outside of reception (where it was now raining cats and dogs) and smiling, poured him more whiskey. *Oh yeah, she's one hell of a good-looking broad. I daresay Shane Rowland's a happy man. But if he's got a woman this smoking hot in his bed, why'd he go about sniffing around Summer?* He smirked. *Not like the damn fool's ever gonna forget tonight's infidelity! Damn, I'd have paid a thousand bucks to have seen his face when she pulled her dick out!*

"What I don't get," he said, picking his words carefully, "is . . . why'd you keep the monster here in Raynham? Why not ship it away to some top-secret government facility where it can't harm anyone?"

Shane shrugged. "Dude, I dunno. That bit always baffled me too. Maybe a bureaucratic screwup, or maybe—"

Then Lance saw that Mrs. Rowland was pointing a shotgun at him over the reception desk.

Her husband looked equally shocked. "Dusty, what are you doing?"

Lance didn't bother asking her a similar question. He went for his own gun.

He'd just got it in his hand when Mrs. Rowland fired.

Boom!

Oh, shit! The shotgun blast hit him right in the belly and flung him back off his stool and across the lobby to crash on the floor.

There Lance lay on his back with a bleeding fire raging in his gut, wondering what the hell was going on.

***

Boom!

The recoil from the shotgun flung Dusty back against the slots where they kept the motel files and room keys.

Dusty had never shot anyone before. For an eternity afterwards, it seemed like the thunder outside was rumbling in her ears. Her right shoulder felt like she'd shattered it.

(Unbeknownst to either Shane or Lance, Dusty had been keeping a watchful eye on the rain-hued night sky. Just as she lifted the shotgun—bang on cue—she'd seen a distant flash of lightning. She'd waited a second longer then pulled the trigger, perfectly synchronizing the motion of her finger with the accompanying-but-delayed boom of thunder.)

Then the fury and the noise were over and the smoke everywhere was clearing and her shoulder only ached, and Shane was staring at her in horror, and she was realizing that shooting someone wasn't actually as hard as people always made it out to be. You just disliked them enough, or had another good reason (in this case, both), and you pointed the gun at them and pulled the trigger.

The shotgun in her hands felt wonderfully warm and solid.

"What the hell did you do that for?" Shane was asking her.

Before replying, Dusty first looked over the reception desk to ensure that Lance was no longer a threat to them. He clearly wasn't: he lay on his back groaning and twitching, with a bloody hole in his belly. His revolver lay a yard to the left of him.

Dusty looked back at her husband, who still had his mouth open. "Shane, stop gaping and get his gun!"

Shane slowly nodded, then ran around the desk and picked up Lance's gun. Then he leaned over the front of the reception desk and resumed gaping at Dusty.

Outside, the rain was now heavier than ever. Dusty pointed out at the cascading water. "It's coming down so loud and hard out there, no one can have heard the gunshot."

To her relief, Shane got it. "And if they did," he said once he understood, "they'll imagine it was just another thunderclap." Then he winced and pointed over at Lance. "He's not dead yet, Dusty. What're we gonna do about him?"

By now there was a widening pool of blood forming around Lance.

"No problem," Dusty replied. "We'll throw him out in the rain. All this bleeding he's doing will surely attract Brainchew."

"Noooo!" Lance groaned loudly, lifting his head off the floor to glare at them both. Then a spasm of pain ripped through him and he collapsed again.

Shane furrowed his brow and chewed his lower lip a bit while looking out at the rain himself. Dusty waited patiently for him to get through with deciding to do what had to be done. In the meantime, she cocked the shotgun and kept a cool eye on Lance, in case he miraculously got back to his feet and she had to blow him away again.

Finally Shane nodded at her. "Yeah, that's a great plan—let's do it."

She walked around the desk to join him. Then they both walked over to stare down at Lance.

"He ain't gonna last too long," Shane said. "His guts looks like that bolognaise sauce you always put on our spaghetti. The sooner we put him out into the rain, the better."

Lance was staring up at them with a world of pain in his eyes, and that seeping, chewed-up red mess in his belly. Oddly enough, now that he was dying, he somehow looked handsome to Dusty.

"Don't do . . . !" he started saying. But then a stream of blood poured out of his mouth and he fell silent again.

After a quick glance at Dusty and a shrug, Shane tucked Lance's revolver into his belt. Then, with Dusty keeping her shotgun pointed at Lance's head, he grabbed the man's wrists and unceremoniously dragged him towards the front lobby door, leaving a red smear behind them.

As he was pulled away, Lance's cellphone slipped out of his pocket onto the floor. Dusty kicked it towards the door, where it broke apart.

Oops, she thought immediately afterwards, *that could have shattered the glass.*

"We know you're a damn crook," she hissed unsympathetically down at Lance as they neared the door. "So we're gonna tell the cops that you tried to stick us up and we shot you in self-defense."

She stepped quickly in front of Shane, pulled the glass door open, then got out of the way.

As the first wash of rain blew in over them, Lance managed to gasp some words out: "N-n-no, please . . . Kat'll . . . pay . . . you. We've got . . . lots . . . of cash."

"Yeah, yeah, man," Shane replied. "*We know* you've got money. Why the hell do you think we shot you? It'll be easier to get the money off your wife now that she's all alone in your room."

Leaving Lance to think that over, they dumped him out in the rain for the demon to get.

***

Lying on his back on the gravel by the front steps of the reception building while the rain came down on him in sheets, Lance Somerset knew that he was dying; it was simply a matter of how soon he'd expire.

Those bastards! he silently raged. *All that while when we were palling up, they were planning an ambush and I never suspected it? How the hell could I be so frigging dumb? The bitch shot me! Aw, hell, this goddam hurts!*

And just how sour could one job go? This was either Kat's 'bad luck' premonition coming to pass with a vengeance, or else a whole lifetime's worth of bad breaks happening in one night. *What I gotta do now is somehow warn Kat to get the hell out of Room 8 before those bastard Rowlands get over there.*

Dammit—where's my phone!? Then Lance remembered that his phone had dropped out of his pocket and that that evil bitch Mrs. Rowland had kicked it. The phone's battery had actually hit him in the eye when it shattered. *And even if I had the goddam thing, this goddam rainfall . . .*

The unceasing fall of water on him was temporarily keeping him from passing out, stopping him from making that final trip over into oblivion. (The hammering of the water on his shredded guts was an indescribable agony.) But with the amount of blood he'd already lost, Lance doubted he had more than fifteen minutes of life left.

Shit, they put me out in the rain for Brainchew to get! Lying on the floor like he was, he was easy pickings for the creature. And he didn't even have a weapon!

By sheer exertion of willpower, Lance forced himself up to a sitting position and quickly looked around through the driving rain. The monster wasn't anywhere in sight. When Lance looked up towards the lobby, he saw that Shane Rowland was still by the lobby door. The bastard seemed to be having some trouble getting it shut again. Then finally, the sliver of light inside the rectangular frame vanished and Shane stalked off out of sight.

Anger filled Lance. He wanted to charge up the damn steps and grab his gun and shove it up Shane's queer ass and fuck him hard with it—finish off what Summer started.

But he'd lost way too much blood now and the pain in his gut was as fierce as if he was being stabbed with hot pokers, and he slumped back down onto the wet gravel again. And the rain just kept beating on him and soaking him worse than a rat in a flooded sewer, filling him through and through with cold, and not letting him die.

His anger against the Rowlands just made him hurt more, so he concentrated all his energies on turning himself over onto his belly.

A long pause after that—when the raging inferno consuming his insides had reduced to smoldering embers—he began crawling over towards the front block, pulling himself over the gravel inch by painful inch.

I gotta warn my darling Kat.

Fifty or sixty yards, that's all he had to travel. He could do it. He'd warn Kat to get the hell out of Raynham. Kat was sure to start screaming and carrying on, and want him to come along too, but no way in hell did Lance see that happening. *Sorry, babe, but I'm done. The Wise Guy in the Sky has definitely dialed my draft number for Heaven's Army tonight.*

He'd just reached the front block. He rested his head on the walkway to catch some strength. He wasn't sure if it would be easier crawling up on the concrete walk where there was less rain, or if he should just remain down on the lot and endure the relentless drenching.

Yeah, Kat'll be okay, he thought, and the thought gave him renewed strength. *With that fifty-five grand we got from Thomas's safe . . . and she still has Mr. Drake's diamonds. . . . But why the hell hasn't Bella turned up yet to collect them for him? But still . . .*

Finally opting to stay down in the rain (as it seemed to be keeping him alert and alive), Lance resumed dragging himself along. Soon he'd passed Room 3, where the earlier snoring—additional thunder at the storm's disposal—was as loud as ever. Damn, that guy needed soft palate implants for sure!

The night was blacker than death and Lance felt its entire weight pressing on him; like it was beckoning him to become one with its darkness. It was a miserable, cold summoning, one he had to resist for as long as he could.

Room 8 wasn't far off now. And Lance suddenly understood that *he was* doing the most sensible thing in this case. Once he got Kat safely out of here and the cops found him dead, the cops would have an open-and-shut case. They wouldn't be able to pin the robbery on Kat, because she'd not entered Thomas's house with them. He was also certain that once the stolen money was gone along with Kat, the Rowlands would adjust whatever tale they told the cops to exclude her—they wouldn't dare chance Bella Novak's wrath after all that hush money she'd paid them.

So Kat would definitely be okay. No, with two-fifty grand assured from tonight and all their savings to add to that, Kat would be better than okay. She'd be sitting prettier than a robin on a high branch. *It's just a shame I won't be spending it with her . . . oh shit, I love that woman so much—I just want her to be happy.*

Yeah, Lance felt better now. He didn't hurt so much anymore either. He'd just arrived at the passageway in the middle of the block—pitch dark because he'd smashed the light bulb—where they'd left Summer.

He pulled himself past it. It was a damn shame to have to leave her in there, but it couldn't be helped now.

Then, blood spilling over his lips, he grinned. But . . . Shane's secret would be out! Everyone was gonna know that he'd been assed by a tranny!

Lance had to laugh at that, though it felt like a rake going through his guts. *The son-of-a-bitch never even appreciated that I was doing him a favor!*

Still laughing, he crawled on. His singular intent now was to make it to the door of Room 8 and see his beloved Kat one last time. And to tell her that he loved her before dying. Maybe even expire in her arms while kissing her soft and beautiful lips.

Then, all of a sudden, something felt wrong to Lance. It took him a moment to realize what the problem was: Yeah, it was still raining, but . . .

But the rain *wasn't* falling on him, and he was still out on the lot amidst the relentless downpour, staring at their gray Ford Focus just twenty yards off. The rain was falling all around him, but . . .

Shit! He turned his head up and saw that Brainchew was bent over him, and that the rain was beating on the monster's back instead of on his, and then running off its sides.

He collapsed onto his side and gaped at it, its form revealed clearly by the walkway lights. *My god, it's even uglier that the Rowlands said it was.*

All he could really focus on though, were its sunken red eyes—eyes like telescoped lakes of lava—and its massive tooth-filled mouth, which was both open and grinning at him with a sort of diseased psychotic pleasure.

Lance thought fast. *I can yell for Kat from here. I'm near enough to our room now that she should hear me. But if I do, and she comes out and this abomination catches her . . . Ugh!* An utterly revolting vision of Brainchew, with its toothy maw and thick rubbery lips wrapped over his darling wife's head and biting down, filled Lance's mind. *Oh, hell no . . . But I also need to warn her about those goddam murdering Rowland assholes . . . but if this thing catches her . . . but . . . !*

And then it ceased to matter what Lance was going to do, because Brainchew covered his mouth with a hand and bent lower and began sucking on his bleeding guts so that his blood didn't go to waste.

And Lance now found that though he really, really, really, really needed to scream, he couldn't. And it was simply horrible to be in that much agony and unable to vocalize it.

He also discovered that he'd badly misjudged how long he still had to live. The agony went on for a very long time. And to his horror, the driving rain seemed intent on keeping him awake and alert for as long as it could.

CHAPTER 23

Shane & Dusty

"It's got him," Shane announced in celebratory tones from the lobby door. "Yes, it's sucking on his guts right now, while he's flailing left and right in pain. I think it's trying to make him wet himself."

"Great," Dusty replied from behind the reception desk. "Look, baby, lock the damn door and let's have a council of war. We need to work out how best to get the money from his wife."

"We'll have to wait a bit," Shane said. "Brainchew's still over by Room 6."

"We can't wait *too* long," Dusty pointed out. "It's a miracle that Bella hasn't arrived yet."

Shane looked back from the door. "Most likely her limo got a flat in the rain or a tree fell over and blocked the road or something."

"He said they've got a lot of money on them. How much do you figure?"

"A lot less than they're gonna get from Bella Novak."

Dusty felt celebratory too. "Be serious, baby."

"I am being serious. Maybe we should wait till Bella's left after handing over the money?"

"Too dangerous. She might want to see the other members of the gang first. And she's *not here yet*. And why are you spending so much time getting the door closed?"

"It won't shut properly. It started after we threw Lance outside. I thought I'd fixed it then, but now it's even worse. It was open again when I walked back for a look."

Dusty faked a look of worry. "Oh no. Maybe Lance hexed us?"

Shane rolled his eyes. "Now *you* be serious."

"Calm down, I'm just kidding." She waved a glass of whiskey at him. "Look, hurry up and shut it and come have a drink with me, and let's get this all thought out."

Shane shoved the door till it shut again, but gave up after two attempts to shoot the lock. Each time he opened it to see what the trouble was, a fresh gust of rain blew in and drenched him, and he'd had enough.

Besides, now that the adrenalin rush of killing Lance was past, his natural aversion to violence and nervousness around bloodshed had returned. Each time Shane had to look out of the door, he couldn't shake a feeling of worry that Brainchew was lurking just outside there and would grab him. It was easy for Dusty to talk about making plans and be so optimistic about robbing Lance's wife—she hadn't seen the creature in action yet. And even now, he could see that she wasn't making any moves to come and watch Brainchew savaging Lance over by the front block.

(If Shane had been less nervous and had checked properly for the cause of the problem with the door, he'd have discovered that the metal battery cover for Lance's destroyed cellphone had gotten stuck inside the door's lower hinge.)

So Shane left the door sort-of-locked and tramped over to accept his drink from Dusty. He took a sip, then regarded his wife sullenly. "The plan?"

"The obvious one, we need to rouse Ambrose to come kill Brainchew again."

Shane nodded. "How do we . . . ?"

Dusty kept her voice deliberately calm, she had to convince Shane to do this. "Okay, I'll keep watch at the door here, to make sure Brainchew remains occupied with Lance. While you . . ." she looked at him hard, her brown eyes focused on his soul to fill him with courage, "you exit by the back way and run down to Ambrose's room and wake him up. Tell him to bring the stone knife and come kill it again."

For a moment Shane gaped at her in disbelief. How could she even ask such a thing of him? Then he shook his head. "Forget it, use the damn phone."

Dusty rolled her eyes. Her right hand straightened out tangles in her dark hair; her left hand stroked the shotgun, which once again lay on its shelf in the rear of the desk. She was keeping a good watch on the front door too.

"Shane," she patiently spelt out for him, "all you have to do is hurry down to the end of the middle block and bang on Ambrose's door. Look, take the shotgun with you, just in case. Give me Lance's pistol."

Shane appeared to consider it, then he shook his head again. "Uh-uh, forget it. Not with that thing out there; the shotgun won't kill it. Besides, baby, it's eight-past-two in the morning, Ambrose'll never let me in."

Dusty knew Shane knew why she'd suggested they take the more dangerous approach to rousing Ambrose. But she told him again anyway, enunciating her words with ladylike clarity: "Shane, you know damn well that my brother don't ever answer the phone when he's either drunk or fucking, and we know he's with that whore Crystal Parr again, so he's sure to be either fucking or fucking drunk . . . or both." She pointed to the phone. "You wanna try and rouse him, go ahead. You'll have better luck waking the dead."

Knowing that Dusty was right, that *it was* a total waste of time to do, but not ready to voluntarily stick his head in Brainchew's mouth, Shane picked up the lobby phone and dialed Room 26.

Beside him, his wife grimaced and watched the rain fall.

CHAPTER 24

Crystal

To her surprise, Crystal found that she couldn't stop crying.

She figured her blues had a lot to do with the rain also. The storm just kept on and on—erratic flashes of lightning that lit up the motel room like God was taking divine paparazzi pictures of her, and then the unpredictable thunder that kept startling her, keeping her jumpier than a grasshopper. Damn, some of those thunderclaps sounded like gunshots, like demon gangsters blowing themselves away. They honestly sounded that nearby, giving her the creepy feeling that God might be getting ready to shoot her too soon. Heaven knew she'd sinned enough in her life.

So the rain fell outside and her tears fell inside. The weeping sobered her up, as though it was the beer she'd imbibed running from her eyes.

Finally, unable to cope with herself any more, she got out of bed and walked into Ambrose's bathroom, got under the shower and turned on the cold water.

Ambrose had now begun snoring. And, boy, was he loud tonight! Ordinarily, she'd not have cared. Now though, with her impalpable patina of sadness hugging her, his pig-like nasal grunting irritated her. She felt an intense need to be far away from him. Even if it was ten-past-two in the morning.

The puke had caked on her skin. Showering it off took like forever, but she persevered. The cold water helped clear her head a bit more.

The phone out in the front room rang while she was soaping herself between the legs. She ignored it. Who the fuck called at this time of the night, when all well-behaved drunks were fast asleep? Whoever it was should know that there was absolutely zero chance of Ambrose waking up to answer them.

After toweling herself dry, Crystal returned to the front room.

Opps, she thought, staggering, then just managing to collect herself before she collapsed on top of Ambrose, who was now snoring in time with the phone, which was still ringing. God—the damn assholes were filling her head with noise! And the goddam rain was still coming down in that pitter-patter like a million rats were trying to break into the room!

She scavenged her clothes off the floor, then sat on the edge of the bed and pulled them on. Dressing while standing up was a no-no. Her mind may have cleared up, but her body still had serious coordination issues. The floor in particular looked wobbly, so much so that she considered staying back and enduring Ambrose's snores.

Finally, however, she decided to chance the drive home. It was only a short distance to her house on lower Prospect Hill Street, and besides, it was 2:27 a.m. now: at this hour she was unlikely to encounter anyone on the road that she could kill by drunken driving.

She shot a last glance at Ambrose, who now lay on his belly with his naked butt up in the air and the stink of a recent fart filling the room, then grabbed her purse off the nightstand and let herself out.

She shut the door behind her, relieved to be out of the irritation zone of the doggedly ringing phone. Her car was parked directly facing her, with the rain doing carwash services. The red Volkswagen Beetle was taking such a liquid beating that she again considered not leaving.

Crystal paused on the edge of the walk for a few seconds, swaying and trying to get the parking lot floor into clear focus. The rain wasn't helping matters any. In addition to wetting her feet (she had no idea that she'd forgotten to put on her shoes) it was blurring the ground into a gray river.

Her tears had ceased in the interim, but her eyes were swollen and aching and she still felt exceptionally depressed.

Finally she stepped down off the walk and was relieved that she didn't immediately sink out of sight and drown in the running water everywhere. With the rain drenching her, she made her unsteady way to the driver's side door of her car and after some fumbling with the key, got the door open.

Then she sat in the driver's seat for a while, not caring that she was soaked through and through, trying to slot the starter key into the ignition.

This ain't really such a hot idea, is it? she thought after the fifth failed attempt. *Ya know, maybe I really should just climb back into bed with Ambrose and fuck him again. At least if he's awake he can't keep me awake . . .*

But on the sixth attempt she got the key inserted and the engine turned over.

Great, she thought, slipping the gear into reverse, *I'm outa here.*

Then she drove off, spinning the Volkswagen around the right end of the front block and homeward.

Just exiting the motel was one hell of a wobbly ride. The entire parking lot in front of the red car seemed to be at first nearby, then far off. And though Crystal was trying her absolute hardest to keep on a straight path, the front block on her left and trees on her right kept shifting their differences from her: one moment the building was closer, then next, the trees were almost within touching distance of her fingers.

I'm gonna kill myself tonight, she thought sadly. *I'm really gonna do it. I'll be in the news tomorrow: 'Raynham's Best Prostitute Totals Herself in Fatal Car Crash.'*

It was such a poignant obituary that she started crying again.

And Crystal now realized that she really should have turned on the windshield wipers before starting out. But for the life of her, she didn't remember where their control was. At least she had her headlights on! The world could see her coming at it!

So, with her already bleary vision reduced yet further by the downpour, the red car kept veering left and right through the lot, till she somehow reached the driveway at the end of it and made a successful right turn out towards the main road.

At the foot of the driveway she survived another right turn onto Carver Street, then stomped fiercely on the brakes just before she wrapped the car around a tree.

In fact there were quite a lot of trees on her right hand now, a green wall of them. There were even a few on her left too.

She collapsed forward on the steering wheel and wept a little more.

When Crystal sat up again, she realized that she'd driven up and over the sidewalk and onto the grass lawn which separated the motel from the main road. Here the rain coming through the trees was broken up into areas of dry air and miniature waterfalls, and she could see ahead better.

She burped. *Alright, now where's the goddam road? Oh, alright, here it is out in the rain on my left! Now, let's get movin', shall we? Alright, car, now we're hitting the home stretch. When I count 'three,' you move your metal ass, O.K.? One . . . two . . . Hey, what the goddam fuck is that!?*

Caught in her headlights like a blinded rabbit was . . .

Oh, my frigging God, is that Brainchew? And who the hell is that guy that it's dragging after it? Then she blinked. *Nah, I'm just dreamin', Brainchew's down in the graveyard where my loverboy Ambrose sent it, ain't it?*

But then, the monster in her headlights pulled the man it had been dragging along up to its mouth and took a massive bite out of the back of his head.

Crystal watched entranced, a dumb smile on her face. *Yeah, it is fucking Brainchew!* Then her face turned ashen, and her smile inverted into a worried frown as fear crept into her thinking. *Hey, it's thrown that guy away and it's looking at me! Hey, no! And it's coming my way. Oh my God—it's coming to eat me! OH NO! It's RUNNING towards me!!!*

In a panic of desperation, Crystal put the car in motion and drove it straight at Brainchew.

Machine and monster met and machine won. With a massive crunch the pair collided—red car and gray skin and yellow headlights and black teeth and green leaves and crimson eyes and the transparent rain and the white haze in Crystal's head.

"Fuck you, monster!" She kept her foot down hard on the gas. "You ain't having *my* brain for dinner!"

The last that Crystal Parr saw of Brainchew was its ugly gray face howling in frustrated rage as it spun head-over-heels away through the greenery and back in towards the motel after bouncing off her right front fender.

Then she was up over the sidewalk and back on the street, temporarily sober enough again to make the drive home without killing herself.

***

Suspended upside-down amidst the lower branches of a mulberry tree, and powerless to halt the red vehicle's escape, Brainchew angrily watched it vanish into the distance.

It was unhurt but now doubly frustrated. It had attacked the car because it had smelt Ambrose on the woman inside it. A LOT of

Ambrose!!! Almost like she was his mate, the woman had smelt of overlapping layers of Brainchew's most hated enemy, as though she had been painted with him at many different times in her life, and as each coating of Ambrose faded into the past, he applied a fresh one to her skin. That was the best way that Brainchew could understand it. But the woman had been a very strange woman—she had smelt of many other men besides Ambrose, some of them crystal-clearly, others well-faded. But Ambrose had been her predominant male smell.

In frustration, Brainchew bared its teeth at the darkness. Eating the escaped woman's brain would have been almost as satisfying as eating Ambrose's.

It slowly extricated itself from the tangle of branches and clambered down the tree trunk to the floor, its claws tearing white lines in the bark.

The rain was starting to reduce now, which was good—rain dulled its sense of smell.

Back on the ground, Brainchew quickly forgot its frustration over the escaped woman. Brainchew was happy. It was feeding well tonight, and there were still many more people to kill in the 'Sunflower.' And best of all, Ambrose was still in there . . . sleeping.

Brainchew laughed with joyful malice. Let Ambrose sleep. It would only wake him to face its wrath when there was no one else left alive to eat in the 'Sunflower.' He would awake to the feel of its teeth locked to the back of his skull.

CHAPTER 25

Shane & Dusty

"If she doesn't kill herself tonight in a car crash, it'll be a miracle," Shane said as Crystal's red Volkswagen turned the end of the motel driveway. "You'd think that with the rain this heavy, even a drunk hooker would stay in bed."

"So long as she ain't around to spy on us," Dusty said.

Shane nodded to that, looking away from the lot and back at his wife. They needed no witnesses to what they had planned. True, with the way the red car had weaved its drunkard's route left and right across the lot, lurching every few meters like it was stalling, there was scant chance of its driver remembering anything she'd seen, or of her even being considered a credible witness if she did. Still, it was best to be as inconspicuous as possible.

"So remember," Dusty continued, "*I'm* the one who'll confront Kat Somerset. You just watch the door in case Brainchew shows up. If it does, you shoot the piece of shit to give us time to run back here."

Shane had the shotgun; Dusty had Lance's pistol. "Honestly, baby, we should both be inside the room with her."

She smirked at him. "Man up and stop being such a wimp. First you refuse to go call Ambrose to come kill Brainchew, and now you don't even want to watch a door? What is wrong with you?"

Shane grimaced. "You don't get it, do you?" He pointed outside the lobby, where the rain was still heavy, though not like it had been when they'd shot Lance. "Dusty, *one* mistake and we're both gonna be dead. What good will the money be then?"

Dusty first regarded him with hard eyes. Then her cold, pissed off expression softened into a smile. She walked over and stroked his cheek lovingly.

"Trust me, darling," she said gently, "absolutely nothing can go wrong with this plan." She pointed over at the red liquid smear that marked Lance's passing. "We're on a roll tonight." Then she laughed. "Think about it: How much trouble can Mrs. Somerset be? You heard for yourself how worried she sounded on the phone. All we have to do is tell her that her husband's hurt. She'll freak out and do whatever we say."

Shane nodded at Dusty, though his eyes were still troubled. "And afterwards? We're not gonna be able to claim self-defense in her case too."

Dusty leaned forward and kissed his lips. Then she stepped back and shook her head. "No need to kill her, baby. I'll wager you a hundred-to-one that the money on her is stolen. So long as we don't call the cops on her, she'll keep her yap shut."

Shane nodded. "You've got a good brain, Dusty. I'm lucky as hell to be married to you." He pulled her to him and kissed her hungrily.

She pushed him off her when she felt his crotch swelling. An erect penis wasn't what she needed now. She wondered how he could be aroused at a time like this . . . the thrill of danger? But even as they separated, she grabbed his crotch and massaged it, keeping her grip firm on the swollen manhood. Her female instinct assured her that if he was aroused he was less likely to be afraid.

Herself? Of course, she was scared too, but this opportunity was too good to pass up. This was their chance to secure a solid nest egg for their future, and without handing the IRS a cut of it either.

She'd lied to Shane. If necessary, they'd kill Kat Somerset—sit her in a chair, put Lance's revolver in her mouth, and force her finger down on the trigger, so it looked like she'd committed suicide from grief over her husband's death. The cops were certain to be too confused from cleaning up Brainchew's leftovers to really care in what sequence the deaths had occurred, or if they'd been staged.

Dusty grinned to herself. Better yet, after helping Kat shoot herself in the head, they'd leave the door open for Brainchew to dispose of the evidence.

"What's so funny?" Shane asked.

She came back to herself and found that she was still holding his penis through his pants, and that it was still hard—a meat gun she could shoot herself with if she so desired. *And, oh yes, I do desire to wound myself with it.*

A sudden intense desire to yield to her husband here and now swept up over her and she felt faint.

She let go of his erection and staggered back against the desk, putting a hand to her temples and gasping though a vision of him making love to her naked on the floor, plunging his lust-hardened self deep into her wet depths while they both slid over Lance's spilled blood.

Shane was looking at her with grave concern. "Dusty? Honey, are you okay? Answer me."

Getting a grip on herself, she smiled weakly back. Her crotch felt warm with the rush of her sudden desire for him. Oh, how she loved him all of a sudden! Even the blight of his screwing Summer Wallace didn't matter any longer—thankfully the big-titted bitch was dead now. Served her right for not keeping her pussy in her panties.

"Yes, I'm fine," she replied. "It's just all the tension of tonight making me dizzy." She glanced down at his crotch. Oh, he was still hard with desire for her. She leaned forward and gripped his shoulders, fighting to keep her breathing even, to not to give away how horny she was. Her knees were instantly weak again. She avoided touching his manhood, knowing that if she dared do so, next thing she'd be unbuckling his belt and taking the male stiffness in her mouth and sucking for all her life was worth on it. And their get-rich-tonight plan would be thrown out of the window because she'd be getting it like a dog on the floor.

Finally, Dusty's knees found some strength and she staggered away from Shane. Frowning coolly, she pointed at his crotch. "Business before pleasure, baby. How 'bout we both take of business first and when we come back, I'll take care of pleasure for you?" She winked seductively. "And I mean, I'll *really* take care of it."

He hefted the shotgun and grinned back. "Sounds like a damn sexy plan to me, baby. Let's go."

"Get ready to get drenched," Dusty said with a scowl. "I've misplaced the umbrella again."

"Forget it. We'll survive."

They walked towards the lobby door. True to Shane's word, the door had once again clicked back open, letting in gusts of rain like puffs from a spray can.

"Shit," Shane said, "I really gotta work out what's messing with the lock. If Brainchew . . ." Then he abruptly stiffened. "Hey, Dusty, can you smell that?"

She stiffened beside him. "Smell what? I don't—"

Then the faulty door burst inwards, and in a gray blur, Brainchew was there in the lobby with them.

Husband and wife were both caught completely off guard.

The monster first headed for Dusty, but Shane recovered quickly and whacked it in the head with the barrel of the shotgun. Howling, it let go of her and came after him instead.

He backed away from it, raising the shotgun to fire as it charged. But then it lunged forward and swiped at him, and while trying to duck its sharp claws he lost his balance and fell sideways, and the shotgun discharged as he fell. And next thing, he hit the floor, smacked his head hard on the tiles and stunned himself, and the shotgun spun away out of his grasp . . . away across the room . . .

And lying there on the floor, Shane could only gasp in disbelief at what he'd just done. "Oh my God . . . Noooo!"

He'd blown Dusty's head right off.

Her body still stood upright in a semblance of life. But she had nothing above her shoulders except for two thick gushing jets of blood, like she was a living lawn sprinkler system.

Then as her headless corpse began toppling forward, Brainchew grabbed it and clamped its mouth over the red gusher her neck had become.

Over the sound of the rain, Shane heard the creature smacking its lips and swallowing.

Shane was utterly horrified and fighting back tears. *Oh, my God, no! I fucking killed her!* Dazed, but still understanding the amount of danger he was in, he rolled over onto his side and looked desperately around for the shotgun. He couldn't locate it.

He looked back again at Brainchew and his dead wife. Both were now entangled in an obscene parody of a romantic embrace, while the monster sucked away at her neck, its mouth and shoulders completely stained red with her blood.

Dusty's pistol lay between her feet, and the monster had a gray foot pressed firmly on it.

Shane realized he had no way to fight Brainchew. His only chance of survival now was flight. He turned towards the door. It was open, with the rain blowing in in erratic gusts. He tried to get up, but his mind was too wooly to stand him upright. So he began crawling instead, dragging himself towards the door.

The tears filled his eyes as he passed his dead wife and the monster. *Oh shit, Dusty. I didn't mean to, honey! I didn't mean to shoot you, honey! It was a damn accident! Oh, God, why? Oh . . . oh . . . !*

He was right in the doorway, the rain showering down on him, when he heard it behind him.

Before he could fling himself out into the rain, he felt its weight on his back.

Next, it had a hold of his head. Then there was a wrenching pain in his neck and he suddenly found that he'd lost all control of his limbs, and that while his body was still sprawled belly-down on the front steps, he was somehow looking back and up at Brainchew, staring into those horrible red eyes like parasitic fruit stuck in badly molded Plasticine, and at its bloody mouth full of reddened teeth.

The monster grinned at Shane, then next it wrenched his head all the way around, completing the 360-degree turn; and then Shane felt its warm wet mouth cover the back of his head.

And then, after a sudden blinding pain . . . it was all over.

***

Brainchew fed with great satisfaction; the man's brain was delicious.

But even now in its deep pleasure, it discovered a new source of irritation. This room stank of Ambrose too. Ambrose was everywhere, like he was the god of this place.

There were yet other people in the motel to eat tonight, but they were all behind doors. Even Ambrose was behind a door, but it must find a way to open that particular door. Ambrose!

In its HUGE head its tiny brain screeched the words it couldn't vocalize: *HATE HATE HATE HATE HATE HATE HATE HATE HATE!!! I . . . MUST . . . KILL . . . AMBROSE!!!!*

Brainchew decided it had waited enough. It would kill Ambrose next.

But first . . . first . . . it had two fresh bodies to drain the urine from. And now it knew how.

CHAPTER 26

Ambrose

Ambrose was having a more pleasant dream:

This time he was in the shower with Nina. They were soaping each other up and down and Nina was playing with his penis and scrotum and they were both giggling and then Nina was kneeling down to suck on his penis and then there was a loud gunshot and . . .

Ambrose woke up groggily. The dream gunshot bounced between his ears as if his brain was surrounded by mountains. It was so real that he looked around, expecting to see his dead wife beside him.

"What the frigging hell was that?"

He sat up. Slowly . . . *very* slowly. The rush of blood out of his head left a hangover in its wake. He was used to hangovers: they were a lush's mental shipwrecks—one just drowned them in additional liquor.

Slowly the world made a drunk's sense to Ambrose. The myriad objects around him fit into more-or-less logical shapes.

Hey, Crystal's supposed to be here with me, ain't she? And . . . what the godawful hell is that godawful noise?

The noise was a combination of the rain and his ringing cellphone. The rain on the roof sounded like a stampede of horses. The cellphone was playing *Paranoid* by Black Sabbath at full volume, with Ozzy sounding particularly upset tonight. Ambrose now wished he'd used *Stairway to Heaven* instead.

Who the hell's calling someone at this hour?

He was going to ignore the damn phone, but it kept on ringing. It just went on and on and on, till its heavy metal drone was replacing the echoing gunshot in his head. So, naked and with vomit on his chest, he rolled out of bed and got the phone out of his pants pocket. He accepted the call and lifted it to his ear.

171

"Hey! Who're you? Stop bugging me at . . . what goddam time in the morning is it anyway? A quarter-to-three? . . . Crystal? . . . Hey— is it you baby? Why's you callin' me if your shoes are still here? Have you locked yourself in the bathroom?"

There was a sudden loud yell of "AMBROSE, SHUT UP GODDAMIT AND LISTEN!!!" over the speaker.

Ambrose stopped talking and stared perplexed at his phone, wondering why Crystal was shouting at him. Then he realized that she was still speaking, just at a lower volume and in a nervous rush, so he put the phone back to his ear and tried to decipher, through a filter of Jack Daniels and Coors Light, what she was getting at.

Finally he made sense of her scared rambling: "You saw Brainchew eating someone's head? Brainchew? Here at the motel? . . . Shit, Crystal, don't tell me that smelly motherfucker's back in town. Someone killed him, didn't they? . . . it was me? Nah, it wasn't . . . Yeah, okay, if you say so—it was me. But stop shouting, please. . . . I gotta stop it? Why the hell me? Why? Look, I just wanna get some shuteye! My head aches like a race riot's happening inside it."

Then Crystal started weeping again and making little sense and Ambrose flung the cellphone on the bed. He got a fresh bottle of Jack Daniels off the top of the fridge, then went and sat by the coffee table. After some fumbling he got the bottle open and took a couple of long gulps.

He felt better now. Yeah, that really hit the spot. A man needed a drink at a time like this.

Then he leaned back in the armchair and stared out at the rain and thought about Crystal. Not about her frantic phone call—women were always getting frantic about something or other—but about Crystal in particular and women in general. (In Ambrose's mind the desperate seriousness of Crystal's message was already dissolving into alcoholic insignificance.)

"Damn," he growled aloud after another long gulp of liquor to warm his insides, "that's the problem with all these goddam women. You screw 'em a few times and they think they own you. Then they start sending you on all sorts of errands: 'Take out the trash, Ambrose,' or 'Walk the dog, Ambrose,' or 'Mow the lawn, Ambrose,' or 'Baby, I forgot to buy us some steak from the store for dinner, do you mind picking some up for me?' And now, there's a new form of female domination: 'I'm scared, Ambrose, can you please kill

Brainchew for me?'" He smirked. "Listen, bitch, this is America, not some third-grade banana republic. You got rights here—if a monster's trying to eat ya, buy a fucking gun and shoot the fucking thing in self-defense!"

While speaking, he drank a bit more to steady himself. About a third of the bottle of Jack Daniels was gone now, and the booze was helping Ambrose think clearer.

Yeah, chicks were right bitches. Who the hell did they think they were anyway? God's gift to men? As if putting one's dick in them gave them the right to run a guy's life.

Ambrose looked reflectively down at his exposed penis. It looked pathetic now, a bit cold and shriveled up, and he knew from experience that it didn't drink, so he got up and put his boxers on—both inside out and turned front-to-back.

He regarded his crotch again. *There, that's better. No woman can get at it now and try to suck the life outa it. Not even that slut Crystal, that public wife . . . and I like her a lot . . . yeah, I really goddam like her . . . a whole damn lot . . . ever since Nina died she's been here for me, drinking with me, and she's my only friend . . . but still, even if I love her, I'm not gonna let her boss me around and send me on dumb midnight errands.*

He took another gulp of whiskey.

While thinking, Ambrose had been preparing to flop down in bed and drop off again; at least the goddam thunder or gunshot (or whatever it had been) and the phone rings had stopped. And Crystal had better not call back for her damn shoes tonight or he'd slap the juice out of her pussy.

But then, he smelt it . . . Oh, heck!

Even drunk as he was, Ambrose both remembered and recognized that smell—that stink like rotting meat and maggots and wet soil with dead worms in it.

He grimaced. *Dammit, he came here lookin' for me? What's the goddam son-of-a-bitch's problem, huh? I wanna get some sleep!*

He had another drink. The bottle was about half gone now.

The hated smell was thick in the air. And now, he heard a loud scratching sound against his front door, like someone was writing on its other side with a stone, or like a huge roach was trapped inside a paper bag and looking for a way out, or . . . like someone was trying to open the door but didn't know how.

Very annoyed now, Ambrose went to open his front door.

He was really pissed off to see Brainchew there. Shit, the goddam creature was red all over, like it hadn't had a bath since he'd last seen it in that pig barn on McKinney's farm, and . . . yeah, in addition to its grossly oversized head, the bloody thing needed a dentist really bad. It was dripping blood on the walkway and making a damn mess in front of his room.

And the thing was just staring at him (which was irritating) like it was gonna say something, but it had forgotten what it was gonna say and was trying to remember. So it didn't say anything, but it moved back slightly into a crouch like it was gonna jump into Ambrose's room, which Ambrose wasn't having. Oh no, he didn't want any more company tonight.

And its goddam bloodshot eyes were staring at him angrily.

"Aw shit, dude, not *you again!?*" he said finally, when he got tired of waiting for it to open the conversation. He belched a cloud of alcohol-infused breath at it. "Alright, hold on a minute, I'll be right back."

Then before the monster could force its way into the room, Ambrose slammed the door in its face and scuffled back over to the nightstand, all the while muttering, "Damn fucking Brainchew. Can't the goddam motherfucking jerk stay dead? I mean, am I gonna spend my whole fucking life killing it?"

While grumbling loudly, Ambrose began searching through his messy nightstand drawer. His vision kept tunneling in and out and the occasional thunderclaps sounded like they were in his head again. *Oh, God Almighty and Jesus, why'd you have to make bad hangovers along with good American whiskey?*

Outside, over the sound of the rain, he could hear Brainchew's constant scratching at the door of his room, then a pounding as it tried to get in to him. A moment later, he saw it peeking in at the window, then it moved out of sight and back to scratching at his door again.

Ambrose took a long pull of his whiskey, then growled back at the door, "Hey, hold your goddam horses, wilya? I said I was coming!"

Finally, he located what he'd been looking for—the stone knife, once again wrapped up in the leather skin with the writing no one could decipher. Back then, the cops had wanted to take the knife from him, but Ambrose had refused to let them have it. And thank God for that!

"AHA!!" he exclaimed in triumph. "Now that stinky son-of-a-bitch'll stop bugging my ass!"

He unwrapped the knife, dropped the leather manuscript on the nightstand, and, carrying his bottle of whiskey along with him, made his unsteady way back across the room to his front door.

After another quick drink, he opened the door.

The monster was still out there waiting for him.

Very angry that it insisted on disturbing him tonight, he extended the stone knife at it.

"Hey!" he said blearily, the bottle of booze gripped tight in his other hand. "Look, this is what you want, ain't it?" Point first, he pushed the stone knife at the lunging monster. "Here—don't be so goddam impatient, just goddam take it! Go find someone else to kill ya!"

He belched again, bemused because the monster had suddenly gone all stiff and straight like a goddam statue.

But, annoyingly, it still wasn't showing any signs of leaving. It wasn't even attempting to take the stone knife from him. And the rain was blowing in on them both now, and some of it was even getting inside his room and wetting his carpet.

"Alright, now bug off and leave me in peace," Ambrose growled. "I got a hangover like the sky just fell on my head!" Then his bleary eyes narrowed threateningly. "Dude, no comprende ingles, mi amigo? I said—goddam fuck off! Leave town, emigrate your stinky ass to Boston, where they won't notice your smell 'cos of the smog. Hasta la vista, motherfucker!"

To make his point, he leaned forward and shoved Brainchew. "Alright, friggin' git! Git!"

Now, to his surprise, the stiff monster toppled over, falling backward off the walkway and out into the rain.

And there, the stone knife rolling away to one side of it, it lay all still like it was dead. It didn't move an inch even with all the rain falling on it.

From being pissed off with the creature, Ambrose was now worried.

"Shit, man, don't faint *here!* My sister Dusty'll be mad! She'll think we've been drinking together."

Bottle in hand, Ambrose stepped down off the walkway. He was very careful while taking his steps: the water in the parking lot looked really deep.

He knelt beside Brainchew. "Aw, c'mon, man, you can't go to sleep here. If Dusty and Shane see ya—they'll start carrying on that I'm trying to ruin business for them by freaking out the guests again."

While talking, he kept rocking Brainchew to wake him up, while the rain beat on them both like Alex Van Halen playing a drum solo. "C'mon, man, don't do this to me. Gimme a break here. Shit! It's happened before . . . and damn, you shoulda heard the hell they raised that day."

He paused for a long gulp of whiskey. "I mean, and it wasn't even my fault—it was the girl's. Just like today, it was rainin', and Sandy says she wants to sing and dance in the rain, and I say sure, why not, ya know? . . . Now how'm I supposed to know that she was coked up to her eyebrows and she meant that she wanted to sing and dance naked? So off Sandy goes running and howling all the way around the front block in her birthday suit . . . shit . . . all the way round to reception . . . and Dusty and Shane had a rich couple and their kids just about checkin' in at the time, and Sandy scared them off and . . ."

A miserable look on his face, the rain running in his beard, Ambrose paused and stared down at the petrified monster. "Anyway, dude, so that's the scene here. Sometimes my sister treats me like I'm useless, ya know?" Then he laughed. "Here, buddy, have a drink too. C'mon, sit up. Alright, it's cool, you can stay with me till morning in my room, then you leave town. Just don't come back this time."

When that didn't work, he tilted the bottle down to the frozen seam of the monster's lips and tried to pour a trickle into the slit there. "Here, have a nip yourself. Yeah, that'll see ya right."

But the rain kept washing it all away so finally Ambrose quit before all his whiskey was gone. Besides, his head had begun spinning really badly again and he felt like he was gonna puke and . . .

Oh, my good gawd, horseshit . . .

Ambrose threw up all over Brainchew. He puked and puked, till it felt like his goddam gut was empty.

Then, simply too tired to remain upright long enough to walk back into his room, he collapsed out there in the lot, in the pouring rain. He managed to crawl up onto the walkway, but there his strength gave out completely.

Ambrose Duggan fell asleep there in front of his open motel room door, with the rain washing over him, and his loudly snoring face turned towards the monster he'd just defeated again without realizing it.

Every now and then he hugged his bottle of whiskey tightly to his chest like it was a baby and grinned in his sleep.

CHAPTER 27

Kat . . . Two Months Later

Kat Somerset sat in a Logan Airport bar with a Dry Martini in front of her.

It was late evening. She was waiting for her flight to Paris to be called: Air France, Flight 333; from Logan Terminal E to Charles de Gaulle Terminal 2E, by Boeing 777-200. 8 p.m. to 8.30 a.m. (Jet Lag Standard Time).

6 hours 30 minutes spent floating up amidst the clouds.

Outside, she sensed the throb and rumble of monster engines, and the rush of thousands of people coming and going from everywhere to everywhere.

It would soon be her turn also.

She looked down at her Martini. It was almost time for another refill. (She'd picked a table from which she could easily signal a waiter when her glass was empty.) Hopefully she wouldn't be so drunk by the time she got on the flight that she'd make a nuisance of herself.

It had been a long and ragged two months for Kat since that tragic night in Raynham. Alcohol had helped her get through it. While she understood that for her own good she'd need to stop drinking so much soon, at the moment the booze was helping cope with a whole lot of things.

***

That night, Bella and Rafael had arrived at a quarter-to-three, an hour after Lance had called her from the lobby. By then she'd been crawling the walls in her nervousness.

They'd been delayed by flash-flooding. The downpour had rendered Interstate 290 completely unmotorable around Auburn, and they'd been forced to backtrack and retrace their route.

They'd both been as surprised as she to hear that neither Lance nor Summer were answering their phones. While Bella remained with her and examined the stolen diamonds, Rafael had gone out to investigate.

He'd returned with the horrible news that everyone was dead. Not just Lance and Summer, but both of the motel owners also, and . . . that *something* had eaten the backs of all their heads and their brains too.

Lance dead? How was that possible? When he'd called her he'd said he was fine and would soon be back.

Kat had almost had a complete nervous collapse there and then, but Bella and Rafael had forced several stiff drinks into her. Then Bella had calmly explained to her what she had to do:

Kat had to be the one to call the police to the scene. And it was best that she did so using the phone in the motel reception. Her story would be that she'd woken up in the middle of the night, and, unable to find her husband, she'd gone out to look for him. Then she'd found Summer and the motel owners dead. Also, even though Rafael had found Lance's body amongst the trees opposite the front block (along with another, female, corpse), she was to insist that she still had no idea where her husband was.

Then all she needed to do was, keep calm and claim she had absolutely no idea of what, if anything, her husband and his friends had been up to tonight. Mr. Ellis Drake would handle the rest.

Kat had nodded through her tears. "But what about all the money?" she'd enquired in a lifeless voice. She'd pointed first to the bag with the money from Thomas's safe, then to the black attaché case that Bella had brought with her, with its $200,000 content. "It's a dead giveaway. It links me to everything."

"Don't worry about it," Rafael said. He'd walked over and picked up the bag containing Thomas's stolen money.

Bella frowned at Kat. "We'll pay the money into a bank account for you, along with tonight's payment. That way, there's no chance of anyone connecting you to anything. Just remember, wait ten minutes after we leave, then—"

Rafael shook his head at her. "Make it thirty—we may have to erase some of the CCTV footage from the lobby cameras."

Bella nodded. "Okay, thirty minutes, then you walk down to reception and call the police. It'll take them some time to get over here at this hour anyway, so we'll be long gone by then."

Kat nodded her agreement. The alcohol in her system was already working as a warm buffer against the shock of her loss. She wasn't sure how long it would last though.

Bella and Rafael Marquez left. Kat sat staring at the wall clock for half an hour, then she got up and headed down to the motel reception building to call the cops.

Okay, so Kat had already known that both the Rowlands were dead, but still, she hadn't expected the scene of total carnage that greeted her there in reception.

Shane Rowland's body lay just inside the front door, with the back of his head missing and his lower belly ripped open. And his wife had no head at all, just a mess of blood all over her shoulders, and her belly was all slashed up as well . . . and there were little bits of her head—hair, eye-mush, ears and teeth—splattered all over the reception desk.

Kat almost turned and fled then. But she'd managed to tame her fear long enough to run over to the reception desk, pick up the lobby phone and (after brushing one of Mrs. Rowland's ears off it) dial 911. (The lobby clock had had the time as exactly 03:30.) She'd had no need to playact her horror to the operator who took her call. Even to herself, she sounded utterly terrified while explaining what she'd found in the motel lobby.

Then she'd walked outside and sat on the lobby steps, not caring how hard the rain beat on her. It mingled with her tears and she was crying a waterfall anyway.

Fifteen minutes later, the Sunflower Motel was swarming with police. She sat there in a wash of approaching headlights as the squad cars pulled up in the rain and urgent men in raincoats dashed to and fro past her.

Then finally, they seemed to remember her and took her inside for questioning.

**

Kat sipped the last of her Martini, holding the mingled liquor on her tongue for an extra moment before swallowing it, while her eyes ranged outside the windows, bearing witness to a mob of people in intricate motion in every possible direction. The magical product of a hundred interrelated and synchronized arrivals and departures from the world's most exotic cities. And beyond and mixed in with the endless throng, the sound and thunder—fed through the bar's reinforced concrete floor into the soles of her feet—of the giant metal birds, the modern-day chariots of the gods that brought in and took away more humanity every few minutes.

Oh yes, it was very true what they said: Boston *was* the hub of the human universe.

Too bad she was leaving it for good today.

Realizing that she'd finished her cocktail, she stirred the lemon twist in the V-shaped glass with a finger and signaled to a waiter for another. That made four now; she'd best wait till she got aboard the plane and could drink to her heart's content. One good thing about travelling first class was that she would also have the privacy to sleep off her latest drunk.

Across the room she noticed a man looking her way. He was seated at the bar and was handsome, with longish brown hair. He seemed about her age, early-to-mid-thirtyish. He was trying to catch her eye, but then the bartender placed his drink in front of him and he looked away again.

Kat smiled. He looked alright; maybe he'd be good company. But there was very little probability that they were headed the same way.

***

She'd been surprised at how smoothly things had worked out. Bella had been true to her word—her employer Ellis Drake had taken care of everything. All Kat had had to do was to insist that she had no knowledge of any robbery having occurred that night, and afterwards remember to stick to her denial.

It was largely an open-and-shut case: the bullet that had killed Chuck had come from Mr. Thomas's gun. Similarly, Thomas had clearly been killed by Summer's knife—his blood was found on the switchblade. And the cops figured that Lance had to have been involved in some way too; most likely he drove the getaway car. But seeing as he was dead, that would never be proved.

And as to why Kat's fingerprints were all over the car? The answer to that was simple: it was *her* car. A check of the registration document in the Ford's glove compartment (and a crosscheck with the Massachusetts RMV) confirmed her story.

There were other questions, but she'd managed to either answer them somehow or else she just feigned ignorance.

Finally the cops let her go. There was nothing tying her to either the robbery or the deaths. And Kat suspected that Ellis Drake's money was already hard at work on her behalf by then.

She wondered what it was like being that rich. Maybe now she'd find out.

(Apparently, the whole plan to rob old Mr. Thomas had stemmed from a woman's harmless comment: Ellis's wife Louise had seen the pair of diamonds in a *Vanity Fair* article on fashionable family heirlooms, and remarked that 'they'd make such lovely earrings.' And her husband had decided to make her a birthday gift of them.

And everyone Kat loved had died for something as petty as that? Earring's for a wife's birthday? Just thinking about it filled Kat's mouth with a sour taste.)

The money from the robbery was already waiting for her in France in a Société Générale bank account. $255,000. And there was also the additional hundred thousand that she and Lance had already saved. So, so long as she didn't overspend, she'd be okay.

Kat was done with the dirt of the underworld for good now.

Already, with Bella's help, she'd made a bid to buy a fashionable Paris shoe shop on La Rue du Commerce, just around the corner from the Eiffel Tower. So that was the future.

But . . . oh, the hurt! The incredible pain of losing Lance! It gnawed ceaselessly at her heart, as relentless as a rat desperate to escape a cage as a flood bore down on it. Morning, noon, and night, whatever activity Kat was engaged in got broken up by flashes in which she saw his face; that fierce unhandsome face that she'd loved, with that smug boyishness amidst his roughness that only she could bring out.

***

Kat's fresh drink arrived. She tasted it then looked around the bar.

The handsome man was looking her way again. She made eye-contact with him and smiled. He smiled back, then picked up his drink and walked over. She watched him come. A chance airport conversation at best. Not a romance. Not for her. It was still way too early for that, she still hurt far too much. But a casual friendship—if they were on the same flight—could help ease her pain.

Part of why she still hurt so bad was because it had been a month after the killings before the Massachusetts State Police would release Lance's corpse to her for burial. So it was really only during the past month that she'd had any time to start healing her hurts.

***

There had been major oddity about the deaths that night. Strange claims made and questions raised.

What Bella had told her—and which she still didn't believe—was that Summer and Lance and Shane Rowland's deaths had been caused by a monster of some kind. Something called Brainchew. A magic statue that had come to life, and which, after it had murdered everyone, had been subdued by Dusty Rowland's brother.

Kat didn't believe a word of that for an moment. To her mind, it had to be some runaway zoo animal that did everyone in.

But apparently the Massachusetts State Police believed the story, because they'd kept Lance's body and the others in cold storage for a whole month, carrying out endless research and experiments on them.

One major reason why Kat didn't believe Bella's story, was because she'd also said that, instead of the State Police taking the killer statue away from Raynham, they'd left it there. No, that wasn't it—they'd kept misplacing or losing it. No, it wasn't that either. They'd initially taken the 'Brainchew' statue away, but then it had vanished from their laboratory and turned up back in Raynham again. Then they'd carried it away *again,* only to have the same thing ridiculous 'E.T. go home' nonsense repeat itself twice more, so they'd finally given up on moving it out of Raynham. The statue seemed to like the town.

It was something like that; one of those three versions anyway. Kat had been drinking at the time and hadn't too clearly heard that bit of their conversation. And since she didn't believe the story anyway, she'd not later bothered with finding out which was the correct misheard version of events.

But then, there was also that funny story which Bella had told her on the phone a week later, about her employer Mr. Drake trying to buy the Brainchew statue from the people of Raynham and move it to his house. As if anyone in their right senses wanted anything to do with something that could kill them.

Apparently, the Raynham folk were mentally sound though, even if the bidding billionaire wasn't. Bella had said that the Raynham Town Administrator and Board of Selectmen were seriously considering selling the statue to Ellis Drake.

But of course, if the third version of events that Kat had heard about Brainchew was the correct one—if the statue kept returning back to Raynham no matter what anyone did—how in the world was Mr. Drake going to get it permanently away from there anyway?

***

He'd reached her now, her handsome suitor from across the room. He smiled, his teeth strong and white.

"Bonjour, mademoiselle. Je m'apelle Thierry . . . Thierry Toussaint."

Oh, so *he was* going to France too then? Slowly she tried to remember enough French to decipher what he'd just said. *Hello . . . my name is . . . Thierry Toussaint . . . ?* Yes that was it. 'Mademoiselle' meant that she'd forgotten to wear her wedding ring again.

"Moi c'est Kat Somerset. Enchantée," she replied, suddenly pleased with herself. Oh yes, this trip wouldn't be bad at all. Up close, Thierry was handsomer than she'd thought. With her woman's instinct, she felt inexplicably drawn to him, as if he would understand her suffering and not demand more from her than she could give until she was able to.

She gestured to the chair opposite her and he sat.

She tried to say more in French, but couldn't construct anything coherent in her head. Maybe it was the Martinis dulling her thoughts, maybe it was the warmth of his smile, or just the swimming-pool-clear bright blue of his eyes.

She quit on it, realizing too that she was smiling honestly for the first time since Lance's death. "Dammit, man, if your American is as bad as my French, we've crashed even before takeoff."

He smiled. "Ah, désolé . . . I try Anglais then. I see . . . you . . . very beautiful." He kissed his fingers at her. "I like know you better . . . very much better."

Kat understood then, that the old saying was true: life always went on. You lost the one you loved with all your heart, and you thought you were going to die, but you didn't . . . one never did . . . you just floated in emotional limbo until someone else's gravitational force sucked you in.

"Delighted to meet you, Thierry," she said happily, extending her hand to shake his and holding on just a moment too long to let him know she appreciated his interest in her.

Then, suddenly high on life, she pushed the undrunk remains of her Martini away and laughed aloud . . . at herself, at Thierry, and at the whole damn world.

The End.

ABOUT THE AUTHOR

Wol-vriey is Nigerian, and quite tall.

He currently resides in a state of uneasy stalemate with his threatening-to-thin-beyond-redemption hair, and believes there actually are things that go bump in the night.

Wol-vriey recycles the ridiculous into reasonable reality for the reader.

His WEIRRRD philosophy?

WEIRRRD = Warp/Write Everything into Realistic Ridiculous Readable Distorted Dream Dimension Descriptions.

Wol-vriey blogs at:

http://oddityfarm.wordpress.com

WOL-VRIEY
BIZARRO AND TRANSGRESSIVE FICTION

BOSTON POSH (BUD MALONE #1)

In 2028 AD, the USA is a nation ravaged by hungry dragons and dinosaurs. In Boston, Massachusetts, private eye Bud Malone is hired to rescue a kidnapped heiress. But nothing is as it seems.

Malone works to unravel a tangled web involving Boston Chinatown, a 200-year-old woman with a 9-year-old body, white robots, a human-liver-eating psychopath, a golem, a porcelain dragon, and a snake goddess with a crush on him. There's also a woman obsessed with chicken sex. Then Malone meets Posh Lane, a gorgeous call girl who's desperate to quit her pimp.

Romantic sparks ignite between Posh and Malone, but Posh's past suddenly catches up with her in a BIG way. To save Posh, Malone agrees to run a quest for Earth's new rulers, the Forks. But, Malone has no idea that agreeing to the Fork's odd request will send him on the weirdest trip he's ever been on in his life.

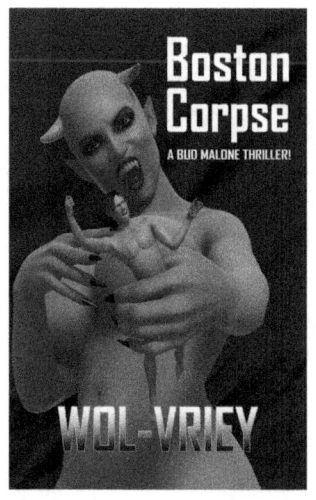

BOSTON CORPSE (BUD MALONE #2)

MAGIC CAN BE MURDER! - Drag queen Lucy Tang is back in Boston, and is hell-bent on settling her vindetta against casino owner Sookie Ling. And suddenly, Bud Malone, PI, has the case of his life to resolve.

When Boston's robot police force are baffled by a mind transfer case, they come to Malone for help. The one person who can likely help Malone out here is the witch Soledad Bathory. But Soledad seems to know a lot more than she's telling him. It's a case not made easier when Malone meets Soledad's beautiful cousin, Josephine 'Slave' Bailey. Slave has her own plans for Malone, most of which involve teaching him BDSM and making him her new Master.

Oh, and Rick Rogers owes Sookie Ling a whole lot of money, a gambling debt that's going to be literally Hell to pay!

BOSTON CORPSE - Not your average detective novel!

Burning Bulb
PUBLISHING

WOL-VRIEY
BIZARRO AND TRANSGRESSIVE FICTION

BOSTON LUST (BUD MALONE #3)

"Bless it, Father, for she has sinned."

Seven murdered gay women, all their bodies completely drained of blood. All also with large parts of their bodies dissolved away like acid has been pumped into their veins.

Bud Malone has to find the female vampire preying on Boston's lesbian population.

Then Malone meets the beautiful Trudi Carmen and the case gets even more tangled. Trudi needs Malone's help in recovering a ring that's gone missing. But how in the world is one little black ring related to either the dead women or their killer?

Resolving this case will lead Malone deep into Lucy Tang's legacy—The Abstracta. And then to the city of Genesis.

Boston Lust—Just when you thought Bean Town was safe to visit again.

HELL DANCER

Six people find themselves trapped in Detention, a nightmare realm where the demonic Schoolmaster is hell-bent on reforming them . . . until they die.

Porn superstar Venus Deluxe came to Springfield, MA to party, and next found her life hanging by a thread. One wrong answer will mean her death.

Suspended BPD detective Tanya Rockford was trying to stop one kind of violence, but found a terrifying another. With her and her companion's lives hanging in the balance, it's going to take all of her courage and resourcefulness to escape this hell she's stumbled into.

Porn stud Chad Cannon has made a career from his ten-inch penis. Here in Detention, however, it's his brains that matter. He'll soon be hoping all the pot he's smoked over the years hasn't completely messed up his memory.

The three students, Sherri, Jordan, and Mike? They were all just in the wrong place at the right time. Will anyone survive Detention? The evil Schoolmaster doesn't plan on letting that happen . . .

Burning Bulb
PUBLISHING

WOL-VRIEY
BIZARRO AND TRANSGRESSIVE FICTION

VAGINA MUNDI

Rachel Risk is a professional thief with super-strong hair that can stretch like tentacles to manipulate objects. Ashley Status has both a digitally augmented brain, and 'muscle-purses' in her arms and legs in which she stores inflatable objects—cars, guns, rocket launchers, etc.

When Raye is framed as the fall girl in a jewel robbery, the pair flee Chicago's vengeful robot gangsters and take refuge in the Hotel Bizarre, where the gorgeous 'vagina singer,' Femina, is performing for a week.

But the Hotel Bizarre is even stranger than its name suggests, and very soon Raye and Ash are involved in an deadly adventure, a struggle for survival the likes of which they'd never imagined possible—with loads of deviant sex, drugs, music, and violence at every turn. And just what is the old woman in the skin desert really doing with all those cats glued to her walls?

VAGINA MUNDI—a Bizarro Hymn in praise of WOMAN!

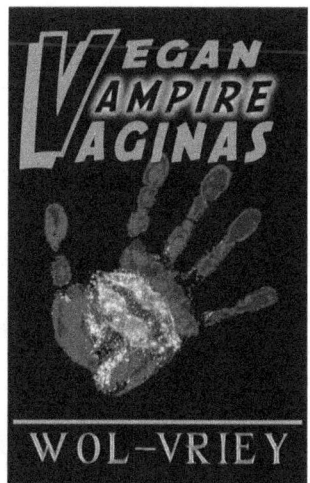

VEGAN VAMPIRE VAGINAS

The biggest bank heist in US history. And Tom Palmer can't remember pulling it off. And no, this isn't your standard case of amnesia. After a one-night-stand gone horribly wrong, Boston salesman Tom Palmer wakes up with a vagina implanted in his left hand. Then his day gets worse.

Tom is transported across space-time to a nightmare version of Boston, one where the Bizarro virus has transformed half the population into cannibals. Worst of all, Tom discovers that in this new Boston, he's the infamous gangster Pussypalm, wanted for robbing the Federal Reserve Bank of Boston a year ago. He also learns that the vagina in his hand is prophetic, i.e. it talks . . . after sex.

With 130 people left dead during his bank heist and six billion dollars missing, Tom knows he's living on borrowed time. It is in his best interests not to remember anything. Because once he does . . .

Burning Bulb
PUBLISHING

WOL-VRIEY

BIZARRO AND TRANSGRESSIVE FICTION

Dr. Orgasm

Courtney Taylor is young, intelligent, beautiful, and successful. She also has a boyfriend who loves her deeply. The problem is, no matter what Courtney does, she can't climax during sex.

When Florence Rigid's communist forces destroy the city of Metaphor, Courtney and her friends Teresa, Highball, Miki, and Heather are cast into the midst of a quest to find the only person able to save the land of Innuendo—Dr. Carol Orgasm, wanted by the communists for developing the O-Pill, a wonder drug that grants women sexual ecstasy on demand.

The communists will do anything to get their hands on the O-Pill and prevent its reaching the millions of Innuendo's women. But Courtney desperately wants that pill too. And so it's now a race between Courtney and the communists to find Dr. Orgasm first.

And Courtney has no choice but to win this race. She must win it: For her own orgasm . . . and for the freedom of female sexuality everywhere.

PUSSY TRANSMISSION

Pussy Transmission were the most decadent Pop Art ensemble of the 90's. Led by the beautiful painter Isis Lynch, the trio revolutionized the art world. Then suddenly, without explanation, Pussy Transmission vanished into historical obscurity. Now, twenty years later, three women come to Lynch Place. Lily and Nina are journalists desperate to interview Isis Lynch. Raven, on the other hand, wants to find her boyfriend, who's gone missing inside Isis's house. Raven's worried—she's heard that Pussy Transmission broke up because Isis began dabbling in black magic . . . with devastating results. All three women will shortly wish they'd never left home. Particularly once the rats in Lynch Place start warning them that they're going to die . . . and Raven meets Betty Butcher, the bouncy supernatural psycho who's intent on chopping her into bits. Pussy Transmission, Baby! Just because . . .

Burning Bulb
PUBLISHING

WOL-VRIEY
BIZARRO AND TRANSGRESSIVE FICTION

VEGAN ZOMBIE APOCALYPSE

In the post-apocalypse worlderness, zombies rule the earth. They're allergic to meat, and brains literally make them explode. Zombies now eat blood potatoes, parasitic tubers grown in the flesh of humancows corralled in maximum security farms. Two fugitives meet in the ancient ruins of Texas. The first is Soil 15-f, a womancow who's escaped her farm a week before she's due to be killed and her blood potato crop harvested. The second fugitive is Able Kane, former head necros food technician, now sentenced to death for heresy. But Soil is no ordinary humancow.

Unknown to herself, she's the vegan zombie agricultural revolution, and the zombies desperately want her back. And the necros equally desperately want Able Kane dead. He's fled with a forbidden discovery which will reshape the world for the worse if used. And Able is just hardheaded/misguided enough to use it.

MELANIE NEMESIS CATCHPOLE

In Springfield, Massachusetts, Melanie Catchpole is hired to fetch back a magic teddy bear worth millions of dollars from a warehouse across town. Problem is, the warehouse is down in Springfield's O-Zone-that totally weird sector of the city where Bizarro fell to Earth. The 'O' is a fairytale land, a place where dreams and nightmares literally live and breathe.

Worse still, the gingers—mutant cannibals—prowl the O. The gingers have already eaten everyone else Melanie's employers sent to get back the magic teddy bear.

Accompanied by the handsome but ruthless Doug Fisher (who she finds sexy but doesn't dare entrust her heart to), Melanie enters the O-Zone. Melanie and Doug are instantly caught up in an adventure they'd never have believed credible even if written as fiction . . . and Melanie's used to experiencing the very weird as the norm.

And now, additionally, there's a mystery to unravel: What does the dark, freezing-cold being called The Fixer want with Mary, the barkeep's daughter?

Burning Bulb
PUBLISHING

WOL-VRIEY

BIZARRO AND TRANSGRESSIVE FICTION

BIG TROUBLE IN LITTLE ASS

From Bizarro master storyteller Wol-vriey comes a truly weird western tale that will leave you awe-struck and on the edge of your seat...

In the town named Little Ass, tight-assed prostitute Rosa overhears a gunslinger's plans to assassinate rancher Edison Bennett. Once the badass Bennett learns of the plot, he ensures there'll be hell to pay for any attempt on his life!

Yes, it's going to take all of gunslinger Jude's shooting prowess, his eclectic collection of strange firearms, a trusty horse that requires an owners' manual, and the help of the lovely and invigorating Nell (who's EXTREMELY odd when the going gets weird), to survive the Bizarro hell that Edison Bennett unleashes in order to hold onto the land that he'd stolen from Madam Zizi.

BIZARRO 101 (A BASIC PRIMER)

Welcome to the strange place:

A collection of 37 flash fiction stories designed to introduce one to the Bizarro/New Weird Genre.

Weird, dreamy, nightmarish, absurd, sad, surreal, humorous . . . this collection of tales is all this and more.

***

"This primer is the very essence of any and all styles and types of Bizarro writing. Wol-vriey collects, distills, and bottles up these 37 tiny stories for your sensory enjoyment. This is an absolute must-read for anyone new to the genre, because it demonstrates the scope of what Bizarro is, and what it can be."
            –Teresa Pollack, Bizarro commentator and blogger

Burning Bulb
PUBLISHING

WOL-VRIEY
BIZARRO AND TRANSGRESSIVE FICTION

GIRLS ARE NOT SMILING

Welcome To The Road Trip From Hell

Pagan is demon-possessed.

Lori is suicidal.

Britt is just terminally pissed off.

Meet three young Boston women on the run from the law, each with problems that will fuse into more than the sum of their individual parts, becoming a holocaust of sex and violence and terror, a literal rain of blood and horror and gore and evil.

And if that wasn't already bad enough, Pagan's pet demon is slowly transforming her into something both unspeakable and unholy. Truly, these girls aren't smiling.

BRAINCHEW

It was supposed to be a simple jewel heist, but it went badly wrong. Chuck got shot and died.

Lance hid his friend's corpse in the Pleasant Street Cemetery. But that was a big mistake—there was something undead, something extremely hungry . . . something eXXXtremely horrible, buried in the Pleasant Street Cemetery.

And Lance had just woken it up.

They called the monster Brainchew because it ate brains. Human brains. And it preferred those brains fresh from the heads . . . of the living.

And now it was awake again, Brainchew planned on feeding big-time tonight. Oh hell yes, it did.

Burning Bulb
PUBLISHING

OTHER GREAT TITLES FROM

Burning Bulb
PUBLISHING

WWW.BURNINGBULBPUBLISHING.COM

BELLY TIMBER

From the writers of Darkened Hills, Detour to Armageddon and Night of the Living Dead comes a novel unlike any other...

In the 1800's, ordinary people learned the secret of the Kala and undertook extraordinary measures to rid the earth of this evil. This is their story.

For John McCormick, life on the Indiana frontier held nothing but promise. His settlement along the White River would soon become the crossroads of America. Friends and family from back in Ohio and other points east were all making plans to see what all the fuss was about in the newly-formed city of Indianapolis. Yes, things were good. John had his general store and his friend George Pogue had his blacksmith business. Claims were being staked and relations with the native Indians were amicable. The town was growing and nothing could be better... or so he thought.

In Ohio, an evil was brewing. The Lecky Family, a group of ruthless Mongolian nomads, had made their way to America and were practicing their cannibalistic religion of Kala with reckless abandon. No one was safe, not even John McCormick's family.

Burning Bulb
PUBLISHING

ANTHOLOGIES
BIZARRO AND TRANSGRESSIVE FICTION

THE BIG BOOK OF BIZARRO

The Big Book of Bizarro brings together the peculiar prose of an international cast of the most grotesquely-gonzo, genre-grinding modern writers who ever put pen to paper (or mouse to pad), including:

NIGHT OF THE LIVING DEAD horror writers John Russo & George Kosana; HUSTLER MAGAZINE erotica contributors Eva Hore, Andrée Lachapelle, & J. Troy Seate and established Bizarro genre authors D. Harlan Wilson, William Pauley III, Wol-vriey, Laird Long, Richard Godwin and so many more!

From Alien abductions to Zombie sex, The Big Book of Bizarro contains OVER FIFTY STORIES of the most outrélandish transgressive fiction that you'll ever lay your capricious and curious hands upon!

WESTWARD HOES

Nine outlaw writers rode into town from obscurity to pen nine tantalizing tales of horror and fantasy, and leaving once they branded their own personal marks on the weird western genre and became living legends of the American Frontier experience.

Like drunken Indian scouts, the writers fervidly tracked down and captured the Western genre, tore off its fashionable veneer and ravished its exposed essence.

So belly up to the bar with your favorite soiled dove and enjoy perusing these thrilling tales of Old West debauchery, danger and desire; compiled by the publisher of The Big Book of Bizarro and featuring the bizarro novella *Big Trouble in Little Ass* by Wol-vriey.

Burning Bulb
PUBLISHING

ANTHOLOGIES
BIZARRO AND TRANSGRESSIVE FICTION

THE BIG BOOK OF BIZARRO SPECIAL KINDLE EDITIONS

OTHER AWESOME COLLECTIONS

 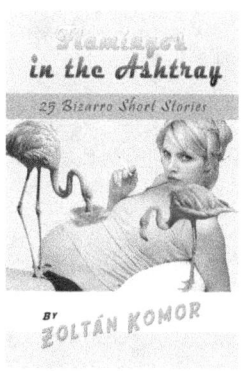 

Burning Bulb
PUBLISHING

GARY LEE VINCENT'S
DARKENED
THE WEST VIRGINIA VAMPIRE SERIES

DARKENED HILLS

When evil descends on a small West Virginia town, who will survive?

Jonathan did not start out his life to become a rambler, it justworked out that way. William was a troubled youth with something to hide. Both were from Melas, a small town tucked away in the West Virginia hills... a town where disappearances are happening more and more frequently.

After the suicide of a wanted serial killer, the townsfolk thought the nightmare was over. But when a centuries-old vampire is discovered they find out the hard way it's just getting started. Dark secrets can only stay hidden for so long and when the devil comes to collect, there will be hell to pay. Can Jonathan and William find a way to stop the vampire before it's too late? Find out in *Darkened Hills!*

DARKENED HOLLOWS

In the heart-stopping sequel to the award-winning *Darkened Hills*, Jonathan and William must return to West Virginia to face possible criminal charges stemming from their last visit to the damned town of Melas, where both had narrowly escaped the clutches of a vampire seethe.

And as livestock start mysteriously getting murdered with all of their blood drained, worried farmers are searching for answers - leaving the local Sheriff and his deputy racing against time to learn the cause before a more violent crime is committed.

Burning Bulb
PUBLISHING

WWW.DARKENEDHILLS.COM

GARY LEE VINCENT'S
DARKENED
THE WEST VIRGINIA VAMPIRE SERIES

DARKENED WATERS

When the world goes to hell, the chosen must arise!

As Talman Cane orchestrates a flood of epic proportions in this third installment of the *Darkened* series the towns of Melas and Tarklin are caught completely off guard by the deluge. Hell-bent on finishing what they started, the evil brothers return to the lunatic asylum to take care of the witnesses and add to the ever-growing army of the undead.

Aided by Lucifer himself and the insane vampire demon Legion, the stage is set to channel all of the forces of hell to come forth. In an all-out race to survive, Jonathan, William, and Amanda soon discover they are up against impossible odds as Lucifer opens the Gateway to Hell, ushering in the zombie apocalypse and the End Times.

Find out who will survive this cosmic battle of the ages in *Darkened Waters*!

DARKENED SOULS

Melas and the Madison House are about to be rebuilt.
True evil is about to be reborne!

Young ex-priest and vampire-killer William is drawn back to the West Virginian town that almost killed him, where his vampire arch-enemy Victor Rothenstein still stalks the earth.

The town of Melas lies destroyed after the battle of the End of Days. But why is wealthy Jackie Nixon so eager to rebuild it using the bone dust of murdered souls?

Terrible evil has visited before, but the Gateway to Hell is about to be reopened in a horrific climax. And this time – it's personal.

WWW.DARKENEDHILLS.COM

Burning Bulb
PUBLISHING

WEST VIRGINIA-THEMED HUMORROROTICA
BY RICH BOTTLES JR.

HELLHOLE WEST VIRGINIA

From the heights of Mothman's perch high atop the Silver Bridge in Point Pleasant to the depths of Hellhole Cavern in Pendleton County, evil lurks within the shadows as the sun sets upon the haunted hills and hollows of West Virginia.

Bizarro author Rich Bottles Jr. blows the coffin lid off horror genre clichés with this tour de force cast of Eco-friendly vampires, beach-yearning zombies and sex-starved she-devils.

LUMBERJACKED

If you are easily offended or do not possess a truly depraved sense of humor, this story may not be the light summer reading fare you desire. As for the four feisty female freshmen stranded on top of West Virginia's third highest mountain, they have no choice but to experience the sick, twisted debauchery and perverted mayhem described deep inside the tight unbroken bindings of this horrific missive.

Lumberjacked takes the reader to a nightmarish world where character development and aesthetic integrity are prematurely cut short by the swinging axes of maniacal lumberjacks, who are hell bent on death and destruction in the remote forests of Appalachia. And at the climax, when paranoia crosses over to the paranormal, Lumberjacked makes Deliverance look like a family raft trip down the Lower Gauley.

THE MANACLED

What happens when twin brothers lease out the former West Virginia State Penitentiary with the false purpose of filming a documentary on supernatural phenomena, but their true intention is to make a pornographic movie?

Chaos ensues as the disturbed spirits of murdered convicts, along with the reanimated dead from the neighboring Indian Burial Mound, take their vengeance on the unwary and undressed trespassers.

Zombies, ghosts, mobsters and porn collide in this bizarro tale from horror author Rich Bottles Jr.

Burning Bulb
PUBLISHING

ZAKARY MCGAHA
BIZARRO AND TRANSGRESSIVE FICTION

SEA OF MEDIUM-TO-HIGH PITCHED NOISES

The zombie apocalypse is changing; the world is coming to an odd demise; and a serial killer tries to change his ways and redeem himself before it all goes away. Now, Crabby has entered the world he left behind; the world of the undead. And things are changing. Everything will come to an end. In this new wave of the apocalypse, everything changes every five minutes. And death would be an absolute luxury. Psychological torment meets physical bloodletting in Sea of Medium-to-High Pitched Noises.

PARK MASTERS

Bad breakups, Bigfoot costumes, ghost bears, and more. Park Masters is a wacky, intelligent, quirky comedy about the power relationships have on people, good or bad. Also, it's just plain fun!

Burning Bulb
PUBLISHING

DAVID J. FAIRHEAD

THE FALL

Hopelessness... How do you protect your loved ones when Hell itself opens its insidious mouth?

Horror... Nightmarish Creatures invade your world and there is nowhere to hide.

Blood... How long can you hold out before they come for you?

Pain... Where do you run to avoid being eaten alive by monsters with a voracious appetite for your flesh?

Screams... While you selfishly run for your own life.

Questions... Who is to blame? Where did they come from? How many people survived...and how does the human race find the means to fight back?

THE FALL OF TOMORROW is man's last tale of desperation told by those that are striving to salvage some hope against a ravenous bastion of evil beasts bent on ruling our world.

DWELLING IN THE DARK

From David J. Fairhead, author of the FALL OF TOMORROW, comes DWELLING IN THE DARK- A soulful anthology of creeping terror to keep you up in the small hours with horror set in the past, present and future. Overlapping bits of puzzle fitting each other, before and after The Fall of Tomorrow.

A place where three children facing a monstrous foe can only pray that their bloody summer would just come to an end. Go back to the 1960's- THE COMMUNE where overindulging hippies use a mage's diary to control the end of the world, only to see first-hand that their drug induced visions have horrific ramifications. Where a young boy's visit to a haunted house becomes a lesson in RESIDUAL morality. The story, DEEPER- plunges two brothers into a sinkhole only to find they were being hunted by an insidious creature from its depths. Visit the old west as hero Dekker Collins battles evil gunslingers in DEMONEYE.

And so much more...!

Burning Bulb
PUBLISHING

WWW.*FairlyDarkProductions*.COM

EVERYTHING HERE IS A NIGHTMARE
Collected Works Vol 1.

"Pyles makes it look easy. His characters come instantly alive with the cocksure verve and swagger of rock stars."
> *- Daniel Knauf, creator of HBO's "Carnivale,"*
> *Executive Producer/Writer, ABC's "The Blacklist."*

The critically acclaimed author of Demons, Dolls and Milkshakes returns with fifteen tales of horror and suspense with Everything Here is a Nightmare.

From zombies in the old west, to a young boy tempted by the Devil. From vampires with romantic longing, to an abandoned lighthouse haunted by vengeful spirits. From a serial killer getting unholy justice, to a haunted English race car, Nelson W Pyles invites you to explore a landscape of fear, suspense and horror.

Take his hand and hold on tight. Remember that whatever you find here, whatever you see, no matter what you might think it could be... know this: Everything Here is a Nightmare.

Burning Bulb
PUBLISHING

RISE OF THE DEAD - a collection of seventeen tales of unspeakable zombie terror. Featuring a foreword and short story by John A. Russo!

www.TheJohnRusso.com

Burning Bulb
PUBLISHING

NIGHT OF THE LIVING DEAD

Why does Night of the Living Dead hit with such chilling impact?

Is it because everyday people in a commonplace house are suddenly the victims of a monstrous invasion? Or is it because the ghouls who surround the house with grasping claws were once ordinary people, too?

Decide for yourself as you read, and the horror grips you.

All the cannibalism, suspense and frenzy of the smash-hit move are here in the novel.

www.TheJohnRusso.com

THE BOOBY HATCH

With NIGHT OF THE LIVING DEAD, John Russo helped blaze a path in the horror genre that has never been equalled. In this hillarious erotic novel, he blazes a path through the wild, zany Sex Revolution of the 1970s.

Sweet, innocent Cherry Jankowski works for Joyful Novelties, where she tests sex toys ranging from the ridiculous to the sublime. But she can't find love or peace of mind and her efforts are hampered by a Peeping Tom, an exhibitionist, a cross-dressing boyfriend, a quack psychiatrist, and even her own product-testing partner, Marcello Fettucini, who can't get it up anymore and is scared of losing his job!

www.TheJohnRusso.com

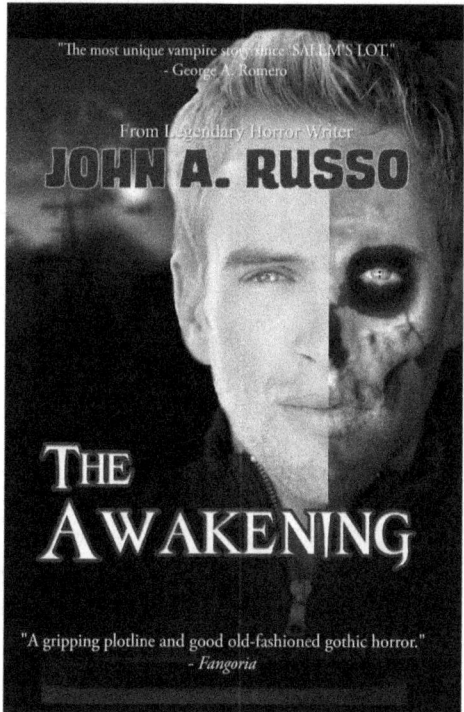

THE AWAKENING

For two hundred years, he has rested. Now he rises. Now he will be satisfied. Nothing can stop him. No one can resist him.

Benjamin Latham is young and handsome, his eighteenth-century mind wakened to a bizarre twentieth-century world. And there is the need deep within . . . an animal need, frightening, murderous, unholy . . . a vital need that must be fed.

And with his need comes a power over men and women to do his bidding, to quiet his dark craving . . .

Until the murders begin. And the inquiries. All suggesting the same hideous truth.

Now Benjamin must find a sanctuary: a lover, a partner, a friend. Someone who can share his darkness. Someone he can lead to . . . The Awakening.

www.TheJohnRusso.com

Burning Bulb
PUBLISHING

From Legendary Horror Writer

JOHN A. RUSSO

LIMB TO LIMB

SUCH A PRETTY GIRL . . .
Tiffany Blake was a beautiful long-limbed dancer with a glorious future and
the backing of a rich benefactor. Then a monstrous accident severed her leg
at the hip.

SUCH A COLD, CRUEL KNIFE . . .
And now her fellow dancers are disappearing without a trace. One by one
they fall victim to a dark and deadly pattern of evil – caught by the bloody,
brutal logic that would have them pay with their lovely bodies for the cruel
fate of another . . .victims of the sadistic madman whose flashing knife will
make them writhe a gruesome new dance.

www.TheJohnRusso.com

Burning Bulb
PUBLISHING

"A sense of infectious fun, straight from the author's pen."
– Nightmare Library

From Legendary Horror Writer
JOHN A. RUSSO

LIVING THINGS

"Russo carries his talent for the horrific neatly over into the novel form."
– West Coast Review of Books

LIVING THINGS

Beneath the shimmering Miami sun sprawls one of the Mafia's biggest empires, a glittering worldof lavish beachfront mansions, neon-painted nightclubs, beautiful women, expensive cars—and absolute control over the state's billion-dollar drug trade. But, one by one, its ganglords and henchmen are falling prey to a new rival. His powers are fueled by monstrous ancient rituals; his hellish undead legions slaughter mobsters and innocent citizens alike, his unholylust for power is virtually unstoppable.

Now a burned-out ex-detective and a brilliant anthropologist must enter a gruesome, nightmare world to fight this master of malevolence and illusion. Their time is short, their weapons few, and they face an ultimate, terrifying choice - annihilation or the loss of their souls to the eternal torment of those who never die. . .

www.TheJohnRusso.com

Burning Bulb
PUBLISHING

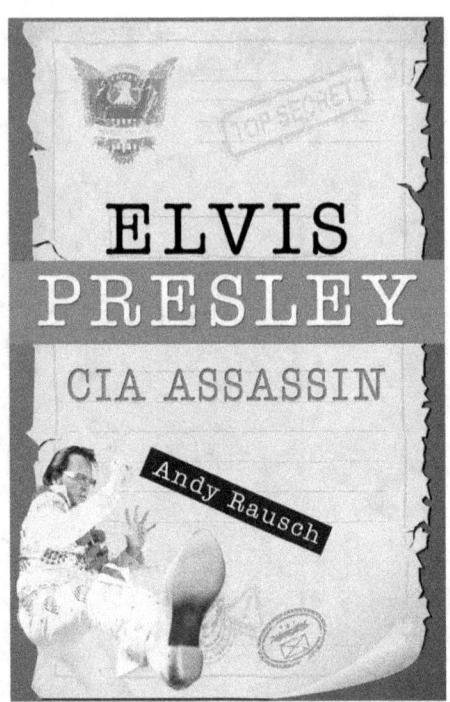

ELVIS PRESLEY, CIA ASSASSIN BY ANDY RAUSCH

"I can guarantee you. Read this book and you'll never look at Elvis the same way again!"
~ Douglas Brode, author of ELVIS CINEMA AND POPULAR CULTURE

SOON TO BE A MAJOR MOTION PICTURE

In 1970, singer Elvis Presley secretly met with President Richard Nixon. This new comedic novel imagines that Presley became a Central Intelligence Agency operative, eventually moving up through the ranks to become a skilled assassin.

Presented in an oral history fashion, the book tells us about Presley's secret transformation by the people who knew him best.

Did he fake his death in 1977? Was Presley involved with the Watergate scandal? The Iran hostage crisis? Communicating with aliens?

Read this book to find out the answers to these and many more questions.

Burning Bulb
PUBLISHING

MAD WORLD BY ANDY RAUSCH

"*Mad World* is dark, twisted, no-holds-barred fun."
—Jason Starr, author of *Bust*, *Slide*, and *The Max*

EVERYONE'S PLAYING AN ANGLE IN THE CITY OF ANGELS

Mad World tells the stories of a black hitman who doubles as a university professor, a Catholic priest who longs to be a gangster, a would-be author from Kansas, a gay phone sex operator who claims he's straight, a group of rich twentysomethings playing a deadly game of life and death, a vicious Mafia boss, and a sleazy Hollywood movie director. As each of their stories intersect, the body count piles up and the action comes nonstop in this tense, white-knuckle thriller by first-time author Andy Rausch.

"A wild ride. If you like it gangster, *Mad World* delivers."
—Daniel Birch, author of *Get Some*

Burning Bulb
PUBLISHING

BLOODLETTING: A TALE OF REVENGE BY ANDY RAUSCH

"Relentless… Addictive… The kind of nightmare you don't want
to wake up from."
—Heywood Gould, screenwriter of *Rolling Thunder*

He was just an average Joe. But when he finds his family held at
gunpoint by merciless thugs, he's told he must murder a Mafia
chieftain if he ever wishes to see his loved ones again.

Against all odds, Joe keeps his end of the bargain, but the criminals
don't. Now at his wits end, Joe is pushed beyond his breaking point
and forced to exact bloody revenge against those who've done him
and his family wrong in this powerful and violent novella by author
Andy Rausch (*Mad World*).

"Andy Rausch has a tight noir style that combines gritty, realistic drama
with a cinematic flair that makes for a powerful, compelling (somewhat
Stephen Kingesque), authentically visual reading experience."
—Stephen Spignesi, author of *Dialogues*

Burning Bulb
PUBLISHING

THE TAILSMAN

From the creators of *The Big Book of Bizarro* and *Westward Hoes* comes a new comic unlike anything you have ever seen!

He's hot on the trail, looking for some *tail*...

Sly Franko was a man of the West, a forger of the wild frontier. Like the Country Western song that would be written years after he died, the words, "Faster horses, younger women, and more money," seemed to be the anthem of this horn dog cowboy.

Franko would ride into town on a blazing saddle, find the closest saloon to wet the whistle, belly up to a good card game, and find him a hot-loving hussy to get his cowpoke on with.

However, Sly might have met his match when a visit to bathroom leads to terror and death. Can Sly and his poker buddies solve the mystery before more of the townsfolk are murdered? Find out in this exciting premier issue of *The Tailsman*!

WWW.BURNINGBULBCOMICS.COM

THE HAGS OF BLACK COUNTY

by Michelle Bowser

Ruled by a committee of Hags, and fueled by toothless rivalries, Black County lurks just far enough out of the way to be completely unnoticed by the rest of civilization. Its inhabitants have been mentally warped for generations and the land itself seems to have the power to drive anyone unlucky enough to visit into ridiculous hillbilly madness. When a construction Company needs to bury a pipeline through its ludicrous hills and valleys, a twisted charm goes to work and every aspect of already bizarre Black County life takes a gory turn for the hysterical. Take a preposterous trip along with its citizens, both native and new, through escapades such as the Hag parade, the grand opening of Madame Skunk's House of Ill Repute, the demolition derby riot and the rabid, zombie clown apocalypse.

THE ABANDONED SOUL

by Daniel Sellers

After spending most of his 20s in a drug and alcohol fueled daze, a young man finally hits rock bottom. Having used up his friends and their good graces, he ends up squatting in an abandoned house. Forcibly sobering he begins to realize that he is not alone in this abandoned house. Left with one last friend and a mountain of regrets, he must decide if this presence is a guilty conscience, or a malicious hunter.

WE WISH YOU A HAPPY KILLDAY

by Jason Heroux

"We Wish You a Happy Killday" is the story of an international b eloved holiday called "Killday" where one day a year everyone over the age of fifteen is permitted to register for a license allowing them to kill one other person. But this year Chad Ovenstock doesn't feel like killing anyone. His friends and family urge him to participate in the festivities, but he can't seem to get into the holiday spirit. On the day before Killday Chad comes in contact with Ambrose, an old friend who suffered a nervous breakdown and is now part of The One Ant Army, a mysterious cult dedicated to making the future disappear. When the holiday finally arrives Chad refuses to participate and tries to survive on his own, surrounded by constant gunfire, countless corpses, and the nagging suspicion that Ambrose may have secretly brainwashed him into becoming a member of The One Ant Army cult.

Burning Bulb
PUBLISHING